Christmas
at
Angels
Landing

Christmas at Angels Landing

A SUGARPLUM FALLS ROMANCE

JENNIFER GRIFFITH

Christmas at Angels Landing

ISBN: 9798562576774

This is a work of fiction. Names, characters, places, and events are creations of the author's imagination or are used fictitiously. Any resemblance to actual persons, living or dead, events, or locations, is purely coincidental.

Cover art by Blue Water Books, 2020.

*For Mom and Dad whose home library is the
best bookstore in the world*

"Pause you who read this, and think for a moment of the long chain of iron or gold, of thorns or flowers, that would never have bound you, but for the formation of the first link on one memorable day."—Charles Dickens

Chapter 1

Sam

As with most December days in Sugarplum Falls, snow swirled outside the office windows at Sugarbear Storage. Sam Bartlett tugged his jacket at his neck. Good thing he'd worn his lined boots because this was frostbite weather already. There would be plenty of driveways in need of shoveling tomorrow morning.

A dozen more people crammed themselves into the small office. At least the heater was blowing in here. He'd warm himself up before heading out to the units. Sam checked inside his wallet and counted the bills. *It'd better be enough. I hope no one outbids me this time.* One of those abandoned units looked like it had been designed for exactly Sam's needs.

He was winning this one. For once.

"Welcome, everyone." The Sugarbear office manager greeted the people who stood shoulder to shoulder in the warm reception area. "If you're here for the auction, Mr. Behr will be with you shortly. If not, please come see me about whatever business you have."

Everyone was there for the auction. Familiar faces packed the small room, the usual crowd for these kinds of events: Jordan McNair, the former Olympic biathlon medalist who owned Frosty Ridge Lodge and ski resort; Shelby Forger, a councilman's wife who couldn't resist a bargain; a few regulars from the estate sales circuit. Oh, and Lisa Lang, the mayor of Sugarplum Falls. What was she doing here?

Uh-oh. Sam had seen that gleam in the mayor's eyes before, like she was hunting for victims for her civic projects. The Hot Cocoa Festival had to be on

1

her mind. He stepped behind Mrs. Forger, a sizable shield. Maybe Mayor Lang wouldn't notice him.

"You have enough cash on you to splash out and win one of these bidding wars for once?" Jordan McNair asked, his shoulder wedged against Sam's in the too-tight office.

"I win sometimes." Sam suddenly doubted the depth of his wallet's stack of twenties. But he had to win this unit. He'd seen the flier advertising it—the photo showed every box labeled with the word *books*. And if ever an owner of a used bookstore needed an infusion of inventory, it was Sam Bartlett.

For the first time in memory, his store, Angels Landing, could potentially lose money at Christmas unless he kept up with demand.

"You haven't won recently. Not from what I've witnessed." Jordan tilted his head to the right. "I see your perennial competitor is here, and she's got crazy-deep pockets at all these things. Is someone bankrolling her?"

Oh, brother. Seriously? Not Tabitha Townsend.

Who tipped her off about this auction?

Sam's usually thriving bookstore had just one problem right now: lack of inventory—thanks to Tabitha's aggressive bidding at every estate sale for the past four months.

"Cute as a bug's ear and deadly as a bidding rival." Shelby Forger, member of the city council and one of Sam's driveway scraping recipients, inserted herself in their discussion. "You'd better watch out."

Ugh, did everyone in Sugarplum Falls know about his losses? Fine. Tabitha had offered large sums at a couple of previous events, so it would make sense that news had spread.

"What could she possibly want with the contents of an entire storage unit?" Sam muttered. Maybe she was just out to sink him personally.

This was the woman who came to Angels Landing Bookstore every single day and asked the same question—*Got any new vintage holiday novels?*—possibly just to irk him, but what was she searching for in all these estate sales and auctions? Sam looked away before she caught him staring. *Again.*

"What do any of us want with the contents of an entire storage unit?"

Jordan guffawed. "Everyone knows you only put stuff in storage that's not valuable enough to want on hand in your actual home. I mean, I can see why this particular auction's a draw for *you*, at least in one of the units up for bid. You have a bookstore, and all clues point to books."

"Fingers crossed."

"The rest of us are nothing but thrill junkies. We could get that from a James Bond movie. Hey, remember that one time you found all the old movie reels?"

"Sure, I remember." There had even been a copy of *Dr. No.* Since they hadn't been a good fit for Sam's bookstore, he'd offered them to Jordan.

"Did you know we projected them onto the snow-packed mountainside? Best event of the late season up at Frosty Ridge."

"If I end up winning any more old films, Double-Oh-Seven or otherwise, they're yours."

Jordan lit up. "Generous."

"Call it the Christmas Spirit." *Or the sight of that woman who makes me feel both shaken and stirred.*

Sam stole another glance her way, then forced his traitorous eyes back to where they belonged, on Mr. Behr.

He got his traitorous thoughts back under control as well.

Tried, anyway.

In his pocket, he pressed his good-luck charm between his thumb and forefinger.

"Welcome, ladies and gentlemen." Mr. Behr had to stand on his desk chair to be seen. He was more teddy bear stature than grizzly. He and his sister ran this place together. Good people. "Thanks for coming out to support my auction today. We have several units available." He described the three delinquent units. The other two had lawn and garden equipment and large furniture respectively, stuff Sam couldn't use. "We'll start with the one I'm calling the book trove. If you'll follow me outside."

They all exited through his office's back door to the outdoor storage area and the biting cold. Each unit resembled a garage bay with a roll-down metal door.

3

Guess who fell into step beside him through the snow? Her long, dyed-red ponytail swished back and forth, the color of candy apples and Santa's suit.

Tabitha Townsend gave him a saucy smile. "Well, if it isn't Mr. Bartlett of Angels Landing, my old nemesis."

Sam's heart-rate probably only upticked due to tromping through snow. She was pretty. Her nose was upturned, like a pixie's. *Nothing like Adelaide, though.*

Then his thoughts caught up with the conversation.

Nemesis. Ha! "Ah, the honorable Miss Townsend. We meet again under familiar circumstances." He gave her a slight bow.

"Indeed." She gave a similar bow of the head. "Old battles revisited. Old rivalries rekindled."

Kindled was right. Something definitely blazed within him at the sight of her. But on a day like today, with books at stake, he'd better keep his eye on the prize, not the girl who had outbid him at the last several estate sales, yanking the inventory right out from under him over and over. And for what reason? It wasn't like the owner of a personal shopping business could offload that many used books.

"Trust me: today there will be an unfamiliar turn of events when the battle begins. You won't outbid me for Mr. Behr's *book trove.*"

She narrowed her eyes and put up her hands in a martial-arts fighting stance. Not pixie-like. More *cute ninja-like.* "Ah, so you say, but honorable Mr. Bartlett, I sense your kung fu is not strong."

Taking her cue, he sliced the air with the side of his hand, as if breaking a board in a single strike. "I have come prepared for battle today, Miss Townsend." He bowed, patting the money clip inside his wallet *and* the loose little vintage typewriter key he carried in his pocket today for extra good luck.

It bore the letter "A" for Adelaide, his wife for a month, his girlfriend for years prior to that brief period when he was her husband, when she'd listened to his stories and clung to his hand.

"A" for his A-game.

"Your kung fu cannot match my preparation, owner of Twelve Days." His martial arts movie accent was terrible. "My bookstore fu will outshine your personal shopping business fu this time."

"Regardless of your preparation"—her accent was even worse than his—"I will be the victor, as I proved when we sparred at the Kynaston estate."

Yuzu-lemon juice in his wounds! "No, Miss Townsend! I will have Mr. Behr's book trove."

Up walked Jordan McNair. "What is wrong with you two? Everyone's listening. Have you been watching a Bruce Lee movie marathon together?"

Sam glanced around. Lots of the bidders were staring at him and Tabitha. *And I was shamelessly flirting with her, as if Adelaide never existed. Bury me in snow right now. Let a big pile slide off the roof and encase the whole of me.*

A merry sparkle danced in Tabitha's eye, however, as if she didn't mind being called out for delaying the auction for everyone else.

She makes me feel like I did when reading adventure stories as a kid.

Mr. Behr cleared his throat. "If I have your attention now"—he side-eyed Sam, *ouch*—"I'll roll up the door. You'll have three minutes to inspect, but no one is allowed inside the unit, or to cross this line." He dragged his foot to make a line in the snow and then rolled up the metal door on its track, making a clatter louder than Santa's reindeer on a rooftop. "The clock starts now."

Mr. Behr stepped aside, and the patrons moved forward. It wasn't a pushy crowd. They all knew each other, more or less. This was Sugarplum Falls, after all. Some acted bored, and who could blame them? It was basically floor-to-ceiling boxes marked *books*. Such a sight could bore anybody but Sam Bartlett.

For Sam, however, the sight set off a similar reaction as when he'd once held a first edition of *Tom Sawyer*. Books, books, all the books!

Even better, some had labels noting from which room they hailed. Living room books, bedroom books, kitchen books, kids' room books, piano room books, parlor books. Library books—hopefully meaning the library in the book-happy home, and not the forgot-to-return-to-the-town-library library.

Bless whomever had left this storage unit unpaid. They'd be missing quite a stash of old friends. How far back into the unit did the book stacks extend? Clear to the back? He couldn't tell.

That was the problem with these auctions—no prior inspection. No one really knew what they were bidding on. Beyond the front wall of boxes, what lurked? *Please say more books, and not some heinous collection of velvet tapestries featuring leopards and rock bands.*

Oh, Sam was getting these. Out of respect for the labeler of the boxes, he'd treat them with honor—besides doubling his inventory. *Yes!* Visions of book-joy danced in his head.

Maybe he was getting ahead of himself, considering he still had a considerable battle yet to fight. He turned to size up his short but fierce competition.

Where was she? Not mashing her way to the front, nor standing on either side of him.

A soft whirring passed his ear, like the beating of a bee's wings. He swatted at it, ducking by instinct. A little giggle erupted from behind him. He turned, and—

"Sorry." Tabitha's mouth quirked, and she shrugged a shoulder. What was she holding? A remote control? "Didn't mean to buzz the tower, there, Crouching Tiger."

It took a second, but the second round of whirring caught his eye. Hovering just outside the unit, at the height of the boxes, a small drone floated. It maneuvered slowly into the storage unit, a light pointing downward from its belly. Did it have a camera?

Sam whipped back around. Sure enough, Tabitha was watching some kind of screen attached to her controls.

Hey. That was cheating. Or, maybe not. Dang-it, maybe it was *smart*.

Tabitha's kung fu *was* strong.

He sidled up to her. "What do your superior Hidden Dragon senses tell you is behind the boxes of books?"

She angled the screen away from his view. Blast.

"That's for me to know, sensei, and you to wonder until after the bidding ends." She wrinkled her face into a smile but didn't look up at him, eyes trained on her target.

Sam kicked himself for not thinking of a drone camera. But—who did think of that? The stakes had just risen.

"Just tell me whether it's going to be worth the bid."

She maneuvered with her thumbs, and the little spy-plane came back to rest at her feet. She scooped it up and stuck it in her purse along with the controls and her phone that had served as a viewing screen. "Good luck. Or as they say in Japan, *ganbare!*"

Fighting was right. Sam had nothing but fighting feelings right now. Who did she think she was, going rogue CIA operative on a matter as vital to his business as this? What kind of person was he dealing with? She couldn't possibly need as many books as were stacked in this abandoned storage unit. No one could. Possibly not even Sam Bartlett, a man with a used bookstore.

"Time's up. Let's start the bidding." Mr. Behr looked over the assembled crowd. "Who'll give me five dollars?"

The bids rolled in, climbing into the fifty-dollar range before other locals began dropping out. When the price scaled past a hundred bucks, only Sam and Tabitha remained sparring.

"Who'll give me a hundred and ten?"

Sam raised his right hand, while pressing his left thumb into the indentation of the little round letter A key in his pocket. *Come on, lucky A.*

"A hundred and twenty?"

Tabitha placed that bid without blinking.

"Do I hear one thirty?"

Sam and his good-luck charm made the offer.

It went on, until the numbers started to pinch a little in his money-clip. "You can't possibly want all these," he hissed to her while Mr. Behr took a breath. "Drop out."

"Two hundred dollars. Who'll give me two hundred for all these books?" Mr. Behr looked between them expectantly. Tabitha held the current winning status.

"You want a clue of what's in there?" she asked, and he could see a mischievous one-side-of-her-cute-mouth smile in his peripheral vision.

Sam did want a clue, but he gritted his teeth and made his bid. "Two hundred." Then he halfway turned to her. "Did you see it with the drone?"

"Mm-hmm. Does the name Inglewood mean anything to you?"

It certainly did! This was Mrs. Inglewood's storage unit? The woman with notoriously exquisite taste in everything? Was that what Tabitha implied?

"Two ten," she said, raising her hand.

"Two twenty," Sam jumped in immediately. "Two fifty."

"No sense bidding against yourself, buddy." Tabitha chuckled. "And thanks for the clue *I* was looking for—with your reaction." She raised her hand. "Three hundred dollars."

Ouch! Sam's kung fu apparently needed a major tune-up.

"I'm out," he muttered. Three hundred was all he had in his wallet for this acquisition. "It's yours." Talk about hidden dragons. Not even three hundred bucks and his lucky letter A could match Tabitha's so-called powers.

Tabitha beamed. "Until we meet again, Crouching Tiger." She pressed her palms together at her chest and bowed.

Jordan McNair clapped, and some of the other bidders let out smug guffaws.

Ha. See if Sam offered them merchant discounts next time they came by his store. Okay, fine. He still would. But ugh!

Neither of the other two units interested him. Tabitha Townsend's cuteness did not currently outweigh her irksomeness. Sam tightened his scarf around his neck and headed back out to his truck.

"Hey," Jordan called after him. "Better luck next time, eh?"

Grrr. "Yeah."

With a final holler, Jordan asked. "Who's coming as your author guest this year for the Christmas Eve sale at Angels Landing?"

"It's a surprise." To everyone, even Sam. Which was another raspberry seed in his wisdom tooth today. Sam should try to be more chummy, but three different authors had committed and then backed out. It was shaping up to be a disaster of a seasonal sales report at this rate.

His truck's engine roared, and Sam steered his way down Orchard Avenue toward the bookstore, parking in the back and stomping off his boots before heading in through the nearly empty storeroom.

"Did you get it?" his shop assistant Mrs. Milliken asked the second he set foot through the doors from the storeroom into the warmth of the main shop of Angels Landing. With its garlands and bows, its cherry and spice candles burning, and the sounds of Bing Crosby's *White Christmas* on vinyl filling the store, the place oozed Christmas charm.

Which brought in the customers, making Angels Landing a Christmastime destination for every soul in Sugarplum Falls.

Mrs. Milliken practically pounced on him, ignoring a bevy of customers at the glass counter. Her gray curls pushed their way out from under her crocheted Christmas hat. "Do you need George to come and help you unload? Or were there too many for one trip? Should we rent a U-haul?"

George was her husband and the other assistant in the store. Two former school teachers, they knew everyone in Sugarplum Falls—and what they liked to read. Angels Landing would be gasping for breath without them. But, at least until this year, it was nothing short of a unicorn: a brick-and-mortar bookstore that turned a serious profit in days of digital dominance. He could also thank the people of Sugarplum Falls for their loyalty.

"No U-haul required." His boots left tread-shaped chunks of snow as he walked over the polished hardwoods through the shelves. "Maybe next time." When he beat Tabitha's bidding strategy. If he could stay in business without good inventory such as the top-quality merchandise like that which must lurk in Mrs. Inglewood's stash.

Not that Sam would ever know.

"Aw, dear." Mrs. Milliken frowned and simpered, dogging his heels through the children's section toward the front of the store. "What kind of heartless Scrooge would outbid the bookstore owner for his inventory at Christmastime?"

He looked at her darkly.

"Don't tell me. The Townsend girl?" She tsked. "And you took your lucky letter A and everything."

Fat lot of good a lucky talisman could do against spy tactics and endless stacks of twenties. "Adelaide is probably looking down on me in disappointment." He reached in his pocket to grab the loose typewriter key that had brought him no luck today.

Except …

It was gone!

9

"Not disappointment, dear. She'd never be disapp—what's wrong?"

Sam turned and jogged back to the storeroom, where he fell to his hands and knees, patting the concrete floor. "Do you have a flashlight nearby?" he called to Mrs. Milliken, who'd followed him to the back again.

"George! Come quick. Bring the flashlight. The good one." Mrs. Milliken dropped down beside him. "Did you lose a contact lens? I'll be extra careful. You need to slow down. Those things break."

Sam wore glasses, not contacts. "I can't lose it."

Mr. Milliken charged in, waving the lit flashlight. "What's wrong? What are we finding?"

They weren't *finding* anything yet. "It's my typewriter key. The one from Adelaide." He crawled toward the door. He took off his coat and shook it upside down.

Mrs. Milliken gasped. "Oh, dear. Slow down. It'll be all right. We'll locate it."

But they didn't. It wasn't in the storeroom, and it wasn't in Sam's truck, or in the snow between the truck and the back door of Angels Landing.

He slapped the side of his face and ran his hand down his cheek hard. It must have fallen out of his pocket into the snow at Sugarbear Storage.

"I'm heading back over there." He shoved his arms through the sleeves of his coat and shrugged it up onto his shoulders. "Sorry to leave you guys in charge of the store again."

"That's fine, dear. I have to be here to sign for the annual flower delivery from Poinsettia Hill. But, say. Maybe you can help Tabitha load her winnings into her U-haul."

Coals. Heaped on his head. Thanks a lot.

Outside, it was snowing again. Hard.

Sam motored and muttered toward the storage facility. By the time he arrived, all the other cars from the auction-goers that had filled the parking lot earlier were gone. Except one—the small red sports car that probably had a trunk bursting with nun-chucks and Chinese throwing stars.

"Hi, Mr. Behr." Sam greeted the owner inside his warm office, with the wall-mounted heater blowing at full blast. "Okay if I look around the yard? I think I dropped something earlier." He nearly asked whether someone had turned it in, but of course it wasn't the kind of thing someone would assume had value. Anyone who saw it would leave it where it lay or else toss it in the trash as litter.

"Sure, Sam. Go on ahead. Sorry you got outbid, but there are worse things than putting a triumphant grin on the face of a beautiful redhead."

Sam blinked a few times. She'd smiled?

Well, of course she'd smiled. She'd won the prize *du jour*. Maybe the prize *du decade*, if the rumors about the Inglewood estate held true.

"Thanks." Sam checked the floor of the office, glancing in the corners and along the baseboards. No, he'd had it with him out in the yard. "I appreciate it."

A new inch of snow covered the ground, precluding any possibility of easily sighting the typewriter key. Dang it. He would probably have to wait until the spring thaw before he found it again. *If he ever found it again.*

"Fruitcakes!" a woman's voice shrieked from somewhere in the maze of storage units, followed by a growl. "And mincemeat!" The shouter sounded ready to commit arson.

Sam headed that way.

Uh-oh. The hollering originated from none other than the Inglewood unit.

"Hey, there." Sam stepped gingerly toward the commotion. Whoa! What the—?

No fewer than fifty boxes lay torn open, their contents dumped in the area in front of the open roll-up door. Books spilled into the snow, scattering hither and yon.

Tabitha?

Chapter 2

Tabitha

Tabitha tugged the packing tape from yet another box of ... No! Not Bûche de Noël! "This many cookbooks is just wrong!"

Those stinking labels written in marker on the sides of the boxes had sent her hopes soaring with words like *Christmas books* and *favorites to read again.* Not a single box, however, contained anything useful, let alone the sole book Tabitha needed.

How crazy-hard was it to find the sole copy of a vintage novel written by a one-time author? This crazy-hard. Boxes' contents strewn everywhere in the snow crazy-hard. Flying a drone to examine the contents of a storage unit crazy-hard.

Talking—more or less yelling—to herself crazy-hard.

"If I see another box of books entirely dedicated to *fruitcake,* I'm going to break something!"

"It looks like you already have."

Her head snapped upward. Someone was here? Oh, no. Not Sam Bartlett. His glasses were slightly fogged, but the blue of his eyes still pierced through the lenses and into her soul. Mmm, and that tousled fair hair in slight need of a cut. He had the hot, absent-minded professor thing down to a science, and it nearly made her forget her mountain of a problem.

Tabitha shrank down and hid behind a disheveled pile. "I've got this. Never mind. Just go on your merry way."

What was he doing here, anyway? Had he come to crow over her colossal failure? *I'll bet he knew this unit was worthless. He was just trying to bid me up! Make me spend my cash. I should have guessed from the way he dropped out of the bidding the second I offered my last dollar.*

She looked around in dismay at what had become of her three hundred bucks. Nothing! Not a single novel in the whole place, let alone *the* novel. Mrs. Barnes was going to be disappointed. Again.

Sam stepped over a pile and wedged his way into the dim enclosure. "Slow down, before you hurt yourself."

Oh, she was already hurt, or smarting at least. "In the last hour, I have opened at least one hundred boxes, and not one of them has contained a single book other than Christmas cookbooks. How many recipes for German *Stollen* Christmas cake can there possibly be? I ask you!" She took a book on soufflés by its spine and held it up as if ready to hurl it like a boomerang.

"Too many, it would seem." Sam reached for the French cookbook, lowering her arm. "Are you all right?"

"It probably looks like I'm throwing a wild temper tantrum." Which she was at this point, but it hadn't started out that way. "I promise, the mess in the snow out front happened when ten open boxes toppled. I didn't dump everything on purpose."

He glanced out at her giant mess and tugged at his earlobe. "Well, could you use any help?"

From the funds-muncher himself? "That's not necessary." Okay, she wasn't really angry with him, and he didn't actually look like he had come here to make fun of her. "Why are you here?"

"I thought I dropped something and came back here to look for it. But seriously, are you all right?" His brow furrowed and he looked genuinely sorry. "I've got time to help, if you need it."

"I'm sorry about the way it looks like I've treated these books." He must be mourning for the death of the books. "I know you really wanted them."

"Sure, but …" Concern marked his visage. "Are you all right?"

Seriously? Did he sincerely want to know? Fine, she'd tell him.

"I can't believe I fell for another red herring." She exhaled, the tension falling away from her shoulders. She shook her head. "I really thought this place would have what my client needs me to find, but as you can see …" She waved her hand around at all the open boxes. Sure enough, every single exposed spine contained titles about cooking. "Granted, some of them are holiday-related, so it wasn't a complete miss. But still, who has this many

13

cookbooks? It's obsession. It's insane."

"Collecting things probably is a mild form of insanity. But it's benign and can be charming."

Charming. Pah. "Not today."

Sam's laughter filled the metal room, echoing around. "If I were in your shoes, I'd probably feel that way, too." He scratched his head and smiled.

Speaking of charming. That smile! The Sam Spark crackled behind her ribcage, just like it had ever since the first time she'd seen him secretly shovel Grandma's driveway years ago, the winter after Grandpa Larry died. And every time she'd encountered him since then. Spark-a-thon today, though, during that auction. Potential for an actual blaze.

"I meant it when I offered to help. What are you planning to do with all these?"

"Burn them?" Because hauling them load by load to the dump in the back seat of her Miata wasn't a stellar use of time while Mrs. Barnes expected delivery of her long-sought book, *Angels Landing,* before Christmas as a gift for her sister.

Tabitha owed Mrs. Barnes every effort to find it. Even to the point of expending all the remains of her bank account, which—*voila.* Mission accomplished.

"Very funny. Have you opened them all?"

She'd opened enough of them to teach herself a lesson—that if the first hundred and ten or so boxes contained only cookbooks, the last five or six weren't likely to change. Especially since *those* boxes were actually labeled *Cookbooks.* "Yeah," she said. "Now that you know what's inside them, you're not even sorry I won the bid. Unless you were thinking of turning your shop into a niche vintage holiday cookbook store."

No one would do that.

"As it turns out …" Sam looked down at his fingernails. "That's one of my bestselling sections in the store."

He was lying. He had to be. But why? "You're saying you'd buy the contents of this unit from me?"

"For the right price." His eye glinted—igniting that darn spark again.

14

So that was how he was going to play it. Was that gleam in his eye greed or triumph or ... not flirting. *Wishful-thinking alert. The brilliant bookstore owner is never going to fall for a scatterbrained, uneducated, business-tanking mess like me.*

"Fine." She huffed, collapsing against the metal wall. "Name your price."

"Fifty."

Fifty! But she'd paid three hundred!

He elbowed one of the many, many heavy boxes. "That's my price for emptying the unit for you."

"You're saying you'll charge *me?*" Of all the—

"I've seen what you drive."

That sports car would never work with all these useless books. "I'll manage." If it took fifty trips, she'd figure it out.

"Perhaps you're aware that Mr. Behr auctions these units with a clean-out requirement. If you don't clean it out, he charges a hefty sum."

"How hefty?"

"Fifteen hundred bucks."

"That's highway robbery!" And more than she had in her bank account.

Geez. This was what came of allowing two startups to go under in five years' time. The third and final, Twelve Days, still seemed like a surefire winner. Tabitha even had some happy clients already, but no other success could compensate for not being able to deliver the obscure novel to her benefactress.

"That's not highway robbery. That's business."

Business. The very word was salt in her wounds. Tabitha closed her eyes. Gurgles rose up her throat and she looked up at the cobwebbed ceiling. "You got me this time, Crouching Tiger." She dipped her chin, narrowed her eyes, and gave him a pointed martial arts movie line. "But I'll be back."

He made a little fist and bumped her upper arm. "Don't be so glum, Hidden Dragon. You haven't even let me make you an offer for the contents. How does fifty dollars sound?"

"A zero-sum deal?" Tabitha squeezed her eyes shut. "Basically, you're letting me walk away from my stupid mistake." It was actually really generous.

Compared to the clean-out charge, she was getting off easy.

"As long as you help me re-box the books that fell over in the snow out there, yeah. I'll come back and clear it all out of here tomorrow. You'll sleep well tonight, and your back will thank you."

Freedom called to her. Loudly. "Done—on the condition that you guarantee no one bakes me a German *Stollen* cake from any of these recipes." She offered a handshake for the deal. "I'll even write you up a receipt."

He removed his glove to shake her hand. It was warm, hot even. Then, his gaze met hers, and dang if it didn't shoot her full-to-bursting with sparks.

"Merry Christmas," he said, his voice suddenly lower, resonant, creeping into the crevices of her soul.

"Merry Christmas." She pulled her hand away before the sparks and gaze started making her say and do things he might find unwelcome, like impulsively touching his hair, or telling him what sexy snow-shoveling skills he had—which he obviously wanted kept secret, based on his ski-mask and the fact he ran off anytime Grandma tried thanking him.

I'll keep your secret. I'll keep all your secrets. Swoon.

"Ahem." She woke herself up. "Let's get repacking." She practically hurdled over the nearest two stacks of boxes.

In no time, she'd cleaned up the mess on the ground outside. "All done."

"That was fast. Not bad." He gave an approving nod.

"Your receipt, sir." Standing on the new-fallen snow, she scavenged in her purse for a pen and scrap of paper, where she wrote up and signed a makeshift receipt.

That way, on the outside chance Sam Bartlett didn't follow through and Mr. Behr came after her for the cost of the clean-out, she'd have written proof of their transaction.

"Put your *Sam Bartlett* on the dotted line." She offered him the pen.

"Turn around."

"What?"

"Just turn around." When she complied, he used her back as his desk for signing. As the pen moved over her coat, it sent more of those tingles. She let out a long exhale, the steam floating and forming ay little heart-shaped mist.

16

Not really. But it could have if she lived in a kung fu cartoon.

Sam finished, and she turned around to accept her pen back.

"Pleasure doing business with you," he said.

"We'll have to do more business in the future." If she winked, would she look sexy or stupid? She lost her nerve.

"Bye, Tabitha." He did wink. And it wasn't remotely stupid. In fact, it was more like a love-potion-tipped dart to her heart. "See you tomorrow." He stayed in the unit, probably to bask in the mincemeat recipes.

"Yeah. You will." She'd keep going back to the Angels Landing Bookstore, her only concrete lead on the book of the same title. Which she had to find.

If not, I'll have to pay Mrs. Barnes back all the money she fronted me to start Twelve Days. Plus probably some kind of pain and suffering compensation for what happened with Soccer Ball.

If only Tabitha hadn't lost that little black and white dog, she wouldn't be stuck in this impossible predicament right now. Winces rippled over her face, just like every time she remembered that awful day. Tabitha had to make things right by finding that *Angels Landing* book for Mrs. Barnes in time for Christmas, even though it meant spending her last dime.

She started her car and waited for it to warm up so she could head back to Grandma's to regroup, but her phone chimed. She checked the text.

You have received three hundred dollars in your account.

From Sam? Her breath exhaled in a huge cloud of steam—one that could have made a heart to fill her entire car. That would bring her account balance to right around three hundred bucks, thanks to Sam. Yeah, he maneuvered himself into first place.

Sigh. That smile. That kindness. That handsome-but-off-limits professor vibe that made it hard for Tabitha to concentrate on anything else when he was in the room. But, even if he did flirt with her a little, there was some kind of shield around him. Emphasis on the *off-limits* part of the aura. Like he was interested but would never act on his curiosity about her.

Not that he necessarily should, considering that Tabitha was a total mess.

Maybe Poppy knew what Sam Bartlett's story was.

Chapter 3

Sam

"No sense doing this all yourself." George Milliken hauled a double-stack of boxes from the storage unit toward the back of Sam's nearly full truck bed the following afternoon. "But clear up one thing for me: I thought Gracie said you lost the auction."

"I did. But it turned out the bid-winner made a mistake, so I made her an offer she couldn't refuse."

"Wheeling and dealing, eh?" George winked. "Turned on the old Bartlett charms, I'll wager. The girls fall for it every time."

"Whatever." He hefted another box into the back of his truck. The final dozen boxes would have to be wedged in the back of Mr. Milliken's town car.

"Come on. You can't tell me you don't notice the fact that every time you help a female customer you make a tidy sale."

So Sam was a good salesman. So he could read what a customer needed and match it with a product. So what? "They come into the store ready to buy. It's not personal."

George snorted. "It might not be personal to you, but trust me. The ladies of Sugarplum Falls are taking your attention very personally." His low chuckle expanded, filling the air of the parking lot of Sugarbear Storage. "This should go a long way toward restocking the inventory, though."

"Yeah." At least of one genre.

"Say, Sam. Why don't you just tell that Townsend girl you want all those books she outbid you on at those other estate sales? If she doesn't want these, then maybe she didn't want those, either. I bet she'd sell them to you."

Maybe. Or maybe not. She'd mentioned a client. Possibly she had multiple clients, and perhaps they included booksellers in Darlington or somewhere else who asked her to stock their shelves as well. Not of cookbooks, apparently, but she definitely hoarded all the books she bought.

"I shouldn't ask. It's none of my business what she plans to do with the other books she's snapped up." Besides, again, if the people of Sugarplum Falls knew how bare his back-room inventory was, they'd lose confidence in him—like that bank-run incident in the movie *It's a Wonderful Life*. Over the past decade, Sam had built a solid reputation.

No. It was better to just let her have the books. He'd paid for these. This haul would stop a gap for now.

"Let's get the last three loads." Sam marched off through the snow.

Thinking.

Women were definitely not coming on to him at the shop, and he wasn't looking for any to do so. He had his business, his books, and his fire to read beside at night to keep him warm. The fleeting insertion of Tabitha Townsend's smile notwithstanding, Sam was not looking for female companionship.

He'd had it a long time ago with Adelaide, deep love with a nearly perfect woman, and that was enough. *"Life is a book, and we're writing our own stories,"* she'd said first, and then he'd repeated it, and so forth.

Until her story ended, and he'd put down his pen and ink.

I wish I could find that typewriter key. He scanned the snow as he returned to the unit, but to no avail. If he couldn't find it, how was he going to have that oomph it always gave him, the connection to Adelaide he needed if he was ever going to finish writing the book he'd started writing for her when she was sick? *If I'm ever going to write anything, like she assumed I would have done by now?*

Inside, George grabbed one box labeled *cookbooks*. "Stack that next one on top here. I can carry two. Maybe even three."

"It'll block your view as you walk." No sense having a retiree tripping in the snow. "Two's still good." Sam bent and picked up the second box to stack for Mr. Milliken, when—

Kerflump! The entire bottom fell out of the box, spilling books onto Sam's boots and all over the now-cleared concrete floor.

"Shazbot!" George hopped on one foot. "That smarts."

"The bottom of that box must not have been taped, or else it rotted out. Here." Sam took the box out of his hands and set it down while George nursed his foot. "Are you all right?"

"One book hit just right. Smack dab, center of my toenail." He sat on the floor of the storage unit, pretty agile for his age, and began removing his boot. "Well, will you look at that." He reached over and picked up a white book with gold lettering. "I haven't seen this in years."

Sam stopped gathering spilled books. "Is that—?"

It was! The books spilled from his arms. "*Angels Landing*? By Ed Garnet?"

"Yup, and I thought there weren't any more copies around." George pulled open the cover, the spine making a crackling sound, as if the book had never been viewed. "Will you look at that? It's even inscribed. Right there, from the author." He tilted the book for Sam to see. "Ed Garnet. Check it out."

Sam accepted it gingerly, almost reverently. "I never thought I'd …" What? See a copy of his favorite book in the world ever again? Read the words that, as a young man, made him aware of his destiny as an author someday? Or—

Wait a second. He flipped to the back of the book, his heart in his throat.

It couldn't be. But it was!

This wasn't just any copy of Sam's favorite book. This was *the* very copy he'd read as a young man. For, right there between the last page and the back cover was the Sugarplum Falls Library stamp, beside the small yellow manila book pocket, where the signatures of the patrons who had checked out the book were listed, as well as the due dates for return.

Samson Bartlett, due December 31, it read. His signature was youthful, much rounder than his current penmanship.

Sam shot through a time machine to that Christmas season when he'd devoured the story four or five times before being warned by the library that they'd consider it lost and he'd have to pay for the copy if he didn't turn it in by New Year's Eve.

"Have you read it?" Mr. Milliken asked, breaking the spell. "It's a good

20

one. Especially the part where the angel guides the hero out of the brambles and helps him survive the blizzard long enough to save the girl he loves."

"I love that part, too." Sam swallowed hard. "I'm ..." He looked up at Mr. Milliken. "I'm not going to sell this one."

"Oh, no! No, no, no. It's too rare. Gracie will agree. Plus, it's got the same name as your bookshop. You'll have to keep it on principle."

Angels Landing. Not just that, but the very copy he'd read! He caressed the cross-hatch fabric of the white linen cover, ran a fingertip over the gold-embossed title and gorgeous outline of the angel. As a kid, he'd thought it was made with gold leaf.

Maybe it was.

Either way, it was worth more than gold leaf to him.

What would Adelaide do if she were here? She'd be laughing that trilling giggle of hers. She'd hug his neck and then tell him it was a sign that he needed to glue his behind to his chair and put some words on the page! A sign he should finish the story he'd begun for her.

But how could I finish that book? I wrote it for her. For my wife.

"You coming?" George asked. "Or are you going to keep standing there until it gets seriously cold?" Then he chortled at his own joke. "As if ten below wasn't definable as seriously cold. Can you believe it? At three in the afternoon?"

Sam blinked and looked around. All the other boxes and books were gone. Apparently, he'd been standing here staring at *Angels Landing* for long enough that Mr. Milliken had completed the hauling and even swept out the storage unit.

"Thanks, George." Sam gulped and shook himself. "I'll meet you back at the bookshop."

Mr. Milliken saluted. "Yes, sir, boss."

"Aw, seriously. You were my high school teacher. Lay off the *boss, sir* stuff." Sam slipped the book inside his down vest beneath his long wool coat. The sun would be setting any minute on ... well, the *best day ever!*

Thank you, Tabitha! She could have no idea how her dislike of cookbooks blessed him.

After this, he might not be able to think of her as irksome anymore, even if she did outbid him everywhere or repeat the same question at his store every morning. Now, since he'd been inadvertently blessed by her, the only right thing would be to do whatever he could to help her find what she wanted to find—wring it out of her so that he could help.

Maybe if I asked her privately. Over dinner... He did have her number. She'd left him her card once, at Mrs. Milliken's insistence. He pulled it out of his wallet.

There was a lipstick stain kiss-mark on the back.

A frisson zapped through his veins. He shook it off. His interest in seeing Tabitha Townsend was about helping her achieve her goal, nothing more. Well, and maybe getting a longer look at her pretty face, up close. The upturned nose. The creamy skin. He could appreciate human beauty, just like he could appreciate a fine painting or sculpture. Tabitha's face merited a little more study.

That was all. He wasn't thinking about anything more than that with anyone.

His phone rang.

"Sam, I need a favor." Mayor Lang. Great.

She was a major reason Angels Landing was a thriving success, thanks to creating an incredible downtown area in Sugarplum Falls. Sam owed her—but in this case, he really didn't want to pay up.

"What can I do for you, Lisa?" He resisted the urge to hang up and pretend the call dropped, since he knew what this would be about. That dumb matchmaking thing.

"Tell me you've already signed up for the hat." She sounded like she was running on a treadmill. The queen of multi-tasking.

"The hat?" Maybe if he played dumb she'd let him out of it.

A hat with some kind of divider down the center with half for the men's names, half for the women's. Whoever was drawn simultaneously became each other's date for the evening of the Hot Cocoa Festival.

Sam had been avoiding it for years.

"Please! It's only on every poster in town, including the one on your business's front window. The Hot Cocoa Festival's famous Santa hat."

"I'm planning on being there. Gotta talk up my author event for Christmas Eve." Which he'd been working on with little concrete success, unfortunately. Every other year, authors had been banging on his door for an invitation—and the event never disappointed, sales-wise. Something like fate must be working against him this time around. "Plus, the hot chocolate is always good. But it's indoors, so I'm not planning on wearing a hat."

"Don't be coy with me. You're one of the desirables. Either you put your name in, or else I lose a whole slew of females for their side of the hat."

"You know I'm not really that guy, Lisa."

Sam wasn't planning on crumbling under external pressure to date again. He'd done that at his family's insistence a few years back, even submitting to setups, but he was done. Hadn't anyone considered that he might be a guy who only ever loves one woman and his quota had been met?

He was really better off as a bachelor, even if technically he was a widower. Quiet life. His books, his writing. Well, not much writing these days. Not as much as Adelaide would have dreamed for him. *Life is a book and we're writing our own stories,* she'd said, but she'd meant it literally in Sam's case. *Get writing.* And he would again. Someday. When he could face it again.

"What I know, Sam, is that you haven't been that guy, but that it's probably time that you became him." Her footfalls on the treadmill sort of sounded like an impatient tapping of her toe. "Tell you what. Think about it for a bit and I'll call you back. But know that I'm not going to be easy to convince with some watery excuse. It'd better be iron-clad."

"And by iron-clad, you mean …"

"The only excuse I'll accept is that you already have a date for the festival."

Chapter 4

Tabitha

Before heading into Angels Landing for her customary morning visit, Tabitha stopped in for a hot drink and a chat with her best friend in Sugarplum Falls, Poppy Peters, owner of The Cider Press and serious barista of all things fruit juice and spice.

"Hey, Tabitha." Poppy fanned herself as she poured a steaming mug. "Here's your hot apple cider with cinnamon and clove add-ins. Do you want a splash of orange in it?"

"Mmm. Yes, please. Thank you. Did you see me coming?" Tabitha accepted the drink and sipped its sweet and tart goodness carefully. The steam temporarily blurred her vision of the surroundings in The Cider Press.

"I know your schedule, more or less. Angels Landing, then you drop in."

"Gotta have my Cider Press fix."

"Cider fixes a lot of things." Poppy and Tabitha sat down together at one of the pub-height tables, and Poppy offered her one of those tiny-circumference straws to sip through. "Like, for instance, whatever is making you a smidgen flushed."

Tabitha lifted a hand to her cheek. It was definitely warm. A memory of the very beguiling Sam Bartlett and letting his eyes dance all over her face yesterday, watching his muscles bulge while he hoisted boxes out of the snow, heated it more.

Poppy leaned in. "How was your trip next door today? Is a certain bookstore proprietor the source of the rosy glow in your cheek?"

"Shhh." The last thing Tabitha needed was for other customers to hear about her crush on Sam, one that grew more desperate every day. "It's not like we're alone in here."

"Yes, it is." Poppy shot a sour look in the direction of the only other customer currently in the shop. "Andrew Kingston doesn't count."

Uh, the gawky but cute lawyer totally counted. Especially since everyone knew Andrew and Sam were good friends. At least, Tabitha knew that they were shoveling buddies, although not everyone possessed that factoid. "Still, shh."

At that moment, the lawyer sniffled and pushed his glasses further up his nose, burying his face in the newspaper.

"He still reads the newspaper," Poppy whispered. "How quaint. Considering he's a viper of the most poisonous kind."

"You're going to have to forgive him eventually, you know."

"Not a chance. I can't imagine for the life of me why he keeps coming in here day after day when he knows I'm going to be here and that I can't stand the sight of his starched collars and his too-curly-for-his-own-good hair."

Surely the guy was hearing all of Poppy's slights. The newspaper rattled in answer, and then he folded it, tucked it under his arm, and left into the snowy day without even bothering to put on his coat.

"Whew." Poppy flicked an invisible crumb toward the exit. "Good riddance." She turned back to Tabitha. "Now, you walked in here in a big enough huff that I paused my Korean drama and came to chat. What's wrong? Did you see Sam Bartlett and he slighted you?"

"Not yet today." But yesterday, a lot. And there'd been a tingle. And he'd flashed her that great smile, making her go all swimmy inside. "Seriously, the only reason I go in the bookstore every day is for work. I have to keep checking."

"Checking him out, you mean?"

Ugh. Yes, but no. "Checking for the item I'm looking for." But Tabitha did want to know his story. What made him flirt but back away so often.

This was not the place to ask that question.

"Does he have *the item*?" Poppy looked back and forth as if they were in a spy movie set in the Cold War, not a cider shop in a small town that was merely cold.

"Not yet."

"But hope springs eternal, I see." Poppy winked. "Who is your client anyway? At least tell me what book it is. I can check my bookshelves."

Nuh-uh. "Can't say either of those things." She'd promised Mrs. Barnes.

"But isn't the clock ticking? It's almost Christmas. Aren't you on a deadline?"

"Very much." When things had gone badly in the search for it all autumn at those estate sales and during online search marathons, Tabitha had begged Mrs. Barnes to think of a different gift for her sister.

No, she'd replied. Again. *You know my sole request. Get me that book by Christmas. It's all I ask of you, Tabitha.*

It was all she asked. How could Tabitha let her down?

"A little hint?" Poppy just put her chin on her hand, as if it would oil Tabitha's jaw.

"Even though I'm going in circles at this point, I gave my word." To keep it confidential, and to keep trying.

"Which explains why you go see Sam Bartlett every single day. Like he could *save* you."

"Please." Tabitha did keep heading back to the local bookstore because it shared the book's name. Because they did share a name. As if somehow the shared name would make that book—*pop!*—magically appear at Sam's shop, even though there was exactly one copy extant in the world, according to Mrs. Barnes.

She dropped her head onto her arms folded on the table.

See? This was how far her logic had sunk! She'd landed in that Broadway musical *The Music Man*, where the crooked salesman is trying to use rhyme as logic to convince people their town has trouble—trouble with a capital T that rhymes with P that stands for pool tables.

Despite the depths she was plumbing everywhere, that book was nowhere to be found. Not in any online search of any bookstore on the continent—or beyond.

"You've got other things on your mind, so don't stress about the thimble for my niece. I'll just get her a gift certificate to one of those junk jewelry shops in the mall in Caldwell City." Poppy got up to wait on a new customer who'd come into the shop.

"No!" Tabitha called, bobbling her cider. "Not when you've thought of the perfect thing for her little shadow box. I will find it for you, I promise."

Again, with the promises. Why couldn't Tabitha help herself from making bold promises when there was no guarantee she could fulfill them?

I do know why. It's a good reason, but it shouldn't be pushing me this far.

Being able to enlist help would have made this whole thing go so much more smoothly. The confidentiality requirement baffled Tabitha. It was as if she thought someone else would beat Mrs. Barnes to the punch and snatch away that rare book the second it was known someone wanted it.

Poppy came back and sat down. "Poppy Peters, at your service. Listening ear, bringer of spiced fruit juice at any temperature you please. Let's talk about your love life."

No. It was too bleak, from start to finish. Fraught with simple misunderstandings that had morphed into complicated breakups and smashed hearts. "Next topic."

"Okay, then we'll talk about mine." Poppy's face broke into a broad, giddy grin. "You're surprised?"

"Yes, I mean—no. I mean, what's going on?"

"I need your help." Now Poppy finally did lower her voice. "There's someone who's been leaving me little things in my shop every day, and I want to reciprocate, but I don't know what to give in return. Can you help me?"

"This is new. Who is it? How long has it been going on?" Someone who left gifts secretly sounded like Tabitha's favorite kind of person. She bounced a little in her seat. "What kinds of little things are you finding, and why do you think they're gifts?"

Poppy launched into her story.

The presents were small, always exquisitely wrapped, and came with a card with her name on them written in a precise hand. They came almost every day, too, and she found them in cute places, like beside the napkin dispenser, or beneath an empty glass cloche on the croissant pedestal stand. "Once it was a pebble, and the card said it came from a pathway near the Colosseum in Rome. Another time, there was a perfectly preserved gingko leaf, pressed flat and laminated. I think it was a bookmark."

"A bookmark? Like, as in from a book-lover?" As in the bookstore owner next door might have given it to her? An irrational pang of jealousy shot through Tabitha.

"Like, as in the fact he somehow knows I'm forever burying my nose in a book—when I'm not watching Korean dramas. The gifts seem to be about me, not about him." Poppy explained she was learning Italian on a phone app and reminded Tabitha that she'd decorated The Cider Press all in yellow fall leaves earlier that year. "It's like he sees who I am at my very essence, but I don't even know who he is."

Hmm. "That will make giving an equally insightful gift difficult."

"Right?" Poppy sighed.

"Don't despair. I'm good at this. I'll think on it."

"Good. Now, back to *your* love life." Poppy grinned. "When you see him today, will you get the spark?"

If only she'd never told Poppy about the spark. "I don't know."

"Which means yes."

Said *spark* had ignited regularly, ever since Tabitha had first laid eyes on a younger Sam Bartlett when she came to Sugarplum Falls as a teenager and walked into his grandpa's general store, now renamed Angels Landing. Sam had been working there when she went in to buy a stack of mystery novels to keep her company over the summer while she stayed with Grandma.

Later that year, after Grandpa Lanny died, he'd delivered a Christmas tree to Grandma's house, setting it up for her without being asked to go the extra mile, instead of dumping it on the doorstep and dashing.

But the clincher came when Sam secretly shoveled Grandma's walk for her on a snowy morning at the crack of dawn, and Tabitha had peeked out from behind her bedroom curtains and seen him at work. He'd left without a word.

Sam Bartlett. A-Number One.

"Come on, Poppy. He's not interested." According to some of the Sugarplum Falls town's talkers, Sam didn't even date. Why would Tabitha, of all people, think she could change that?

"Don't you think it's time to change that?" Poppy's eyebrows went up and her chin went down, as if in challenge.

"Um …"

28

"Hey, Ms. Poppy Peters?" A boy stuck his head in the front door, thank goodness, and took the heat off Tabitha. "You're finally not busy." He came inside.

"Hey, Declan. What's up? You looking for odd jobs today?"

"Nope. Just acting as Mayor Lang's assistant." He handed Poppy a flier, and then passed one to Tabitha as well. "Glad I caught you, too, Ms. Townsend. You're both invited to put your names in the Santa hat at the Hot Cocoa Festival."

Ooh. Cool. "Is that a prize drawing?"

Declan just laughed and hauled his teenage joviality toward the door. "It might be." The door jingled and he was gone.

"Stop frowning, Poppy. What's the Santa hat?" Tabitha looked down. Oh, no. It was a matchmaking ploy. The last thing Tabitha had time for was dating a random guy. "I'm not doing it."

"You've been targeted already, Tab." Poppy folded it and stuck it in her apron pocket. "Once Mayor Lang gets you in her sights, there's really no escape."

***

Of all the bad luck! Tabitha put her Miata in reverse, hit the gas, and sure enough, the wheels did nothing but spin. Her car was wedged in a snowbank on the corner of Orchard Street and Apricot Avenue, still a good twenty-minute walk from Grandma's house.

Where were Prancer and Vixen to fly her little red sled out when she needed them?

If she walked to Grandma's house from here, found the shovel in the shed, and walked back, she might be able to dig herself out before midnight.

But it was snowing again, and she wasn't wearing the best hike-through-snow footwear. Plus, when she'd gone to Angels Landing to check for vintage holiday novels—which she more or less knew wouldn't be there, but Sam might—Sam hadn't been there after all. *Out reading,* his clerk Mrs. Milliken had claimed.

Reading!

Bending over the hood, Tabitha pointlessly pushed the car backward from the front end. Not even a fraction of an inch would it budge.

Down the highway all was dark. Yoo-hoo, Good Samaritan? Secret Santa? Anyone? No other cars or trucks had motored past in the last fifteen minutes since the black-ice incident that landed her up to her front axle in the white mire.

A truck came along and pulled up, its lights on bright, blinding her. Thanks a lot, pal.

"You need a winch?" A guy lighted from the truck, but the glare obscured him.

No, she was not a *wench,* thank you very much. "Excuse me?"

"I can pull you out of there, if you don't mind that I attach a winch to your back axle."

Winch. Right. She blinked a lot more times until the glare-blindness abated. "Sam?" Sam had come to her rescue? "Sure. Yeah, thanks." Her stomach tried out the moguls at the Frosty Ridge ski resort.

Sam took a walk around her car. "I see your kung fu is less strong today. Or the snowy road's is stronger. Is this a rear-wheel drive model?"

She didn't really know. "All I know is I'm not getting any traction."

"If it's rear-wheel drive, and I think this model year of Miata was, all we need is a little weight in the trunk and you'll be able to back out of there easily." He walked around to the back of his truck and returned, toting … a large box labeled *Christmas cookbooks.*

Eye roll. Of all things. "I see you brought salt for my wounds." She opened the trunk for him.

"Keep in mind, salt can be a great disinfectant. It has some antibacterial properties." He placed the box in her trunk, and the car's body lowered slightly on the axle. "Ultimately, it can be a healing balm."

"Maybe, but it hurts like the dickens up front." Poor Charles Dickens, always getting his name used as a synonym for pain. "Thanks for the payment, by the way. That wasn't part of the deal, but I appreciate it."

A lot.

Together they loaded three more boxes into her trunk, until the frame rode low on the wheels. "That should do it. Give it a whirl." He motioned for her to sit in the driver's seat. "I'll go push from the front."

He moved his truck well out of the way and then went around and placed his hands low on the hood of the car. Through her open window, she heard him count down. "One, two, three!"

She gunned the engine, and at the same time, he bent over and pushed her car, his neck veins straining but his face looking super masculine.

The wheels caught gravel, and yes! Out it sailed from its stuckness. Yes!

She put it in park but kept the motor running at a low *putt, putt, putt*. No sense losing the heater's help in this cold. "How can I thank you?"

"You could sell me some of those books you bought at the Lincolntown estate sale. You remember, the one with the extensive collection of Betty Boop jewelry."

"Oh, I remember." Another huge waste of time and money. "I took them to the dump."

"The dump!" Sam's eyes flew wide, as if she'd just told him she'd lost his puppy—which if she were still walking dogs she might do. "How—how—?"

"They all ended up having mold damage. Remember? That house had had a flooded basement."

Sam's shoulders fell and he exhaled. "Moldy books do not make good gifts."

"No. They do not. But you can have the ten boxes of books I bought out from under you at the Guyman estate up in Reindeer Crossing. No mold there."

"You don't need them after all?"

"Nope." She shrugged. "If you can use them …"

"I'll take them." He extended his hand to shake on it. "It's a pleasure doing business with you—this time."

"What is that supposed to mean?"

"It means, I'm not used to getting outsmarted in business deals."

Smarted. Ha. Laugh out loud at that idea. The last thing Tabitha was was smart. Ask any of her teachers. Ask Dad and Pamela. "Sorry about the bidding wars. I've been pretty focused on helping a Twelve Days client by collecting books all autumn long."

31

"Except for cookbooks. Which only crazy people collect."

"See? You get it."

"We get each other."

They did? Ooh, wouldn't that be nice. Tabitha found herself leaning toward him. The steam of their exhalations mingled in the glow of his truck's headlights. "I'm glad we could help each other out." It hardly seemed like enough thanks to give him those books, after the snow rescue. "I should buy you a drink at The Cider Press or something to thank you for this."

"I'd like that," he said. "It's a date."

A date? She hadn't meant it to be a date, just a thank you. But if Sam Bartlett was counting it as a date ... A thousand Sam Sparks prickled through her. "Good. I'll stop by."

"I know you will." His eye glinted again—and her heart squeeze-pounded. Was this Sam-induced, or was this a medical emergency?

"I always do," she managed, despite the cardio workout she was enduring. "But when I come into the shop, do me a favor: don't direct me to your cookbook section."

"Deal." From her trunk, he unloaded the first box of books, and she got the next. "But I owe you the thanks. I love all these European cookbooks."

"Because you like those puddings the English people light on fire?" Like he'd lit her on fire with his handshake the other day at the storage unit?

"Not really, but I appreciate what you did for my store just the same."

It was like he'd read her mind about the handshake memory. He slipped off his glove and offered her his hand to shake. She took hers off as well, the skin of their palms making contact.

Talk about cardio workouts. The spark parade resumed, venturing into fireworks-on-the-driveway zone. He didn't let go, either, and his gaze made a slow stroll around her face, blinking now and then, studying her like she was a puzzle to be solved or a map to memorize.

"See you tomorrow?" he said.

"Uh, huh," she managed, and then kind of floated to her car on the electromagnetic field of levitation he'd activated in her.

Back at Grandma's house, she parked in the garage, when a text sounded.

Please let it be from Sam. But it wasn't. And it wasn't Mrs. Barnes, either. Instead it was from Mayor Lang.

Lisa Lang here. I keep hearing great things about Twelve Days! How can I support it?

Aw, how sweet. Tabitha fired off a response. *How kind! Anyone you may know of who needs a personal shopper for gifts this season, I can help. I can locate hard-to-find items a client already has in mind, or else I specialize in identifying the perfect gift for the perplexed or overwhelmed giver.*

Send. Uh-oh. She'd pressed that button before she thought through the repercussions. She hit send before remembering the flier—or the *hat.*

I'm in! Mayor Lang fired back. *You're hired. I need gifts for everyone on the mayoral staff. Can you have them by the first Saturday in December? The night of the Hot Cocoa Festival?*

Absolutely, Tabitha could. They exchanged email addresses, and Mayor Lang promised to send a list of names, ages, and hobbies of everyone on her staff.

This week was finally looking up! She shot a thank-you text to Mayor Lang.

I appreciate your business. If there's anything I can do to help you or the town of Sugarplum Falls in other ways, let me know.

It really was generous. Tabitha shouldn't be suspicious of the mayor's motives. That flier thing was probably just a coincidence. Declan had gone into The Cider Press to tap Poppy for it, and Tabitha had just been incidentally nearby. Declan was an opportunist, and chances were Mayor Lang paid him by the flier.

Tabitha headed inside.

"Grandma?"

Grandma was in the living room talking on the phone, but she smiled and held up a finger and mouthed *one second.*

Tabitha hung up her coat and came back to the comforting sofa, where she plopped down beside Grandma. The call was still going, so Tabitha pulled her favorite item from the shelf beneath the coffee table and thumbed through the familiar pages. *Mom. Mom holding me when I was a newborn. Mom and*

Dad before things got bad. Mom smiling by the Christmas tree. Mom and Grandma laughing. Grandpa Lanny throwing me in the air while Mom looks on in horror. Me in a little Santa pajama set squished onto this very couch in this very room. So many memories in this house, but all of them saved only in this book, never to be relived with Mom.

Sigh. She closed it and stuffed it back in its place as Grandma signed off.

"It's great to speak with old friends. That was Della Ruskin, my best friend who I haven't seen in ages." Grandma didn't wait for an answer. "If she can get time away from watching her great-grandkids, she's coming to town sometime this holiday. She says she will bring me a plate of caramels. She makes the best caramels."

"Caramels are delicious at Christmastime."

"Della's are the best." Grandma sighed. "She only had a minute to talk, so I didn't get all her details, not even where she's living nowadays." Grandma shook her head, as if memories were piling up. "Oh, Della. She's had a few hard knocks, but to hear her talk now, you'd never know it. Life's good sooner or later, you know? How's your work going?"

Neat that Grandma could say so, despite the love of her life having passed away a decade ago. She lived life well. "Other than a couple of bumps"— enormous, Himalayan-sized bumps—"pretty well. I think I picked up a new client today." The mayor counted, right? Nothing specific yet, but Lisa Lang didn't seem like the type to promise and renege.

"Oh?"

Just as she was about to explain the good news to Grandma, Mayor Lang's number appeared on the screen, a live phone call.

Grandma got a call, too, and excused herself, saying something about either pinochle or pickle ball. So many clubs.

"Tabitha! I'm so glad you offered to help me out. Yes, as a matter of fact, there's something huge you can do for me in return. You've heard of the Santa hat, of course."

"Sure. It's a town classic." Horror classic. Better suited for Halloween than Christmas. A dark foreboding cloud hovered overhead.

"I know what you're thinking. Oh, no. Not the Santa hat. Mayor Lang's public matchmaking event, the terror of every single person in Sugarplum Falls. But it's really just for fun. I can count on you, I'm sure. Bye, now."

A gurgle rose in Tabitha's throat. Wasn't this how innocents got entrapped by the mafia?

"Wait! Can I have some time to think about it?" Eventually Tabitha would be forced to say yes, but she needed time to let it seep in. "Can I get back to you in the morning?"

"Of course, dear. But no lame excuses."

"Just for clarity, what would constitute a lame excuse?" Tabitha gave a hopeless chuckle. "Surgery? A funeral?" Her own, for instance? Really, on some levels she'd rather die than be fixed up on a date in a public square in front of everyone in the whole town.

"Call me in the morning with your decision. But I really think we can help one another out, darling."

If being publicly humiliated was how the mayor defined help, sure. That was spot-on.

Chapter 5

Sam

Sam arranged and cleared shelves, collapsing five other sections of book offerings to create a whole new space on the front shelving for what they were calling *The Inglewood Collection* of holiday cookbooks.

"Some of these books are really rare." Mrs. Milliken sorted through the fifth box, inputting the ISBNs to the system, as well as prices. "I'm seeing them on online booksellers' sites for big dollars here and there. How much did you say you ended up paying for the lot?"

He hadn't said. "Should we make a designated area for the rarest books? Or should we arrange them by topic or author?"

The front bells jingled. Sam's heart hiccuped.

Could it be Tabitha? This was the usual time of day when she stopped in. He tucked in his shirt in the back a little tighter.

"Hi"—he rounded the corner—"Andrew." His snow-shoveling compadre. "You missed our workout this morning."

"Last minute court briefs to file."

"You missed out." Sam placed a few books on the shelf. "You looking for something in particular?"

"You got anything really small?"

"As in, tiny books?" Sam took Andrew to the front counter. "Who's this for?"

Andrew jerked his head in the direction of the wall. Whatever that meant. "Let's just say it's not one of *The Others.*"

Ah. Meaning the kind of women who usually hunted down Andrew for his Kingston last name. One in particular had been notorious, but he lumped them together under the heading of *The Deep-fakes.*

"How's this?" Sam held up a bookmark. "Small enough?"

"It'll do." Andrew handed him some cash. "You? Got anyone to buy gifts for this year? Staying clear of *The Deep-fakes* in your own world?"

"Always."

Andrew scoffed. "We both know *that's* not true."

Fine. There'd been quite a few scheming women who'd tried to get their hooks into Sam over the years. Women who'd taken a look at his thriving bookstore and his ostensibly *single* status and attempted to fake their way into his life. Elise, for one. Fakest faker of all. A deep-fake. He'd almost not seen through her. Andrew had fallen victim to one of those himself. They stung like a Portuguese Man-o-War. But Sam wasn't falling for them anymore.

He was keeping his heart under lock and key. With memories of Adelaide as guard.

Another ring of the bell, and in walked the last person he wanted to see.

"Mayor Lang."

"Just the man I wanted to see." She gave him her firm handshake, albeit with mittens. "What's the verdict? Are you in the hat?"

Right to the point. "I'd like to help you out, but I may go ahead and ask someone myself."

"Is that so?" Lisa's eyes lit up like Mrs. Milliken's, over by the Christmas tree near the entrance. In fact, Mrs. M looked like she might explode with a mixture of curiosity and joy. "As much as I am dying to know, I won't ask who. Now, promise me you'll be in the hat as a last resort, though."

Mrs. Milliken sidled up to him. "Hi, Lisa. He promises." Turning to him, Grace Milliken mouthed *You're dating!*

Mayor Lang beamed. "Thanks, Mrs. Milliken. It's good to have you on my team."

"I'm the head coach of the get-Sam-on-a-date team, in case you're wondering."

Blimey. Everyone was transparently out to get him. No paranoia required.

If she were here, Adelaide would have something to say to these women—but what? And what would she say to Sam about dating and moving on? Probably something about *writing your own story.*

The bigger question was what would Adelaide think if she knew Tabitha

Townsend, a scattered but pretty redhead, was getting a few mentions in the story of Sam's current life?

"Talk all you want, ladies. I'm making my own decisions." Sam left to go shelve cookbooks, while the interfering women took their conversation elsewhere, leaving him in semi-peace. Wow, Tabitha hadn't been kidding about there being an abundance of books on mincemeat. Pretty much every chef in Sugarplum Falls and the surrounding towns could own a book on the topic from this stack and there would still be dozens to spare.

George rounded the corner. "What are you planning to do with these?" He held a half-empty box from yesterday. "Far as I can tell, they're not cookbooks at all."

Sam peered over the side of the box. An odd assortment cluttered its depths.

"That one from this box was special to you, I know."

Sure was. Sam had left for part of the day to read it, and he'd brought it with him to work today in case he could snatch more time to look at it again. "I waited to find it a long time, you know. Read the whole thing last night." He'd mentally rhapsodize about that later.

"Seems to me, this other one might be special to someone else." George extracted a photo album filled with family pictures.

"Do you know this family?"

"Nope, but that's not my strength." Mr. Milliken shoved it away. "Maybe Gracie will know. She's better with faces."

But Mrs. Milliken didn't recognize anyone, either, when she looked a few minutes later. "We moved here forty years back, but these are from before that time."

As to timeframe of when they were taken, the pink aluminum tree was a dead giveaway. Nobody had used those since the *A Charlie Brown Christmas* special on TV had condemned metal trees to *Rudolph the Red-Nosed Reindeer*'s Island of Misfit Toys fifty-some years ago.

"It's a shame." Mrs. Milliken tsked. "Some of these photos are precious. I mean, yearly pictures of Christmas Eve family pageants and Christmas morning joys of children and adults? I can't imagine someone wanting to throw this out. We should try to find the family."

"I'll have to do some research." But how? It wasn't like a bookshop owner had access to facial recognition software or anything. Maybe in the new year if he had time. Someone had been without this book for decades. Another few months wouldn't make any significant difference.

"Just think what a blessed Christmas present for the owner." Mrs. Milliken sighed, filling the air with guilt-inducing wistfulness.

But no. He was swamped. And he still hadn't gotten a solid yes for his author event this Christmas eve. "We'll be sure to get it to the family by next Christmas." After he'd had a year to let it come to the top of his priority list. The grandfather clock in the front chimed the hour.

Mrs. Milliken went to the back room, and George helped a customer who wanted to chat about George's role as mayor of Sugarplum Falls in the town Christmas play. The store was even more swamped than usual for this time of day—except for one glaring exception.

Where was Tabitha? It was past her usual time to come in and ask about her vintage holiday novel. Well, today, at last, he would have something to show her!

Naturally, *Angels Landing* wouldn't mean anything to her. Too obscure. The book wasn't famous like *A Christmas Carol,* or the kid-classic *The Best Christmas Pageant Ever,* or even like the more contemporary *Skipping Christmas.* However, if she was looking for a gripping story of triumph of the human spirit in a holiday setting, she really ought to have a knowledge of the Ed Garnet masterpiece.

And he certainly couldn't allow her to buy it, but at least they could discuss it.

Maybe over dinner. Or a late evening after the Hot Cocoa Festival. Yeah. They'd have a late-night literary discussion, too. Why not?

"So, Sam. What are you going to do with this?" Grace reappeared with his copy of *Angels Landing.* "Hope you don't mind I swiped it off your desk. George told me how precious it is to you. I say it deserves a place of honor, seeing as how it's the same name as your bookstore. I'm guessing that's not a coincidence."

Sam took the book from her, gently lifting the cover and shutting it again. "Finding it again is like meeting an old friend."

"I feel that way every time I re-read 'The Gift of the Magi.'" She offered a swoony sigh. "Sacrifice, true love, an offering from the deepest place in the heart. Now *that's* the meaning of Christmas."

Exactly the reasons he loved *Angels Landing*. "Should I display it?"

"I'm on it!" She snagged it from his hands and rushed to the back room muttering something about spun glass and angel hair and twinkle lights. And a music stand. And spray paint. "I'll give it its due honor."

The front doorbell jingled. Sam's head instinctively snapped that direction, but Mr. Milliken had beat him to the punch. "Can I help you, Miss Townsend?"

Sam's fingertips tingled.

"Um, sure." Her smile was almost audible. "But I'll bet you know by now what I'm going to ask."

"We certainly do. Yes, indeed. In fact, there's a lot of great new inventory in vintage books just now. Heh-heh."

Uh-oh. George was going to spill the beans about *Angels Landing!* Sam rushed to his side to shush him. No matter what Sam had envisioned a few moments ago about sharing the book with Tabitha privately, he'd changed his mind. No one should know about the big acquisition before Mrs. Milliken made her grand unveiling. It wouldn't be fair to her.

"He's right," Sam said, placing an arm over George's shoulder and shooting him a *let me handle this* look. "Would you like to check out our broad new selection of rice pudding recipe books? Some have raisins and cinnamon, while others do not."

"Yes to cinnamon, no to raisins." A little smile toyed at the edge of her Hershey's Kiss of a mouth. "But yes to dried cranberries. Do you allow substitutions?"

"What happens in the privacy of your own batter bowls is your business."

Mr. Milliken ducked out from beneath Sam's arm to go help another customer with the silver handbell selection, leaving Sam with Tabitha's wide eyes. Had they been that green before?

"I have a different question for you today." She suddenly looked shy.

"Oh?" He shouldn't feel disappointed.

"How about going next door for a cup of hot cider sometime?"

"As in when?"

"How about now? I did promise to treat you to one as a thank you."

"And I said it's a date." *Date.* The word created a sizzling sensation in his fingertips and toes. "Sounds fine." Good. He could ask her the next question—out of earshot of his customers. "You okay with running the shop while I'm out, George?"

"If you're going with Tabitha Townsend, you can be gone all day. All week."

Oh, brother.

Next door, they perused the menu board. His date request was on the tip of his tongue, but he was out of practice. Didn't there need to be a *moment* to ask someone out?

"I'll take the number three, Poppy."

"Sure thing. And I've got yours ready, Tab."

Tab, huh? Not just a first-name basis between Tabitha and Poppy, but a first-syllable basis. "You two must be close," he said as they sat down at a table near the front of the shop. Frost flowers painted themselves along the edges of the large plate-glass window.

"Poppy's my main friend here in Sugarplum Falls, besides Grandma Honeycutt. We've known each other since I used to come in the summers and for holidays as a kid."

Tabitha had been around Sugarplum Falls? Sam should've noticed.

Poppy brought their drinks.

"I'm making a little headway on our secret admirer project," Tabitha said, accepting her beverage, warming her hands around it. "You'll have to let me know what you think."

"Deal." Poppy smiled.

Secret admirer, huh? Who did Poppy admire? Or was it Tabitha? A sizzle of jealousy snaked through him. He squelched it.

"You two have a good visit." Poppy gave an exaggerated wink over her shoulder as she left. This town! Was everyone in it an amateur matchmaker? Emphasis on amateur.

Tabitha's hands wrapped around her cup. "Forgive her. She's got an imaginative streak."

"Lots of people in Sugarplum Falls seem to." Sam sipped his drink and burned a spot at the front of his tongue. "Delicious, if a bit too—ouch." He pushed it back and took off the lid to let the near-boiling mixture cool.

"It's not always *this* searingly hot." Tabitha sent a smirk toward the register. "I think we have a *helper* back in the kitchen who wants us to take our time."

Sam's gaze shot to where Poppy was standing. She looked at the ceiling guiltily and ducked behind the counter immediately.

"So"—he lowered his voice—"now that we're out of range of the multiple secret-spy cameras lurking all around my bookstore keeping track of everyone's book conversations, can you safely tell me what book you're looking for?"

She clouded.

"Just nod if I'm on the right track. A first edition Dickens? A copy of Tolkien's Christmas book? Am I getting warm?"

She shook her head emphatically no. "If I told you, I'd be breaching a confidence."

"You'd have to kill me. I get it."

"No, my client would kill *me*. I don't think you want blood on your hands like that."

Fine. "Client, huh? Twelve Days, right? Good name."

"Personal shopper for all your holiday shopping needs."

"Clear something up for me, though. Haven't we entered the age where if someone wants to shop without leaving home, they can? No surrogates required."

"Not everyone can, though. Some people don't have the time, and others get mental blocks when it comes to gifts. Think about it, though: you own a store. You've seen someone experience the thrill of finding the perfect gift for someone they love." When he nodded she went on. "That's my goal, all day

42

every day. Helping others pinpoint what will convey that feeling. It'll sound cheesy, but it's my passion."

Passion, huh? "So you parlayed it into a business."

She looked at the table. "Well, let's say my choices narrowed, and it became clear this was my path."

"Oh?" There was more to this story. Sam didn't prod, exactly. He sipped his drink. "Tell me about it."

Tabitha tilted her head. "You actually want to know about this?"

"Sure, but only if you want to tell me." He downplayed his curiosity, which for some reason was dialed to high. "If you're comfortable."

For a second, she considered. Then she spoke. "I don't have the cleanest employment history. Somehow, things get away from me. I guess I'm prone to making promises I sincerely mean to keep but then can't. For valid reasons. But anyway, a few years ago, after I left my last retail job under a cloud of frustration, I realized I'd better just work for myself."

"Okay." Sam wasn't exactly suited to working for others himself. Not for the same reasons, but still. "You started Twelve Days."

"Nope. I started Classy Closets." She sighed heavily. "A closet organization service." She winced. "Not a great fit for someone who doesn't excel at tidiness. I don't know what I was thinking."

"So, you started Twelve Days."

"Again, no." She pressed the center of her forehead and shut her eyes. "Self-awareness isn't my thing, so I started Peppy Pups, a dog-walking service—which required me to keep a complex schedule, including not scheduling large, lazy, bad-tempered dogs and small yappy, energetic dogs for the same walk."

"Not a good fit?"

"See? You know me already."

Actually, yeah. A better picture of her was coming into focus—of an energetic, disorganized—but determined—woman. "What next? File-drawer clean-outs for hoarders?"

A laugh puffed from between her lips. "If I'd thought of that next, I'm sure I would have tried it, but no. Next came Twelve Days. It took lots of self-reflection and painful honesty, but I finally honed in on my weaknesses and strengths. Shopping? A strength! Figuring out what someone's aching heart could receive that would soothe it—easy! Gifts aren't everyone's so-called love language, but for people who feel most *seen* when they receive the perfect present, I'm ... well, I've got that covered. Thus, Twelve Days."

Slowly, Sam nodded. "Love language." He'd heard of that theory a long time ago. "So, are gifts *your* love language?"

Tabitha toyed with the lid of her cider cup. "I don't know for sure. What would yours be?"

"What are my choices?"

She listed them, with a little stumbling along the way. "Gifts, time, service, words of affirmation, physical touch."

The last one felt like an arrow. *I haven't experienced that in a while.* "I ... don't know either."

"I think there's an online test. Maybe we should take it."

"Together?" he asked. "Sure. That'd be fun." Fun! Sam Bartlett wasn't into fun. He was into reading near the fire. Steady evenings of quiet. Polite solitude. *Or am I?* It might be what he was used to, the only option he'd allowed himself for a long time.

Adelaide would forgive him, right? It wasn't disloyalty or forgetting Adelaide to spend an evening or two with someone he knew from work. A little fun—she'd want him to find that. To live a little, even if she couldn't herself.

Sam steeled his nerves and swallowed hard. "Tabitha? Would you be my date for the Hot Cocoa Festival?"

Chapter 6

Tabitha

"Really? With you?" Christmas had come early. *Getting asked on dates with Sam Bartlett is my love language.* "I'd love that."

He exhaled, as if he'd assumed there was a chance she'd say no.

Never. Not ever. Never ever. If all it took to get Sam to notice her was to let him have all the books in the estate sale, she would have done it months ago.

Her eyes strayed to Sam's mouth. Clean-shaven, the outline of his upper lip was defined. Tempting-looking. Dates could lead to kisses, right? Mmm.

The clock on the wall struck the hour, snapping her back to reality—one where she'd just blabbed all her shortcomings to the one person she wanted to impress. They'd been talking for an hour already? Time flew when she was with Sam. "Thanks for listening to my whole … you know. I had a good time."

"Yeah," he said, blinking as if just coming back from a long trip into his mind. "Yeah, I'd better get back to the store. Mrs. Milliken is creating a special display and she'll want feedback."

"Like a front window for the holidays?"

"Come to think of it, yeah. She'll probably be using the front window." The smile came again. "Thanks for the date."

Date. A prickling of magic filled the air at that word. Or maybe it felt as if something big was about to happen. "I'll walk you back." She stood along with him. "It's such a long way, and I wouldn't want you to have to make the trek alone."

"All twenty paces of it would leave me hopelessly bereft of companionship," he said as they headed out into the cold. "Hey, I was going to tell you. I found something that wasn't a cookbook in that stash of stuff. Unfortunately, I can't just give it to you, since it's really personal."

"Oh? Is it a journal, or something?"

"No, it's a random photo album. Lots of family pictures from Christmas mornings decades ago."

"Really? Whose family is it?" Tabitha's heart twisted. If she ever lost her photo album of Christmas morning with Mom, it would be … *It'd be like Mom never existed.* Sure, she had the journal, with its brief list of Mom's dreams for the woman Tabitha would become, and its infrequent entries other than at the end of her marriage, but otherwise, no memories.

Mom. I'm sorry about not living up to what you want for me yet. But I'm trying. If only she could talk to her, find out what Mom was really like. It was a big, blank spot in her life.

One that Pamela had never bothered attempting to fill.

So the photo album had to do for now.

"I have no idea, and neither does my staff."

"And you think I'll be able to identify them?"

"I'm telling you about the photo album because you ought to know that you weren't a hundred percent duped by that book trove. It wasn't exclusively recipes for mincemeat and strudel."

"Thanks. That actually does make me feel a little better." Like, a thousandth of a percent, but still. "What are you going to do with the album?" They stood on the sidewalk in front of Angels Landing, shifting their weight in the cold, but even though Tabitha should get back on the present-hunting job, she wasn't ready to relinquish his company yet. "If you actually do need help finding the owner, I might be good at that."

"That would be great." The smile came back. It almost buckled her knees.

They lingered in front of Angels Landing. Gracie Milliken was, indeed, working on the front window display. Yards of white tulle hung draped from the ceiling, and strands of twinkle lights stretched down in straight, golden lines. Her narrow frame blocked whatever main attraction she was working on, but beyond that, ensconced in the folds of the netting stood a stylized angel with wings, large and beautiful, white and gold. It was going to be an irresistible window, and perfect for the name of the store. Angelic.

"So, I guess I'll be back tomorrow." She drew a circle in the snow with

46

the toe of her boot. "You know me. I'm always going to check and see if you have any vinta—"

Gracie had just stepped aside from what she'd been working on, and revealed a large, white-painted dictionary stand, made of some kind of metal with scrollwork that featured gold-leaf details. But it wasn't the pretty furniture that yanked the words straight from Tabitha's mouth.

"Angels Landing?" she squeaked, her voice getting higher with each syllable as her throat constricted. After that, her vocal cords failed completely, and all she could do was flail a hand and point at the book on display.

Sam turned around, placed his hands on his hips, and bumped his elbow against Tabitha's side. "Ah, she made it look so nice." He knocked on the window, and when Mrs. Milliken turned around, he gave her a thumbs up and a big nod.

Gracie smiled and curtseyed.

Tabitha fought hyperventilation. Her hand went to her chest, and her other hand she planted atop her head, feeling around to find out if she'd lost it somewhere.

"It's a great book. I've been looking for it for years, actually."

"Wh—where did you finally find it?" Tabitha's voice was scratchy, pained. *Please don't say in the storage unit. Please!*

Chapter 7

Sam

Sam should give Mrs. Milliken a raise. There, in the front window display, she'd set off the novel to perfection, and now, as she placed the large gold-glitter-covered individual letters of the title on the white curtains behind the book, it only got better and better.

He gave her the thumbs up.

"Where did you get that book?" Tabitha's voice caught on a hiccup. Was she getting sick?

"The book on display? Oh, yeah. I mentioned the photo album, but I really should have led with the Ed Garnet book—since it's such an incredible treasure, and so personally meaningful to me. In fact, I should have called and thanked you immediately when I found it at the bottom of the last box."

"The last box," she murmured. "The last box. At the bottom."

"Are you all right?" he asked, changing his focus to her reflection in the window. "You look unwell." He turned toward her.

Her face was red, and she was shaking. "I'll—I'll buy it from you. Name your price."

Ah, no. "It's not for sale. Sorry."

Her eyes widened, and she grabbed her throat with one hand and her gut with the other. "I'm not playing, Sam. Name your price!"

Name his price? She had to be kidding. "I love when someone really values something I cherish. It's great that you can see what a gem that book is."

"Sell it to me, Sam?"

"I'm not selling the book." Not for any price. Not after spending so long never being able to read it. "This is my copy."

"Yours! But you just bought it yesterday."

True, but—"When I say *my* copy, I mean I read this very copy when I

48

was a kid. Come inside and I'll show you." He led her into the warm shop. "Mrs. Milliken? Can I take the book for a moment?"

"Are your hands clean?" Mrs. Milliken asked in her former-English-teacher voice. "The binding is white linen, you know."

"Bring it to my office?" He headed for the back room, and Tabitha followed, after a longing look at the display window. She probably needed to get back to her shopping job, what with Christmas so near. He was wasting her time—especially since he wasn't willing to part with this book, which she clearly wanted to buy.

She'll have to find some other vintage holiday novel.

Except … could *Angels Landing* be *the* vintage holiday novel she'd been looking for?

Not even possible. Almost no one else had even heard of the obscure book, except maybe George. In all Sam's years since turning Grandpa's general store into a bookshop, no one had ever once mentioned the connection with that book's title. Plus, *Angels Landing* could never be as precious to someone else as it was to Sam.

It had to be some other book she was looking for.

Mrs. Milliken stage whispered. "I'm so glad you're willing to share something so close to your heart with Tabitha."

When had subtlety died in this town? Maybe by edict of the Sugarplum Falls City Council it had been barred from entry at the city gates.

In his office, he flipped on the lights, plus the lamp on his desk and angled it onto the book.

"Was this the only copy in the box?" Tabitha's voice was squeaking again. Maybe he could make her some hot lemon juice or get her a cough drop or something. The kind with menthol helped, right?

"You and your obsession with vintage holiday novels." Sam laughed, holding the book out to her—but pausing. "Wait. Let me show you!" He flipped to the back cover, and opened it to reveal the library insert, including the date and his own name on the card. "I was either fourteen or fifteen." Quick math. "Fifteen. This book changed everything for me."

Tabitha's expression softened, and then hardened again. "But—" Her

49

shoulders fell, and she looked like Charlie Brown walking off a pitcher's mound in the rain. "I'm glad it changed your life." Forlorn. That was the word for it.

What on earth could she want this obscure but amazing book for? "I wish I had a second copy—one that didn't have my name inscribed right on it. I'd sell that to you in a heartbeat. In fact, I'd give it to you outright."

"It changed your life, you said, but I'm here to tell you, it needs to change someone else's."

"What are you talking about?"

She bit her lips, like she was holding back information. Again. But then her breathing sped up, and a look of a cornered animal filled her face. "I mean, I did place the highest bid at the auction." She wrung her hands. "Mr. Behr and Jordan Finch and Mrs. Forger and everyone else who was there yesterday will witness to that fact." She looked like she might cry.

"Whoa, whoa, there." He resisted the urge to call her Hidden Dragon. It didn't seem like the moment for it. "You're talking about witnesses, but you did walk away from the purchase. In fact, you sold it to me."

Her eyes were wild. "No witness saw you give me anything for it," she said as if it were a silver bullet to his arguments.

Slowly, and a little fearfully, Sam dug in his pocket, pulled out his wallet, and from it extracted a folded scrap of paper. He'd tucked it in the innermost compartment, maybe because she'd signed it personally, and because her handwriting had such a feminine flair, and he'd been charmed by those loops and curlicues. "The receipt. Remember?"

"Oh." The defeat returned. "And the digital transfer to my bank account." Her shoulders slumped. "Couldn't you just ... exercise mercy?"

He could, but if she wasn't going to tell him anything, he couldn't reasonably capitulate. "If you'd explain, I'd at least be able to weigh my options."

"I can't," she whispered, looking back and forth, her eyes getting watery. "Please, Sam. I'll give you back all the money from the auction. Repay you. And then some. You can have all ten of those non-moldy book boxes for free. I'll promise never to bid against you on a book auction again." Her voice grew tinny, like it was coming to his ears over a taut metal string. "If I could just have that one book."

Had it been any other book, her watery eyes would have done him in. "Tabitha, my store is named for this book. This very copy. It's etched on my heart." Even without the physical copy in his possession, he'd returned to the story time and again in his mind. He'd recounted it to Adelaide while she was in the hospital. He'd used its themes as a springboard for his own yet-unfinished novel, the one he'd been writing just for her. "Now that I have it again, I think I'm going to be able to restart working on a goal I'd lost my way from a long time ago."

Whoa. He hadn't intended to lay himself so bare before her.

"Is there any way you could take, I don't know, energy or strength from the book for a while, and then give it away again?"

Good question, but probably not. Certainly not yet. "I just found it again, Tabitha, after not seeing it for years."

"What if I told you there's someone who needs it more than you do?"

No one could feel as much connection to this very copy of this very book as Sam Bartlett did. "I'd highly doubt that possibility." Impossible.

"There is. I promise you."

"Who is it? A client of yours?"

She nodded, wincing. "But you didn't hear that from me."

So it was a confidential situation, and this really was the novel she'd been asking after all this time, no matter how much he'd tried to talk himself out of it.

She exhaled, dragging it out until her cheeks puffed. "It's a closely guarded secret. So closely guarded that I know next to nothing about it, except that I have to have that book."

"If I were to relent, there's no way I could get another copy, Tabitha." Especially not an equal copy. Not *the* copy that changed his life, and which still meant so much. "It's not replaceable."

Adelaide's soft features flashed into his mind's eye. *If you find it, you hang onto that book,* she'd said weakly, and Sam had replied, *I'm hanging onto you. Forever.* But he hadn't been able to.

51

"Do you think my client doesn't understand it's irreplaceable?" Her voice grew strident, desperate. "Please," she whispered so intensely it penetrated his cell structure.

But he couldn't let that get to him, and he shook his head. Parting with it would be like parting with Adelaide and her dream for him all over again.

Hurt filled her eyes, and she nodded, turned, and left.

Sam held the book in his arms, but for some reason, they felt empty instead of full.

Chapter 8

Tabitha

Tabitha's throat was tight and her fists were curled tighter as she stomped toward her car. Failure. Disaster. Despair! On several levels. Oh, why couldn't Sam just believe her when she said she needed that book?

Disaster, disaster, disaster. The footfalls of her boots on the sidewalk tapped out the chant in rhythm.

The book existed. Great!

Tabitha could never have it. Terrible!

No wonder Mrs. Barnes had been so adamant that her interest in that particular book be kept under tight wraps. Look at reality: the very first person who had laid his hands on it had kept it for his own.

Worst of all, Tabitha had had it in her *grasp*.

What was Mrs. Barnes going to say when she found out? Which she would. The book was going to be *on display* in the front window of the store!

She sat in her car and stared. Disappointment always made her ruminate over past failures, but one in particular rose up on its hind legs ready to scratch her eyes out today—the awful day that had started all this mess.

"Here, Soccer Ball. Come on!" Tabitha hollered toward the freeway overpass on the last exit into Darlington. "Come on out, sweetie."

Mrs. Barnes called, too. "Soccer Ball! Come!" to which the little black and white fur-ball of a puppy finally obeyed. It jumped into her arms, whimpering and licking her face. "You naughty boy. You should not have run away from the nice dog-walker." Despite calling Tabitha nice, Mrs. Barnes's glare looked like it could melt Tabitha's face off.

"I'm so sorry, Mrs. Barnes. When Soccer Ball's leash got tangled with Bruno's, I was just trying to loose him so that Bruno wouldn't ..." Eat the littler dog for lunch. The St. Bernard was a bad decision as a walking-duo for

the puppy. And if Tabitha hadn't been so disorganized, she wouldn't have paired them. Shouldn't have paired them. Ever.

"Good thing I had him chipped. Isn't that right Soccer Ball?" Mrs. Barnes nuzzled her dog, who was cheering up quickly, despite having been lost until sundown. "I hope you don't expect me to stay a regular customer."

No. "Of course not." Tabitha sighed. Today's incident was the third strike. "It'll probably make you feel safer for all dogs in Darlington to know that I'm giving up Peppy Pups for good."

Mrs. Barnes mashed her lips into a satisfied smirk. "Wise. What will you do next?"

Why Tabitha chose to confide in Mrs. Barnes at that moment was a mystery, but it had changed everything else in her life. "If I had enough money, I'd start the business I was working toward opening—personal shopper." If Dad had been willing to loan the money, possibly using the tuition he'd offered if she'd stayed in college. But his disappointment in Tabitha's lack of educational interest locked up his financial support forever. "But I wouldn't start it here. I want to have my business in Sugarplum Falls."

Every iota of Mrs. Barnes's demeanor changed, almost in a rainbow of emotional hues. First, she looked bored, then mildly interested, then horrified for a brief moment, and then, at last, she cleared her throat and said, "Is that right? Personal shopper? And in what town did you say?"

Tabitha repeated herself, explaining briefly her business plan for Twelve Days, and how she'd always wished she could live full time in Sugarplum Falls with Grandma Honeycutt. Then, being a dimwit, she babbled on about her love of giving good gifts, of her near-super-powers of sleuthing out the perfect present, of her online shopping skills.

Mrs. Barnes was quiet for a very long time. To the point of Tabitha considering calling for a ride back home from the freeway overpass, near which they stood. Finally, however, Mrs. Barnes spoke. "I'm willing to overlook what happened with Soccer Ball today."

Tabitha's knees buckled, but she caught herself before falling at the woman's feet. "You'd forgive me?"

"In fact, I'd be willing to help you get your business down there off the

ground."

Wow, she really did think Tabitha should get out of the dog-walking business if she was willing to pay for Tabitha to leave town. "Are you being serious?"

"As serious as can be." Mrs. Barnes walked to the car and stuffed Soccer Ball inside, and at the same time pulled out her checkbook, in which she began scribbling. "Here." She tore out the paper and handed it to Tabitha. "That should get you started."

Tabitha stared at the figure on the amount line. "Mrs. Barnes!" It certainly would get her started. It would pay for a website, business cards, moving expenses, plus some advertising. "This is so generous. Why—how—?"

"Why? Because there's a difficult-to-find gift I need."

"I'm your girl!" Tabitha nearly jumped up and down. This was happening. Really, truly. "Anything. I can get it!"

"I do believe that—and that you're the one person on this earth who can."

In that second, a shiver ran down Tabitha's spine, a shiver that confirmed Mrs. Barnes's words. "I'll do my very best. I'll get the word out this very afternoon. What's the gift?"

"Just a minute!" Mrs. Barnes pulled the check out of Tabitha's hands. "You will most certainly not get the word out." Then, she expressed in no uncertain terms the dire need for secrecy. "Not a word. Not to family, not to a friend, certainly not to a single citizen of Sugarplum Falls. Do I have your word?"

Tabitha gave her word. "Can you tell me the name of the book?"

Mrs. Barnes gave the book's name and title. "And everything inside me tells me it's in Sugarplum Falls. Search every nook and cranny of that town and the surrounding areas. Get the book, and you can keep this money. If not, it's a loan you'll have to repay on Christmas Eve."

"Understood. And thank you!"

Soccer Ball yapped from the back seat, and Mrs. Winnie Barnes handed Tabitha the check.

Taking the check had been a mistake, if today proved anything. However, without Mrs. Barnes, Tabitha couldn't even have begun her dream business, couldn't have moved to Sugarplum Falls.

If I can't get that book, I'll have to pay Mrs. Barnes back all that money. To do that, I'll have to move back to Darlington. I'll have to leave Grandma and the house and Mom's memories. Everything. I'll have to get a real job.

Real jobs and Tabitha didn't mix.

At home, she sat on a barstool at the kitchen island's harvest gold Formica and pulled an entire tray of frosted sugar cookies in front of her and began fog-eating them, one after another, nom-nom-nom.

First, there'd been that jarring photo album discussion with Sam. Lost and found—but found by the wrong person. Needless panic had shot through Tabitha's veins. Pointless. It wasn't like *she'd* lost her lone visual connection to Mom. But the mere thought of someone else going through that potential trauma had sent her into heart palpitations.

Then, the whole *There's the book I need!* elation instantly dashed on the rocks.

The date to The Cider Press had been more like a horrible amusement park ride she couldn't get off.

"Hello, Tabby." Grandma padded across the brown moss linoleum of the kitchen in her velour track suit. "I see you found the cookies."

"Armrmrm." Tabitha tried to comment, but she had to swallow first. "They're extra good. Lots of cardamom. Are they from Sugarbabies?" Mrs. Toledo at the bakery always said she relied heavily on Collette Honeycutt's patronage. Grandma called herself *a patron of the arts—the culinary arts*, and did none of her own baking, but was assigned to take refreshments to several social functions a month.

"No, no. I bartered for them with Mona. She baked those for me, and I put all the ribbon on her Christmas tree. She can never get the grosgrain to twirl just right, she says—which is so crazy, since of all the decorating things it's the simplest."

True enough. "Don't you just hold the spool flat and not twist it at all while you pull downward?"

"See? You know it's that simple. I feel bad taking cookies in exchange

56

for such an easy fix." Grandma nibbled the edge of a cookie. She hardly ever ate a whole one herself, which was probably how she stayed so trim in her sixties. "By the way, speaking of Sugarbabies, I saw Mrs. Toledo at pickle ball, and she said her mother-in-law loved the Christmas present. The electric teapot was perfect, and she'd only read one of the books you chose."

"That's nice to hear." Cold comfort, since Twelve Days was officially on its last gasp. "I'd hoped I hadn't given her all duplicates."

"And everyone on the team wanted to know if you could get them one of those amazing cutting boards. You know, the kind with the laser-engraved recipe in the original handwriting. That was ingenious. In fact, I think they'd like the one Mrs. Toledo gave her mother-in-law, with the original strawberry jam thumbprint cookie recipe, but of course that's personal. Anyway, they all want one for their own gifts. You're drumming up business left and right."

If only she could get her hands on the only gift that actually mattered. Which looked even more impossible than ever. She shoved another cookie in her mouth and washed it down with cold milk, barely bothering to chew.

"What's the matter, hon? You don't seem as pleased as I would expect."

When the man of her dreams, the man she'd been dying to date and who had recently finally noticed she was alive, destroyed everything else she'd been working for in life? No, not pleased at all. Horror-stricken, more like.

"Grandma, what do you do when you have bad news for someone but you know it will hurt them?" Tabitha's sentences came out crumbly.

"You mean, do you wait for the perfect time to break it to them, or do you just *rip* the Band-Aid off and give it to them at once? Band-Aid ripping has always been my preferred method." Grandma pantomimed it, making a *rrrrip!* sound. "See? All done."

Tabitha pictured Mrs. Barnes doing the same thing to Tabitha's head. "What about when it involves a person who ..." *Who I owe money to?* She didn't finish the sentence. Grandma didn't know about the financial infusion from Mrs. Barnes that had started Twelve Days, and she certainly didn't know about the book *Angels Landing.*

"You're exactly right. It depends, dear. Not every situation is the same." Grandma set her cookie down daintily. "Can you tell me about it? I might be able to help you weigh your options."

"I wish I could." Sincerely, deeply, truly.

"Then you have to fall back on your guiding principles." Grandma saluted with one hand and placed her other over her heart. "Truth, justice, and the American way."

What a nut. "Guiding principles. Okay." Slowly, she nodded, weighing them. "That does help, actually." Besides the values Grandma had noted, Tabitha could lean on Mom's list of what she'd dreamed for her baby girl to become.

Someone who gives good gifts.

Someone who keeps promises.

Someone who finds her own path in life.

There had been several more on Mom's list tucked into the back of her journal, but today these were relevant—and could serve as a guide.

Frankly, keeping her duty-bound promise to find that book for the woman who believed in Tabitha combined them all. Not only did she long to repay Mrs. Barnes in the sole way she'd asked, she'd also come through when everyone in Tabitha's immediate family had walked out on her—*here's looking at you, Dad*. Plus, Tabitha had promised to do whatever it took to get the book.

Promises made, promises kept. Those were guiding principles.

"Good." Grandma grinned. "Since I am already late to claim my seats for tonight's performance of the town Christmas play"—she pulled her jacket from its hook behind the door to the garage—"can we chat more later about it? I don't want to miss a second of Tom Kingston starring as Nicholas." Grandma raised and lowered her eyebrows a few times. "All the ladies in my pickle ball league insist it's a sight worth taking in."

"Nah, I think I've got it."

"Sweetie, I'm not remotely surprised." She reached across and squeezed Tabitha's hand and then headed out the door. "You've got a good head on your shoulders."

Tell that to Dad.

The time had come. Tabitha dug her phone out of her purse. There was only a small charge left on it, but those percentage points all belonged to one person. Tabitha dialed the dreaded number.

"Mrs. Barnes, there's been a development."

"By the tone of your voice, I take it you're not talking about a *good* development."

No, she was not. Tabitha explained the situation. She did not omit any portion of her culpability. "The problem is that no matter what amount of money I offer, the current owner refuses to sell the book."

Soccer Ball yapped in the background. Christmas music played, too. Tabitha heard it all because Mrs. Barnes remained silent long enough that Tabitha began to wonder whether the connection had dropped, or if Tabitha's phone's battery had died.

Wouldn't that just be the cherry on top of the unprofessional-ness sundae?

"I won't pretend this isn't serious." Mrs. Barnes heaved a tired sigh.

"Perhaps if you could tell me a reason you need the book, I think there's an outside chance the owner could be persuaded." That was stretching the truth, but he'd probably at least listen.

"No." Mrs. Barnes was not one to budge.

Tabitha searched her brain for any alternative solution. "Have you considered the possibility of contacting the author to see if he has a copy? Ed Garnet, right? From what I understand, the publisher sends the author a few copies to distribute to reviewers. That might have been the case when the book was published."

"No." At least this time she elaborated. "Ed Garnet does not have author copies. Ed Garnet currently possesses or knows the whereabouts of each remaining copy that was printed."

"You have the author's contact information?" That was good news! "If you'd like, I could make contact, ask again—anonymously."

A blurble-gurgle-snurff sounded through the phone. "You have at least located the book, and in all the world, I do still in my heart believe that you were the one person who could do that."

"But you still don't have it. If we asked, maybe the current owner would let you borrow it."

"Borrow it!" It was accompanied by a shriek that sounded as if it were the most preposterous suggestion in the world. "A bird not in the hand is not worth two when it belongs to someone else." Mrs. Barnes's tone went from stern to flat-out desperate. "This is vital to me. It's the one thing I need from you. And I need it this year. Please, don't give up."

It was the desperation that got to her. "I won't give up until the book is yours, Mrs. Barnes."

Chapter 9

Sam

After rereading a few passages just for fortitude, Sam replaced *Angels Landing* on the bookstand, careful not to disarrange any of the fluffs of fabric Mrs. Milliken had so artfully positioned, and then stumped back to his office.

In this mood, he could hardly meet customers.

"Hey, boss." George leaned against the doorframe a while later. "How'd your cider-sipping date with that pretty Townsend girl go? She's a looker. Pert and pretty. Maybe I should use one of those Western twangs to combine those into *perty*."

"It fits," Sam said, but without enthusiasm.

"Feisty, too." George was a walking thesaurus today. "I saw the way she dashed out of here with that pout on her lips. What did you say to her? Did you break your date with her to the Hot Cocoa Festival?"

"It's probably safe to assume my hot cocoa date with Tabitha is off." Whether or not it had officially been canceled.

"Disappointing."

"It's a crying shame, is what it is!" Mrs. Milliken pushed her way into Sam's office, her hands on her hips in some kind of fighting stance. "And I'm not talking about the broken date as the shame. I mean the disgraceful way you treated that girl."

Splutters formed behind Sam's lips. "What are you talking about? I was sympathy itself." Sort of. Probably. He hadn't given in when she'd pressured him, but otherwise, he'd been firm and considerate at the same time.

"Yes, your words were kind. However, when a woman is practically on her knees begging you for help, and you both refuse and offer no other solution, that's where the gentlemanliness ends and the caddishness begins."

"Mrs. Milliken. In all my life, you're the first person ever to use that term on me."

"Cad?" she scoffed. "If so, I'm guessing that's not because you haven't deserved it."

"Gracie!" George grabbed her by the arm. "What's eating you? Sam didn't do anything to Tabitha Townsend. She was being a stubborn mule, refused to answer his questions, and kept throwing temper tantrums in the back room. Do you really expect him to reward that kind of behavior?"

So they'd both been listening? "She didn't throw a temper tantrum. She just asked." Without making any solid arguments, but she'd at least been polite.

Mrs. Milliken's square shoulder-line rounded. "George, why do you have to …" She muttered for a moment. "Fine. That's probably all true."

"So I'm not a cad anymore?"

"I wouldn't go that far." Her mouth twisted to the side. "But you really could have been more compassionate. She was in real distress. She hasn't had the easiest life, from what I know. She's Collette Honeycutt's granddaughter, you know."

"Yeah." He'd somewhat known that. Collette Honeycutt's driveway was on his shoveling rounds. Did Tabitha live there, too? "And?"

Mrs. Milliken just shook her head, her tongue clicking against the side of her mouth. "Shame about Charmaine Honeycutt."

Okay, that was a mystery Sam would have to plumb the depths of later.

"I can accept that I could've been more compassionate. Fine. Give me a second."

He texted Tabitha. *I'll rack my brain. Maybe I can come up with a solution we can both live with.*

He showed Mrs. Milliken his phone screen. "How's that?"

He turned the screen back to himself, and a reply appeared from Tabitha. *So, you'd consider letting me have it? It's not off the table?*

Apparently the only solution she'd accept was the one he couldn't offer. *Sorry. That wasn't the direction I was going.*

Not at all. But he could at least try to contact the author again. It'd been a few years since he'd attempted it, with no result. But he could at least try.

I guess we're at an impasse. I guess you don't want to take me to the festival Saturday.

Sam hadn't said that. But, yeah. Tabitha wouldn't want to be stuck with him as her date with all the tension springing between them.

Maybe we'd better cancel? he responded.

If you think so.

He wasn't sure. Did they have to cancel? Probably. It'd be for the best.

Though she hadn't seen the replies, Mrs. Milliken frowned. "A solid C-minus for effort." Maybe she *had* seen the texts. "Mayor Lang is out there."

Mayor Lang? Not now. Not when he was busy earning failing grades and his gut felt it fully.

"She's not a patient woman, and I've already wasted a lot of her time standing here arguing with you. Do you want to come talk to her, or shall I run interference?"

Bless her! In a million years, Sam could never let Mrs. Milliken retire from Angels Landing. "You'd throw yourself on that sacrificial pyre?"

"Of course. Now, what do you want me to tell her about the hat?"

Ughhhhhh, the hat. "I guess I don't really have another choice right now."

Thus, on the first Saturday in December, Sam would be a slab of meat in the public market. But that wasn't the real kicker. The worst part was that Tabitha Townsend existed in this world, just inches from his side at certain points in the last few days, and he'd breathed her scent, and been the recipient of her heated looks and her gentle chiding and her knee-weakening smile.

And she now wanted him to go jump off a cliff.

Maybe it was better this way. Maybe? Ugh. If only he hadn't lost that typewriter key. *It could tell me what to do right now.*

But it was gone. So Sam had to go with his gut. And his gut said he should try to win Tabitha's favor back, book or no book, because she made him … feel something. And she was different. She intrigued him.

Fine. He was going for it.

Even if it meant putting his ego and his feelings on the line. Even if it meant letting a little bit of his shield down. Even if it meant she might personally drive him to and shove him off that cliff.

Chapter 10

Tabitha

"Did I even wear the right thing?" Tabitha alternately stepped one patent-leather Mary Jane-style shoe on top of the other, as if doing so would hide her candy-cane-striped stockings. If only she'd done her laundry and found a longer skirt! Her thighs were catching a lot more breezes than they were used to, even here in the indoor environment of the Sugarplum Falls Recreation Center gym.

"You look fine." Poppy forged ahead through the crowd of cheerily dressed cocoa drinkers. "Very festive. Do you love the decorations? I can't believe they made an entire night sky out of Christmas lights and indigo velvet. Mayor Lang gets my vote next year."

The room really could pass for the outdoors. With all the fresh-cut firs and spruces around, and the balsam and sage scents, it was like being in a forest in here. "She didn't accomplish this all herself, did she?"

"She had a committee," Poppy said. "Including yours truly. Shelby Forger, Don Rickert, and the other councilmen's spouses were on it, plus some other local business owners. The mayor knows how to lean on people to get her way."

Truer words ...

"As a matter of fact, I'm one of her victims." Tabitha mentioned the tragic name-in-the-hat circumstance, but she left out the part about trading favors with Mayor Lang, that she'd hire Tabitha as a shopper if Tabitha went in the hat.

For the past week, Tabitha had gathered and wrapped and tagged gifts for the mayor's office staff, awesome gifts that would doubtless win the day, but which also made Tabitha a good profit. Finally! That kind of a business contract didn't come along often. It had never come before in her other two businesses. Please say the staff could enjoy the choices Tabitha had made for them!

"I feel your pain. Mayor Lang roped me into this the same way. She lined up a Tuesday lunch club meeting at The Cider Press for every week next year. I couldn't refuse." Poppy lowered her voice. "You never told me what happened to your date with Sam for this shindig."

"I don't want to talk about it." Or to think it. Or think about her bigger struggle of tackling the Sam Bartlett and His Most Precious Possession problem.

"Then we're in it together. Coolio." Poppy held up a hand for a high five. Then she craned her neck, looking around. "Who all is here? I'm fine with pretty much anyone as my hat-line-up—other than that louse of a lawyer, Andrew Kingston." She snorted. "I'll just sing 'I Saw Mommy Kissing Santa Claus' and 'Santa Baby' in front of everyone if fate decrees. Mayor Lang can't make me into that much of a laughingstock."

"Singing? In front of people? What are you talking about?"

"Karaoke. You know. If you agreed to participate and then you flake out, you're doomed to the karaoke stage for the remainder of the night, and pretty soon everyone in the whole town hates you unless you sing like a meadowlark. And I don't."

Tabitha shuddered. She didn't sing like a meadowlark at all. More like a magpie.

"Worse, the only songs on the playlist of the machine are the songs everyone is tired of listening to on the radio by the day after Thanksgiving. You're in danger of getting half-eaten doughnuts chucked at you."

"Like the stocks in medieval times." Wow. "I'd probably get pelted after a single note."

"Don't worry. There's probably no one whose name is in that hat you'll even know, let alone have a bad history with."

A cute couple sang a flirtatious Christmas pop duet. on the stage. The girl looked like a Sutherland. Chelsea, maybe? And the guy was from the bank.

A tall figure loomed up in front of Tabitha. "Hello. Merry Christmas." He held two cups of hot cocoa and offered her one.

"Sam?" Tabitha gripped the hem of her sweater. Gah! This guy! "I didn't think you'd be here tonight." After canceling their date, he would have stayed away from her, right?

"Mayor's orders."

"She got you, too?" And after he ruined her life, she shouldn't have been talking civilly to him. But she couldn't help it. He tilted the cup back and forth at her. She accepted it but didn't sip.

"I'm afraid so. Did she bribe you?"

"More or less. She hired me to shop for her staff Christmas party. You?"

"Huh. Nice. I should have held out for more. She just manipulated me into promising I'd help since I benefit from the efforts of the Chamber of Commerce."

"Dang." And dang, he looked good, sipping from that cup, never unlocking his gaze from hers. It was electric, as was the easy flow of their conversation. He had some seriously strong kung fu when it came to sweeping away her annoyance at him. "Your kung fu was not strong."

"Yeah, Hidden Dragon. Remind me to take tips from you on dealing with the mayor."

"No negotiation tips from me. I'm usually terrible at making deals. I always end up shortchanged." As in her Classy Closets contract with that celebrity in Caldwell City. Ouch. Just the memory stung. "I can't believe I even own a business." And she might not for much longer, thanks to Sam. Frown, frown, frown. Because she'd have to dedicate all her profits from current clients to a fund to repay Mrs. Barnes.

That was the only other option if Tabitha intended to guard her integrity.

Sticking with my principles.

Sam didn't seem to notice her frowns. "From what I hear, you're winning Christmas for everyone. They have less stress shopping, and it's making their seasonal loads better, so I'm sure your business acumen is not nearly as bad as you make it sound."

No, it was worse. He hadn't heard details of her Peppy Pups debacle. "Trust me."

"I do," Sam said softly.

All of a sudden, the air was charged with electricity. He was looking at her like he wanted to please her. To make her understand his heart. Please let this mean there was a chance Sam could change his mind! Hope sprang as if on pogo-sticks all around in her chest.

He may soften!

A kid bustled past, jostling Tabitha's leg.

"Mac, stop it! Give me back my elf plushie!" A blonde girl chased the kid. Two parents bumped through apologizing and calling after the kids.

Unruffled, Sam sipped again from his Styrofoam cup. "Which cocoa are you voting for?"

"Not sure yet. What about you? Chosen a favorite yet?"

He gave her another once-over. "I usually go for the peppermint cocoa, but tonight the pumpkin spice had a little something extra." He sipped again, his eyes landing on Tabitha's—all deep and penetrating, as if he had something to communicate to her, but couldn't right now. The gaze decimated all her bad feelings toward him for a moment, leaving her just staring at the place where his lips met the Styrofoam. "The raspberry fudge brownie cocoa is a close second."

"Raspberry fudge brownie cocoa?" she repeated, stupidly, like she was a breathy teenager meeting her pop-star idol. "You make that sound really good."

Sam took a step closer. "It's luscious." He was less than a step away. His breath may have grazed her cheek. "I really wish there were two copies of that book. See you later."

He walked away, leaving her breathless, inert, and all numb and tingly inside.

"What. Just. Happened?" Poppy's mouth dangled open. "Who was that guy in the Sam Bartlett mask?" She turned to Tabitha. "In all my years knowing the guy, working next door to him, being *related* to him, I've never once seen him put on an act like that for a girl."

"An act?" So it wasn't sincere? All the tingles clocked out for the day. "Oh."

"No, no. Not like that." Poppy led her to a cocoa vendor. "I mean … like acting flirtatious. Sam Bartlett does *not* flirt."

Uh, Tabitha begged to differ. What about his charming banter with her about kung fu? And the way he'd locked eyes with her over cider? Those didn't count as flirtation? "He probably just doesn't do it when you're watching." Duh. Because, face it. The guy was definitely not out of practice. He had flirting skills enough to founder Tabitha's ship on his shoals.

"Trust me. That was unique." Poppy sipped from her cup and handed Tabitha one. "Come on. It's almost time for the hat thing. My only regret is that Kang Jin-Wook isn't one of the guys on offer tonight."

"Who?" Oh, right. The Korean drama star Poppy drooled over. "You don't even speak Korean." Tabitha sipped her cocoa. Mmm. The hazelnut was really good, too.

"Jin-Wook speaks some English. Did I tell you? My secret admirer left me another gift, though. A little replica of the N Seoul Tower, that Space Needle in Korea. It's so cute. I put it right next to my Colosseum pebble and my ginkgo leaf bookmark."

Tabitha really needed to figure out who this admirer was, so that she could peg the perfect gift for him from Poppy. Christmas was only days away now.

"Ladies and gents!" The mayor's voice boomed through the PA system. "Gather around, calling all who belong to the Order of the Santa Hat."

"That'd be you and me." Poppy moved them through the throngs. "Come on. Let's line up with the rest of the suckers."

At the raised platform at one end of the room, Mayor Lang presided over a jumbo Santa hat perched fur-side-up on the table. She waved various people toward her, lining the women up on one side of her, and the men on the other.

"Merry Christmas, folks." A knowing gleam lit her eye. "You're about to get the first gift of the season. Potential true love." There was a cackle next— right into the microphone. It bounced off the ceiling and the floor, seemingly not the least bit muted by the velvet fabric draped above to simulate the night sky.

Tabitha joined her sisters-in-suffering, about a dozen strong, and craned her neck to size up the potential male counterparts, but the lights shut off, and a disco ball at the center of the room reflected the only light beams—red and green for the theme, bless those rays' hearts.

I have rarely been so humiliated.

The DJ struck the holiday tunes, replacing it with that prelude of synthesizer music that always showed up as professional athletes take their places on the field of play. The audience clapped in rhythm.

"Ladies and gentlemen." The mayor affected a deathly serious tone, like those radio announcers when an asteroid is about to hit the earth. "We will now"—the clapping and music continued—"pair our couples using the hat!"

With echoes of Harry Potter and the hat that decided each student's destiny, Mayor Lang drew first from the women's side of the hat, and then from the men's, calling each name as though they'd each just been selected Miss America and the winner of the Powerball lottery.

The crowd cheered. Or was that jeered? Hard to tell with the deafening volume of the sports tension-music.

"Ugh! Andrew Kingston still hasn't been called," Poppy murmured beside Tabitha. "I swear, if he's …"

"Just because he was assigned to prosecute your speeding ticket, it doesn't mean he's A, out to get you, or B, your enemy. It's his job."

"Then he shouldn't have done it so well if he didn't want me to think he's a black-hearted villain for all eternity."

"But you yourself told me you were speeding. Twenty miles per hour over the limit." Criminal speeding, in other words. Plus, he and Sam were buddies, so how bad could Andrew be? They shoveled widows' snowy driveways, for heaven's sake.

"It's nothing but a speed trap. They only have it designated so low in that place to ensnare unsuspecting drivers who have places to be."

"Through a stop sign, Poppy."

"A detail!"

"He didn't pursue criminal charges. You only got the civil charges."

"They still cost me an arm, whether or not he left my leg intact."

Poppy would probably never forgive poor Andrew Kingston. When he

69

came in The Cider Press, Poppy let his drink get cold, or sometimes even threw a piece of ice in his cup just to make it lukewarm for him.

Heaven help Andrew Kingston if his name got drawn out of the hat at the same time as Poppy's.

"Poppy Peters!" Mayor Lang said. "Tonight your date will be the dashingly handsome attorney, Andrew Kingston!"

Poppy's fingernails dug into the back of Tabitha's hand.

"Good job stifling your scream of horror. You're already winning." Tabitha patted Poppy's hand, peeling back the digging fingers. "Now, go forth and earn your Tuesday lunch club meetings for a year."

Poppy slouched her way toward the unlucky lawyer. She'd better not ruin his night—since chances were, he was probably here against his will as much as Poppy. *I wonder what dirt Mayor Lang could have on Andrew Kingston to strong-arm him into putting himself in the meat market.*

Ugh. Speaking of guys putting themselves up for sale, down the long table, only a handful of guys remained. One of whom was … guess who.

Sam lifted his hand to wave when he caught her staring.

Her face flushed like it had been splashed with cocoa. She gave a wave back, but *please, don't let my date be Sam.*

However, the odds were against both Tabitha and Poppy tonight.

"Well, well, well," Mayor Lang chuckled like the Grinch at an unlocked door on Christmas Eve. "Our next couple is Tabitha Townsend and our town's very own eligible bachelor bookseller, Samson Bartlett. Don't forget to shop at Angels Landing for all your reading needs."

The crowd obliged with applause, but the pairings were getting old now, even for the onlookers. Could this night just end, already? As in *before* she started thinking Sam was the most charming man in the world again?

Okay, it was too late for that.

Then again, this pairing up might give her a chance to convince him to loosen his hold and rethink his dug-in heels about *Angels Landing.*

Chapter 11

Sam

Andrew Kingston hung back from his pairing with Poppy Peters long enough to rib Sam. "You and the redhead, huh?"

"You and Poppy." What else could he say to that?

"Just be careful of the out-of-town girls."

"Yeah, yeah." They'd been over that familiar ground. "She's more local than she seems." And not fake, unlike Andrew's bait-and-switch ex. "I've got my eyes open."

"Can't blame you, though. She's looking really festive tonight."

Sure enough, Tabitha's short dress and long stockings did ignite all kinds of celebratory feelings. But—where was she going?

Sam hustled to follow Tabitha as she peeled off from the line at the front of the room. He caught up to her near the beanbag toss of Rudolph's nose. "So, we ended up together tonight after all."

"Coincidence or fate?"

"Christmas magic." He made jazz hands at her, which earned a smile. Wow, she had a good smile. More of that, and maybe in the course of the night he could convince her to forgive him for refusing to hand over the book. "Here." He handed her three bean bags to toss through Rudolph's nose. She made two and missed one. "Not bad."

"Show me how it's done."

"Can do." His beanbag tossing skills were strong. All three went in.

"Winner winner. Do you get a prize?"

"Yup, he gets one." The kid manning the booth placed a Hershey's Kiss in Sam's open palm, where it whispered, *Kiss her, kiss her, kiss her!* through its aluminum foil wrapper.

Yikes. This was a canceled date, not a date. And she would not want him to kiss her, considering everything else going on between them. He shoved the

Kiss into Tabitha's hand. Did that count as kissing her? In some punster's world, probably it did.

"Actually," he said with a clear of his throat, "we win tonight by looking like we're having the best time ever, and by making Mayor Lang look like a genius for pairing us up."

"But the hat did the sorting, not Mayor Lang." Tabitha popped the chocolate into her mouth.

Sam shot her his best *you don't really believe that, do you?* look. "She's a woman with firm opinions about who should be dating whom in her town. Keep that in mind."

"No!" Tabitha's exclamation wafted past him scented with milk chocolate. "It's a sham?"

"The same level of sham as all the scripted dating shows on reality TV. Sham for the viewing public, at least. I wouldn't put it past her to use polling and focus groups to see which pairings the local crowd would want to see most."

For a second she looked appalled, but then she shook herself. "You're funning me. Just for that"—she slapped his bicep—"I'm going to beat you at every single one of these carnival games."

"Not a chance."

"First, I'm going to out-eat you at doughnuts on a string." She pulled him toward that booth. Sam handed the worker a ticket. The kid aimed a bored thumb toward the line of suspended doughnuts hanging on red and green curling ribbon from a festooned length of PVC pipe.

"Pick any doughnut you want. The first to eat it gets to take a fresh doughnut home." It sounded like the kid had said it ten million times in his life already, and one more repetition nearly did him in. "No hands."

"Excuse me, young man." Tabitha stepped toward him, batting her eyelashes.

He looked up from his phone and straightened both his drooping Santa hat and his shoulders as he perused her. *I mean, what red-blooded male wouldn't?*

"Can I answer a question for you, Miss Townsend?"

The skin bunched up at the back of Sam's neck. How did this twerp know Tabitha's name? Oh, right. They'd been announced in front of the crowd—and any red-blooded male worth his salt would have taken note of the woman in the short green dress and the sexy striped stockings.

"Can I choose my partner's doughnut?"

"Sure." The kid had one of those besotted baby deer looks on his face. "Totally."

"Okay, then. I pick that one." She pointed delicately at the lowest-hanging doughnut. "And that one is mine." She winked at the kid, who nodded in agreement as if he'd been hit by a blowgun dart tainted with one of those CIA prisoner-compliance poisons.

Hey, spy tactics should be off-limits! "You do not play fair, Tabitha."

"Hands behind your back, tall man." She pulled a smile with just one side of her mouth.

"I'm going to have to kneel to eat that, you know."

Her eyes flashed with mischief. "I really like doughnuts, and I want to win so I can take one home. What can I say?"

Sam liked to win, too. "Ready? Because I still think I'll win." There were a lot of ways to win. Some of them involved kneeling at the feet of a beautiful woman.

"Go!" she said.

Hands behind his back, Sam dropped to his knees and got in a bite before bumping the sticky pastry with his nose and getting glaze on his eyelashes. Above him, Tabitha had taken several small bites from the bottom of her doughnut, which wasn't swinging at all. Ah, so there was a strategy to this contest.

How was it that Tabitha always seemed to be a step ahead of him? She was challenging, and exciting, and—holy cow. He was almost right at eye level with the hem of her green skirt, right where the skin peeked out at the top of her red-and-white striped stockings.

The doughnut disappeared, as did the disco ball and its beams of light and all the crappy karaoke going on in the far corner of the room. The only thing that existed was that stripe of fair, smooth skin and Sam's need for it.

"Done!" Tabitha jumped up and down. She had half a doughnut in her mouth, but was pulling it in, and chewing it down. "I win!" she shouted through pastry. As she did her victory leap, that already-short skirt raised the tiniest bit, and the band of skin extended a wee bit wider.

No, I am definitely the winner here. He stood up and dusted off his pant legs. "Congratulations." He bowed in praise. "Your pastry-on-a-string kung fu is very strong."

"Sam, I hate to gloat—okay, I don't—but look at that sad result." She waved a finger at his partially nibbled carbohydrate blob. "Not a stellar effort."

"Trust me, I have no regrets." He cleared his throat, if not his mind's eye. "Where do you intend to defeat me next?" Literally and figuratively, he could add.

When did I last have fun? Not just read an entertaining book, but real fun? Easy. With Adelaide. *It's ... not bad.*

The evening progressed through five more booths: a ping-pong ball blown into a waiting cup and a prize claimed; a wheel of fortune where they each ended up winning a lump of coal—which was really just a hunk of black licorice; a ring-toss onto reindeer antlers for miniature candy bar prizes; a naughty or nice knock-down-the-stack game.

Tabitha won them all—and Sam won by watching her bubble over with giddiness at the triumphs. She really did bubble nicely.

"Can I tell you something, Sam?" She sighed heavily as they made the rounds through the cocoa vendor booths. "You're very difficult to dislike."

"Well, from that I take it you're schooling yourself in *dislike Sam* courses, and—"

"Failing. I'm getting a D-minus."

Hmm. "Not an F, then?" He'd much rather she receive an F in that class.

"The fact remains you are breaking my heart by keeping that book."

"Heartbreak? Really?" Did she mean that, or was she being playful? Dark humor often revealed truth. And pain.

"Never mind. Maybe later." She slipped away from him. "So, about that book of yours. Any chance you'd loan it out, maybe lease it?"

He'd waited too long to own it. In fact, he'd inserted it in the store's safe nightly, rather than leave it in the window. "New topic."

"Fine. No elephant in the room for now." She stopped in front of a cocoa booth, accepting a cup and handing him one. "How about that photo album? Any leads?"

"I haven't had time."

"Can I help?"

"Sure." Except, just a second. A big question just grew bigger. "Why are you willing to help me with that when, you know?" *I am breaking your heart.*

"It's a photo album of Christmas mornings." She searched his face. "It's connection to the past and happy times and people we love now or used to love but whom we can't see anymore."

She pronounced the words with tenderness, as if she'd lost someone and couldn't see the loved one anymore.

Shame about Charmaine Honeycutt. Mrs. Milliken's words from earlier floated in the air. Had Tabitha's mother died? Sam rarely saw his parents, since they were RV-ing around the country, but he called them at least once a week. The last person close to him that had died was … Adelaide.

"A photograph is precious." Tabitha hadn't stopped explaining. "More precious than money. Even books can be rewritten. But in case of a house fire, people say they'd save their photo albums first."

Sam had heard that somewhere, too. *What would I save?* "Is that what you'd grab first?"

"I'd save my photo album almost over my life."

Everything about her felt real. Earnest, honest, and without a millimeter of façade. She didn't hold back on her opinions or her feelings. It was refreshing, like reading a P.G. Wodehouse novel after years of economics textbooks.

Their eyes met, and he hoped she believed what he said next. "I hope yours stays safe, then."

She briefly pressed her lips into a line. "I hope we can find the owner of the one you have."

Yeah. Sam, too, now that she'd given him a course in *What's Really Important.*

75

"You're really smart, Tabitha." A lot smarter than she seemed to give herself credit for.

"Not me." She looked at her shoes, her cheeks flushing.

"In the things that matter, you are."

When he'd met Tabitha, Sam had thought he'd been annoyed by her persistence and her quest. But that wasn't accurate. Actually, he'd been annoyed with himself for finding her appearance so irresistible when he'd determined to keep all women off his radar. Plus, she'd of course bought every book in a hundred-mile radius out from under him. That, too.

Now, however, he wasn't irritated anymore so much as bothered—while she inched her way under his skin with how much she cared about people and things that connected them to their pasts.

Maybe that's what she wasn't telling him about *Angels Landing*.

"Mmm." She sipped her current cup of cocoa. When had they picked up this recent flavor? It was good. "Ooh, this one is *good*. I think it's got cayenne in it."

"Which booth did it come from?" He needed another hit of it. "I love spice with chocolate. Hot spice most."

"Is that so?" She crinkled her eyes. "I wouldn't have pegged you for a hot spice guy. More of a warm spice man."

"Don't you mean *Old Spice*?" He sniffed his shirt collar.

"You're the one who was singing the praises of the pumpkin spice cocoa." She laughed and then held out the cup for him to taste. "I have no idea which booth this came from, so here." She offered it a little closer to his mouth. "Go on."

He inched closer. "If you're sure."

The edge of the cup sported a bright red semi-circle of her lipstick. Like some kind of juvenile amateur flirt, he took it and twisted the cup so that his mouth met the lipstick stain, and then tilted it to sip, while keeping his gaze locked on hers. "Delicious."

She gulped visibly, then touched her neck, dragging her fingertip across her collarbone.

Bingo. He handed back the cup slowly, and his fingertips brushed hers as

76

he returned it.

"You, Sam Bartlett, know how to savor a sip of cocoa." She turned the cup and sipped out of the place he'd just sipped. "Consider me schooled."

Not just bingo, jackpot! Did her statement mean she'd fallen from D-minus to an F in her *dislike Sam* course? He inched closer, reaching for her free hand, curling his fingers to brush the back of hers, and—

"There you two are." Mayor Lang burst into the moment. "What a gorgeous couple the hat created, I must say." The mayor turned her sights on Sam. Distant thunder rolled. For a split second, he nearly ducked behind Tabitha to use her as a human shield, but reason stopped him in time. It wouldn't be gentlemanly. And he'd already been accused of caddishness when it came to Tabitha Townsend.

To be fair, during the doughnut moment, he might have deserved the scolding. But also to be fair, he hadn't seized that moment, despite violent urges to do so. Didn't that very fact reiterate his gentlemanliness?

"Sam," Mayor Lang said. "You'll be perfect for what I'm working on next week."

Distant thunder rushed to near proximity. "What's up?" He tried to sound casual, not like a cornered animal. "You need help with a civic project?"

Why was he such a sucker? *Because Tabitha's watching, of course.*

"In fact, I could really use the both of you." She grinned, almost like one of those serial killers in movies, right before they were about to strike.

"Sure," Tabitha bubbled. "Whatever it is, sign me up."

That bubbly, impulsive answer could be getting Sam into a different kind of trouble now. *But it's also getting me out of my pain cave.* And he might like it out here.

Chapter 12

Tabitha

At home that night, Tabitha fell onto her bed and stared up at the ceiling. She hoisted one leg up, peeled off her red-and-white striped stocking, and kicked it into the air. It landed across one of the blades of the old rattan ceiling fan, which set it spinning oh, so slowly.

Just like the slow, dangerous smile of Sam Bartlett.

Gently, slyly, it had sneaked its way into her soul, planting itself, taking root, making a home inside her. My, but he was climbing inside her heart and making a little house there. Even though he wouldn't budge about the book.

The fan spun lazily above, the long stocking dangling in its festive stripey-ness, tugging her through the events of the evening in leisurely replay.

She hit the memory-pause button on when he'd gazed at her over the brim of the hot cocoa cup, his eyes locking on hers, claiming every particle of her as his own.

Ahhh.

And when his fingers had brushed hers, shooting roman candles up her arm, igniting her interest in him all over again. It was like the rush she'd gotten when she'd found the Etsy designer who made the laser-engraved cutting boards. Or when she finally got the bow tied just right on a cellophane-covered gift basket full of perfectly ripened apples from Kingston Orchard to give to Mr. Behr's sister for her birthday last month. Or the delight of accidentally spotting the ideal collar for Mrs. Barnes's pup, Soccer Ball.

She's going to love it.

Except touching Sam was better. Even better.

Tabitha grabbed the pillow from up above her head, pushed it over her face and screamed like a teenager into its muffling feathers.

But the most incredible moment of all was his compliment—misguided as it may have been—that still burned a little glowing hole in the fabric of her soul: *You're really smart, Tabitha. In the things that matter.*

Never in all her born days. Never once from Dad had she heard those words. Never from a teacher in school. Never from anyone. There'd been a peripheral *I think you can figure this out this time* from Mrs. Barnes when she'd cut Tabitha that last check to invest in the website for Twelve Days, but not those magical words outright.

Smart? Tabitha?

Dad would get a belly-laugh out of that. Pamela would smile sadly, but she'd probably snigger about it with Dad later in private. *Their* daughter, well Pamela's step-daughter, bright? Not even. Unlike their full daughters. Those two were destined for educational greatness, to hear it told ad nauseam anytime their names were mentioned in Tabitha's presence.

Humph. Tabitha hadn't even scored *approaches standard* on her report cards in school. It was always the gut-twisting *Falls Far Below*. FFB.

But not according to Sam. In Sam's beautifully skewed vision of Tabitha, she was smart. In the things that mattered.

Ahhh, sigh of delight. Whether she deserved it or not.

Her phone rang, and Tabitha answered.

Poppy launched into auto-rant. "I am going to get back at that fishwife of a mayor for putting me with Andrew Kingston. She'd better sleep with one eye open."

"But if you go attack her at night, you'd miss the latest episode of your Kang Jin-Wook drama. You wouldn't do that."

"There's a reason TiVo was invented."

"As in, for more convenient multi-tasking between midnight assaults and Korean-drama viewing?"

"Precisely!" Poppy huffed once, long and low, and it became a growl. "But seriously. That man is insufferable."

"Kang Jin-Wook?" Tabitha shouldn't tease. But it was so easy.

"Stop toying with me. You know that Kang Jin-Wook is a demigod sent to earth to grace our eyes and flutter our hearts. I'm talking about Andrew Kingston. Do you know, he quizzed me for two hours? It was like I was being interviewed to work for the Secret Service, or something. We were on a *set-up date*. It wasn't an invitation for an interrogation!"

"He's probably good at interrogation and used it on you to impress you with his job skills." Tabitha should not have brought up the sore, sore attorney point. She thought fast. "Or maybe he's into you. Wants to get to know you better."

"By asking me my shoe size? My fastest running time in the hundred-meter dash? The number of teaspoons of sugar I take in my herbal tea?"

It did seem excessive. "Did you answer all of those questions? Seriously?"

"I felt like I was sitting on a metal barstool in a dark room with a single shop-light dangling over my head, answering questions for people whose faces I couldn't see, and who were scratching down answers on yellow legal pads, just waiting to trip me up. I was a sitting duck. I had to answer. I couldn't help myself." She broke into overly dramatic fake crying.

"Stop."

"Okay, fine. He didn't ask all that junk, but he did seem annoyingly interested in my personal life. As if he didn't observe its glorious boringness on a daily basis by loitering in The Cider Press for an hour every morning to read the *Hill Street Journal*. Neanderthal. Why not read it on his phone like the rest of the humans?"

Poppy had harped on this point in the past. "Do you have something against physical copies of newspapers?"

"No, but I am against newsprint. My older brothers had early morning paper routes in junior high, and when they'd come home, they had dirty fingers and wiped the ink on my face when I was asleep. I didn't always wash my face before school, since I was a little kid, and there were these bullies who kept asking me if I slept in the cinders of the fire."

That … was a good enough reason to hate newsprint. "I don't think you should hold any of that against Andrew Kingston. He's not the one who made you look sooty."

"Trust me. I hold *lots* of other things against Andrew Kingston. Newsprint is a drop in the vast, comprehensive ocean of complaints I have about him."

"But you did have some fun with him at the festival," Tabitha ventured to guess.

A brief pause. "Yeah."

Ta-da! *Knew it!* Otherwise, why call at this hour of the night? "Want to tell me about it?"

Poppy did want to tell Tabitha about it. Every detail of their stroll around the indoor festival. From the carnival booths they visited (all of them), to the cocoa they chose to vote on (dark chocolate orange), to the moment he accidentally brushed her feet under the table, and she was shocked at how *not* repulsed she was.

"We even talked about Kang Jin-Wook. Andrew knew who he was—and had seen a couple of the dramas I'm re-watching. Can you believe that? He's just got this … I don't know." Poppy groaned. "I really don't know what it is about him."

"The *je ne sais quoi*?"

"Exactly! And I do know that phrase means *I don't know* in French, and that you're making fun of me."

"I'm not." Maybe a little. "He sounds great. Are you thinking about dating him?"

"No. Although, he did ask me to his work Christmas party at the lodge at Frosty Ridge on Tuesday night."

Ooh. Showing her off to the county attorney's office staff. Sounded serious. Tabitha kept that to herself. No sense adding pressure. "You forgave him for prosecuting your ticket, I take it."

"You were right. He didn't have a choice. They just get assigned to stuff. It's not like they have a personal vendetta most of the time. I can't believe anyone thinks that. Besides, he promised never to prosecute a ticket against me again."

Uh, how did that work? "What if he gets assigned?"

"He won't. He's not working for the county anymore. He took a job as a corporate legal adviser for Tazewell Solutions." She giggled. "You didn't think the county would pony up for a big Christmas staff party somewhere as fancy as Frosty Ridge Lodge, did you?" She giggled again.

Giggling. A sure sign of infatuation.

It seemed like she'd *really* forgiven him for the prosecution thing. "This brings up a question: what are you going to do about mystery gift-giver man? Let him down easy?"

There was a pause. "Oh, no. I forgot! And I left him something *today*."

"Really? What was it?" Tabitha had given Poppy a list of possibilities a few days ago, but they hadn't decided on anything, and Tabitha hadn't started shopping for Mystery Gifter in earnest yet.

"Just something small. Not even personal, since I don't know who he is. A cider-stirrer. You know, those long plastic sticks we hand out? Except this one was pewter and had a little Christmas tree on the top. I figured if he came into the shop, he must like our cider—*and* that a gift like that would make him identifiable."

"Sneaky. I like it."

"But now, I don't know. I don't want to lead him on. I shouldn't have done it. Now I'm stuck."

"You're probably not stuck. We'll think of something. Have you considered the possibility that Andrew is the secret gift-giver?"

"Andrew?" she scoffed. "No. Not a chance. He's really not … Well, I just don't think he's the one."

"Okay."

"Ooh! I'm just getting a text from him. I'll talk to you later. Bye." Poppy was gone in a flash.

Andrew was obviously the gift-giver—at least it was obvious to Tabitha, which made her task of helping Poppy a whole lot easier, once she did a little surreptitious information gathering about the guy. But how? And should she tell Poppy the giver was almost certainly Andrew Kingston?

Nah. Poppy had dismissed the idea too readily. Besides, letting Poppy discover it on her own would be a lot more fun for everyone.

Ooh! The thought of suggesting gifts for Andrew from Poppy sent a little giggle up Tabitha's throat from her belly. This was going to be fun.

A lot more fun than trying to wrench *Angels Landing* out of Sam's grasp. Blah. That said, hanging out with Sam and convincing him to see things her way might not be such bitter medicine. He'd turned her inside out tonight with his smiles, his fun doughnut eating, his compliment on her intellect, his deliciously seductive cocoa-sipping skills, his … everything.

If Tabitha wasn't careful, she was very much in danger of falling for the guy.

Chapter 13

Sam

Monday morning before dawn, Sam loaded up his shoveling gear. As always, he had to get it done before the neighbors caught him. Snow had only stopped falling after dumping close to a foot of white stuff on Sugarplum Falls. Boots on, and his ski mask keeping him warm and disguised, he headed out for his usual route, starting with Mrs. Forger's house. Her husband was on the city council but also in a wheelchair. Then, down the road a bit, he shoveled at the Parrishes' house, who were recovering from surgery. Finally, he circled over to Orchard Street to pick up Collette Honeycutt's drive.

Over a decade of winters he'd done this, ever since she passed away.

Adelaide, it's for you. Because you loved snow but hated driving in it. I'm clearing the paths for those who can't clear their own. I hope you'd approve.

By the time he finished, the sun had come up over the mountain ridge, setting a million-zillion diamonds a-sparkle on the snow-covered fields surrounding Sugarplum Falls.

Sam parked his truck in the back of Angels Landing and unlocked the door to the storeroom, where the safe contained his copy of the book. Twenty-two to the left, eighteen to the right ... He dialed the combination on the lock, and when it clicked, he opened it and removed the white linen-covered tome from the dark depths.

It was time to savor his find again. He'd read it all the first night after finding it, but he needed yet another dose of Ed Garnet's story.

He leaned back in his office chair, the metal of the base creaking, and set his feet up on the desk. First, he pressed his nose up to the pages. Ahh, the scent of an old book. Some wouldn't agree, but to Sam, it was the best smell in the world.

He cracked the spine of the short novel, opening to the title page.

Angels Landing
by Ed Garnet
Based on a True Story.

Sam had forgotten that detail—and the full impact of the content of the book smacked him hard, all over again. The events in the book had actually happened to someone, somewhere.

He thumbed to the preface. Had he ever even read this part? As a young man, he was likely to have skipped it in all the dozen times or so he'd devoured the book.

In our lives, sometimes the extraordinary occurs. It is my belief that unless we are pressed to the extreme, we are not usually graced with dramatic intervention by the Divine. However, we need not experience these events ourselves to accept them as real, nor need we meet an angel to allow one to change our hearts.

Well, that was nice. The angel in this book had certainly made a dramatic change in Sam when he'd first encountered him.

Sam turned to chapter one again. It was amazing to re-experience the short novel as an adult.

Two hours later, at the stroke of ten, the lights came on in the storeroom, and George's whistle stopped abruptly. "Boss? You reading?"

Sam closed *Angels Landing* and swiped at his eyes before the mist in them condensed. "Re-reading." In fact, he'd devoured every word again, whooshing through the pages like his soul had been ravenous for just this prose and these phrases after a twenty-year fast.

"I remember the angel and the hero and the brambles part, but the rest is vague. Like what I ate for breakfast today." George chuckled at his own joke. "How about you summarize for me?"

Gladly, if only to relive it. "Just the Cliff's Notes version, though. If you recall, it starts out with a young woman in desperate circumstances."

Sam touched on the main points: the woman's original destitution as a youth, her abusive circumstances, the fact she mistakenly felt every ounce of the blame and the burden herself. Then, there was the husband, the baby, the surprise turn of the husband's personality from man to monster. Following that, the hopelessness and hunger, with no chance of escape for herself or her infant.

Next, out of fear, the woman takes the rash steps of standing atop the highest bridge in the area, babe in arms, ready to both destroy and to save herself and the little one from the ravages of her life, when—divinity intervenes, and an angel appears.

The woman is shown the outcome of her leap, that she herself will survive but the baby will die—and then that the worm that cankers her soul will never die. Fortunately, the angel presents an alternative future, if the young woman has the courage to seek it. It's left to the reader to decide which end is real.

"Sounds like that Dickens novel, *The Chimes*."

"Yeah? I haven't read it." To Sam, the novel *Angels Landing* always felt like *The Greatest Gift,* the novel on which *It's a Wonderful Life* was based, but with a more intimate setting, and a female character in greater desperation. More of a tear-jerker. Yes, George Bailey was a true icon, but Elda Granite of *Angels Landing* spoke to Sam more poignantly.

"Yeah, short novel, *The Chimes.* Came out the year after *A Christmas Carol.* Not as famous now, but it was in its day. I think that was based on a true event. I think the woman's name was Furley, and when she was questioned during trial about her guilt of infanticide, she said, 'I preferred death for myself and my infant.' Truly wrenching. I recall the same case being related to a poem I used to teach called 'The Bridge of Sighs.'" Mr. Milliken quoted it,

> *"Make no deep scrutiny*
> *Into her mutiny*
> *Rash and undutiful:*
> *Past all dishonour,*
> *Death has left on her*
> *Only the beautiful."*

Only the beautiful. Wow. That fit *Angels Landing*'s theme perfectly, too.

"Unfortunately, in the poem, no angel comes." Mr. Milliken frowned. "Nor did an angel stop the Englishwoman in real life, according to the articles I used to share with my students to give them a sense of the struggles of Victorian London."

"That does sound like a topic for Dickens to address."

Mr. Milliken tapped his temple. "An event, sent to a courtroom, made into a poem, made into a Dickens novel, made into another novel, made into a Jimmy Stewart movie. Then, possibly, made into the book you hold in your hands. How about that?"

Steps into the past, it appeared the book *was* based on a true story, but the angel part must be fictional—which was too bad, since that was the most poignant part.

Real-life angel or no, the book had impacted Sam's life—making him determined to write something truly great someday. Something better than his weak but heartfelt first attempt at a novel, the one he'd completed and sent starry-eyed to a publisher at age fifteen after reading *Angels Landing*. Naturally, it had been roundly rejected as *juvenile*. Looking back, it definitely had been, but the insult still smarted.

Yeah, something better than that. Something with power to break down wrong-thinking and soften even the most hardened heart.

For now, though, he was still mired in the manuscript begun during Adelaide's treatment. A brief chapter a day he'd brought to her side, reading to her the little snippets starring Sam and Adelaide in a fictional future where she was well and whole and they were raising children who loved to dance in the back yard and play in the spray of Sugarplum Falls.

Sam had married her, there in the chapel of the hospital, with her dad at her side, holding her up. Their vows had included some words from the novel Sam was writing for her. A month later, when Adelaide had finally succumbed to the sickness, Sam couldn't type another word.

The unfinished manuscript lay printed on his nightstand, with the only additions since then being a scrawl or two at the bottom of the final paragraphs he'd read to her.

It was only half a novel.

Those who taught novel pacing often advocated for a *false high* at the midpoint. The couple should experience a first kiss, the hero should seem within reach of his Holy Grail—only to have it dashed out of his hands, or for the couple to be separated instantaneously by misunderstandings or a devastating revelation.

Sam's novel for Adelaide ended on the false high.

Then, the angels had taken her.

I still need to write. She made me promise to write. And yet—how?

Especially since he'd lost the lucky token she'd given him after he finished the first chapter, that little round typewriter key featuring the letter A in a silver bezel. How could he have been so careless?

Tabitha distracted me. That's how. Not that he blamed her, not personally.

Regardless, Sam should go back to Sugarbear Storage and look for it soon, if there was a thaw.

No thaws were likely before March.

The bell out front rang several times. Sam should go out and help with the influx of customers. He pushed through the doors into the storefront, and nearly ran into mountain of a man, Owen Kingston, lawyer Andrew's cousin.

"Sam! Just the person I needed to talk to." At Owen's side stood Claire Downing, petite owner of the Apple Blossom Boutique women's clothing shop down the street. "Claire doesn't believe me that a book is the right gift for Portia, but I dragged her into Angels Landing so she could see what you and I already know—that a book is *always* a good gift, since there's a book for everyone."

"There is a book for everyone." But for Portia? Sam hid his wince. "Does she … read?" Of course Portia could read, she had stage scripts she constantly memorized—and recited anytime anyone would give her the spotlight, even in a small room in an intimate setting. "Maybe a celebrity biography? Marilyn Monroe, or Audrey Hepburn?"

Claire pushed a palm to her forehead. "You got me. You're right." She looked up at Owen. "I thought I knew Portia best, since I've been friends with her for"—she looked at the ceiling as if counting the eons—"ever, but a celebrity biography would actually be a great gift." She turned to Sam. "Thanks for settling this dispute. Can I head back to the boutique now, Owen?"

Claire scuttled out into the snowy day, and Mr. Milliken took care of the cash register for Owen's Audrey Hepburn biography.

The crowd had thinned, so Sam went back to his desk. But not for long.

"Hey. There you are, boss." Mrs. Milliken wore a festive green scarf and a Santa hat, her gray curls bursting from beneath the faux fur edge. Her gaze fell on the book on his desk. "Whew! I went to the safe to collect your storefront display piece, and it was gone. I'm so glad you're the one who has it."

"I've been reading it all morning."

"Oh, good for you, dear. I saw you—you came up with the perfect book idea for that poor Owen Kingston."

"Poor!" Sam wouldn't call Owen Kingston poor. His family owned the biggest orchard in the region, and Owen was set to inherit it, since he managed it now, while his dad was ill. Was his dad in a coma? Andrew had said something about his uncle's tragic accident. "How is Owen Kingston poor?"

"Just that he's dating the *wrong woman*." Mrs. Milliken bunched up her shoulders. "He doesn't belong with that *show pony* of a local actress. He's a workhorse type, and he needs someone who will be equally yoked with him." Her eyes brightened. "Like that nice Claire Downing!"

"They're *friends*, Mrs. Milliken."

Mrs. Milliken nodded knowingly. "Well, you'll have to convince me of that as an argument against love later. There's a visitor here for you. It's Lisa Lang."

"Another visit from the mayor?" He brushed off his pants and handed Mrs. Milliken the book to place back on display.

"She seems to think you signed up for a service project. I told her you were neck-deep in service as it was—but don't worry. I didn't say snow-shovel deep."

Good. Sam didn't want anyone to know he was the Secret Driveway Cleaner of Sugarplum Falls. Only Mrs. Milliken knew and that was because, worried for his welfare, she'd come to locate him once after he'd failed to come into the shop on time after a major snowfall.

Out front, Mrs. Milliken went to work on the front window display again, and Sam went to greet Lisa Lang. "Great party on Saturday."

"Indeed, in no small part thanks to you." She winked. She really liked winking. "I must say, you and Collette Honeycutt's granddaughter put on the best show of the night for all the patrons. The lovey-dovey looks? The chemistry? I was all a-swoon." She fanned herself then broke into her cackle. "The hat chose well when it paired you."

Right. The hat.

"Now, about the service project. I'll need you there on Tuesday evening at seven. Not a moment later, or everything will be thrown off. Your store closes at seven, but I've already talked with Gracie Milliken about getting you out the door early."

"Where am I headed?" Next thing he knew, this woman was going to tell him she'd signed him up to donate a kidney.

"Didn't I say? You and Tabitha will be performing three musical selections at the Sweet Haven Nursing Home. You know the place. On Bellwether Street."

"Musical selections?" Sam had to choke back his guffaw of disbelief. "Isn't that risky? You don't even know if I can sing."

Mayor Lang whipped out her phone, tapped a few times, and then twisted the screen toward him. There, in a harsh spotlight and teenage glory was Sam's high school men's quartet's rendition of "God Rest Ye, Merry Gentlemen" in four-part harmony, with Sam on lead baritone.

"Be careful what you leave lying around on the internet, young man." She pocketed her phone. "Choose any songs you like, just keep them light and fun. We're not exactly talking Carnegie Hall here, but recall that all the Sweet Haven residents in attendance will have their hearing aids dialed to high, so try not to hit any sour notes. The current high school men's quartet performed last week, and when one went off-key during that stupid hippopotamus song, Mrs. O'Houlihan had something very loud to say about it." She patted his arm and beamed at him like he was a good child. "But I'm sure you and Tabitha will do just fine. *Fine.*"

Mayor Lang sped out of the shop with a jingle, so quickly Sam's head spun. It had been a long time since he'd done any public singing. A really long time. Like, even longer than it had been since he'd written anything.

"Oh, good!" Mrs. Milliken breezed past with an armload of quilted oven mitts from a consigner. "You have such a nice voice. It should be heard regularly and by all."

"You didn't put her up to this, did you?"

"Please. You don't imagine Lisa Lang requires any help from others in her machinations, do you?"

No, actually.

Mrs. Milliken fanned out all the oven mitts in holiday fabric on the glass countertop. "If it were me, I wouldn't wait until the last second and wing it. I'd need practice."

Sure she would. The woman practically treated Angels Landing like The Met when no customers were in the store.

"If you need a piano or anything, you can come by and use mine. I can serve you both dessert, but you'll have to buy her a nice dinner. I mean, she deserves at least dinner, right?"

Dinner. With Tabitha.

Chapter 14

Tabitha

"There." Tabitha tied the bow atop the cellophane just right, and then stepped back to observe the effect. "Nice."

Inside the gift basket were twelve individually wrapped gifts, one for each of the twelve days leading up to Christmas. Never mind that *technically* that twelve-day period should begin on Christmas and end on Epiphany. Besides, the modern American way of doing it built more anticipation.

"Mrs. Forger is going to be delighted." Grandma fussed with the bow one more time. "Mr. Forger was smart to hire you to surprise his wife. She's always so large and in charge, he can never get ahead enough to surprise her."

Large and in charge did describe City Councilwoman Shelby Forger. "I'm just glad I got to do an actual twelve-day gift, in honor of my business's name."

"It seems like you're getting more and more clients. I'm so happy to see your business taking off."

"It's picking up, but I have a long way to go before I'd consider myself a success." Without the book, she failed.

"But what about all the business you've gained lately, Mayor Lang's office, the other jobs you've been doing?"

"Overhead." To pay back her debt.

Grandma nodded as if she understood. But she couldn't. Telling Grandma about both her previous failed businesses was too wrenching. Grandma didn't need to know about the Classy Closet that turned into a famous person's lawsuit against Tabitha when Tabitha failed to follow the *measure twice cut once* rule and had drilled holes all over the drywall in the woman's closet that had been larger than Tabitha's whole apartment.

Nor did Grandma need to know about the Corgi puppy that was on

Tabitha's schedule to be walked but got missed when Tabitha double-booked a German shepherd at the same time, and the owner came home to a severely hyper puppy and claimed they both had suffered trauma.

Disorganization plagued Tabitha's business past. Bubonic plagued it.

When, oh, *when* would Tabitha figure out how to keep a business from tanking? Maybe this time? Not if Sam refused to help her out.

"Sweetheart, you look truly troubled. What's wrong? Please tell me."

Fine. She could tell Grandma this much. "I have to find a certain gift for someone. I promised. In fact, I guaranteed. And if I don't find it, all my profit, every cent, gets caught up in a repayment fee rather than reinvesting in Twelve Days."

"No, dear! That isn't right."

Maybe not, but that was where duty, honor, and honesty left her. "The thing is, I did find it, but I'm not able to procure it after all. The client is devastated. Worse, I took on some debt"—huge debt, and not just of money— "when I began the business, which means Twelve Days is in the red when it should be turning a profit this time of year."

If Tabitha couldn't turn a profit at Christmas, she never could. Twelve Days would have to shut down. Tabitha would have to look for a regular job. Or, as Dad would say, a *real* job. In Darlington. Or worse, Caldwell City.

I can't work for someone else. I just can't. But apparently, she couldn't work for herself either. *I'm the most undependable person I could have hired.*

Except ... this basket did look lovely. And she hadn't gone belly-up yet. As long as the book existed, there was a chance. "I'll just take this to Mr. Forger, and he can plant it somewhere to surprise his wife." She grabbed her red coat with the fur lining, the one that made her feel like Santa's helper, hoisted the gift basket on her hip, and headed out to her car. When she backed out of the garage and onto the driveway, she stopped.

Someone had shoveled the driveway. The *whole* driveway. All the way from the garage door down to the street.

He did it. I know he did.

She called Grandma. "Did you shovel the driveway?"

"Me? Never. Not since Grandpa Honeycutt died. The shoveling bandit

93

strikes again."

It had been going on this way for years? Her tummy flipped twice before loosing its throngs of butterflies. "Do you know who it is?" *I do. I swear it's Sam.*

"If I did, I'd probably demand he marry me." Grandma laughed. "Whoever it is, I can never seem to catch him. He strikes early in the mornings. I do know he's got to be muscular, considering he never uses a snow-blower, which would be noisy, wake me up, and reveal his identity. My widow friends and I have been trying to unmask him forever. Anytime we chance a glance, he wears a ski mask, and if we approach—get this—he runs away. We don't want to embarrass him, so we agreed to stop trying to find him out."

"That's sweet." Very sweet. *I'll keep your secret, Sam.*

She dropped off the twelve wrapped gifts around the corner at Mr. Forger's house. Mrs. Forger was gone, doing city business, but their driveway was clean as well. Was Sam's handiwork in evidence here, too?

"Thanks, Tabitha." Mr. Forger beamed at her from his wheelchair, hugging the basket on his lap. "Do you know how long I've been trying to get Shelby something she can't guess ahead of time? Let's just say we've been married for forty-five years, and this might be the first."

"Glad to help."

"The thing is, she adores surprises more than anything. But she's too good of a guesser to ever get her wish. I'm so glad I get to make her wish come true for once. Thanks to you." He smiled broadly and dashed at the moisture collecting in his eyes. "She does so much for me. Ever since my accident, I can never hope to catch up. This means a lot. Really a lot. Thank you."

Down in her car, Tabitha hugged herself. Shopping for someone else maybe shouldn't be an emotional reservoir-filler, but it was. A hundred percent.

I want to keep going with this. I don't want to let it go.

Her phone rang, and before she could even say hello, she heard, "Tabitha?" It was Sam. "Let's meet for dinner to practice our songs for tomorrow night."

Dinner sounded great, and like a chance to work on him about *Angels*

Landing. However, "What songs?" There would be no songs. Tabitha was not the least bit musical. In fact, she was the embodiment of *anti-musical,* if such a thing existed.

"Mayor Lang hasn't cornered you yet? Well, she will. Anyway, you can either meet me at the bookshop or I'll pick you up. Unless your grandma has a piano."

"She does. What's going on, exactly?" Then she remembered: the service project. "I signed us up for this, didn't I?" Except, she hadn't signed up for music.

"We're booked to perform at Sweet Haven. The nursing home? Do you play? We may need a backup track. Are you better at melody or harmony?"

Um, neither? "Who all is singing?"

"Apparently just the two of us."

Yikes. Double-triple yikes. "I don't know, Sam." Yes, she did know. It was going to be terrible. "Are there other options? Soup kitchens, warm-clothing drives, barefoot marches in the snow to highlight a social ill?"

"I'll meet you at your house tonight after I get off work. I'll bring dinner, and you start thinking of your three best Christmas songs, okay?"

Three? She'd be lucky if she could gurgle her way through one.

But wait. Did he say he'd bring dinner? "So, does that make this our third date?"

Chapter 15

Sam

For the entire afternoon at Angels Landing, Sam flipped through used holiday sheet music books from the store shelves. Singing could be pretty fun, even though Tabitha had sounded wholly unconvinced.

He'd see her tonight. He rubbed the side of his hand, where it had brushed hers to electric effect. He blinked a few times to try to clear the image of her striped tights. No use. It was stupid to let chemistry dictate how he was going to interact with Tabitha tonight. Just because the caveman in him was grunting *kiss, kiss, kiss,* it didn't mean he had to listen and obey.

He hadn't kissed a woman since Adelaide. And not even Adelaide once she got very sick. Barely a peck on her lips when they married. She hadn't really been up for it.

Sam was way too out of practice to be letting cave-thoughts run rampant.

He silenced them. Totally.

"Did you know we carried this many different collections of Christmas piano arrangements?" he asked George, as Mr. and Mrs. Milliken sauntered out for the evening. Sam was closing up, with late hours for the holiday.

"Don't you have an author meet-and-greet to plan?" Mrs. Milliken said, looking at her wristwatch as if it also contained a countdown clock to their Christmas Eve event. "We really should print the name on the advertising."

"Yeah, yeah." If any of the dozen additional authors he'd contacted would return his calls, he'd get that set up immediately. Including Ed Garnet, who—according to the vast tentacle-like reaches of the internet—did not exist. "What do you think of 'I've Got My Love to Keep Me Warm?' Or maybe, 'Christmas Kisses?' Or else there's always the classic 'Let it Snow.'"

Mrs. Milliken shot a look at her husband. "Sounds like he's got more than Christmas on his mind."

"Those are all quite the romantic options." George cleared his throat. "Most of them are about one thing. And it ain't the Nativity."

"George!"

"I know, I know. I'm a retired English teacher and shouldn't succumb to temptations like *ain't*."

They left. It took all of Sam's willpower to leave the stacks of sheet music to go assist Mrs. Forger as she purchased five of the Inglewood collection's recipe books on Christmas dishes from around the world.

"I really think this is my year to make yummy borscht on the Sunday before Christmas." She grinned. "Don't you just love borscht for the holidays?"

"Your family is so lucky to have you as an enthusiastic holiday cook," he said, still thinking about the various implications of the lyrics of "Let it Snow" and how they may or may not apply to his evening with Tabitha. Frightful weather, delightful fire, kissing good night.

"Would you like these gift-wrapped?" he asked dumbly. Mrs. Forger was getting them for herself. To use before Christmas Day. "Sorry, no. I'm sure not. Well, have a delicious beet soup dinner." Could he sound any more distracted?

"Merry Christmas," Mrs. Forger said, giving him a weird look.

Good, she was gone—but so was the time. The cuckoo clock on the wall sang six times, and he hadn't even ordered their dinner. Sam rushed back toward his pile of songs. Why was he acting like he was sixteen again and going on his first date? Sweaty palms, check. Mild hyperventilation, check. Garbled speech, and thought patterns, check check.

It wasn't like he was going to kiss her. There was no reason to be turning into a melting snowman.

He dialed the wrong phone number for Mario's three times before getting the digits correct and finalizing the order for their cheese manicotti and garlic bread. No—scratch the garlic bread. Just give him some plain breadsticks. Not the soft kind. Those had garlic sprinkled on them. Yeah, the hard stick kind of breadstick. Perfect. He'd be there in ten minutes to get it.

It took fifteen minutes to gather his final selections of sheet music, which

97

he dropped four times, to brush his teeth twice at the sink in the little bathroom with his travel kit, and get out to his truck.

The caveman and I are going to kiss her. Tonight.

Chapter 16

Tabitha

Tabitha cleaned the kitchen, the living room, the powder room, and the front hall like there was no tomorrow. She took all the throw pillows off the rust-orange velvet sofa, and then put them back on. She dusted the pendant lamps and the piano keys. It hadn't been played in years, probably since Aunt Charlene lived here. Not a chance was Tabitha using it for singing practice on her own. The plants would die—faster than if she played really negative acid rock music at them day and night.

And what was she going to wear while she humiliated herself sounding like a drowning frog at the piano? Perhaps a drowning frog costume would be appropriate? The wetsuit from her summer diving class would do.

Never mind. She found a cute black sweater, some fitted jeans and a pair of boots with heels. *He's tall. I want to be closer to his height.*

Uh, what for? No way was he going to kiss her. They had that big vintage Christmas novel looming between them, and neither of them could budge on it. Therefore, no kiss. Enemies didn't kiss.

She was not kissing Sam Bartlett. Nope.

Besides, Grandma was going to be at home in the same room or nearby working on her crafts. There wouldn't be a private moment for anything like a kiss.

"Tabby, honey?" Grandma swept down the stairway wearing going-out clothes. "Well, look at you. You're dressed to kill. Who is your target?"

Tabitha's neck got hot, and it wasn't due to the closeness of the sweater's neckline. The doorbell rang. "I'll get it."

"Just a minute, cutie. I need to just slip out, and I'd rather not be late due to introductions and things." She gave Tabitha's cheek a swift peck.

"You're leaving?"

"Yep. And I'll be out late. Don't watch for me. It's Bunco night, and I'm in charge of the prizes, so I have to stay to the bitter end, which will be later than usual, since it's the Christmas party. Too bad you can't come this time."

Which meant she and Sam were all alone in the house. Tabitha's temperature spiked.

"Sam Bartlett is coming. That'll be him at the door. We have to go over some Christmas music for a service project at Sweet Haven nursing home tomorrow night. Mayor Lang roped us into it."

The bell rang again. Grandma blinked a couple of times. "Tabitha, be careful."

"I will. He thinks I'm an obsessive lunatic, so I'm not in any danger."

"No, I mean for *his* sake. He's the still-waters-run-deep type. Don't hurt him, okay? He's been through a lot." Grandma air-kissed Tabitha and left.

Been through a lot? "Like what?" But Grandma was gone. The bell rang a third time. *I really should have asked Poppy more of Sam's history before now.* But she hadn't. And it was too late to ask before tonight's date.

Well, add another *besides* to why she wasn't going to kiss Sam Bartlett: if he'd been through a lot, whatever it was, Tabitha had to be careful. Kissing wasn't careful.

Armed to the hilt with all her resolves, Tabitha dashed to the door. "I'm so sorry! I was saying goodbye to Grandma, and—" Holy cannelloni. "Sam?"

He looked especially sharp under the light from the porch. His blue eyes were a keener blue, impacting her instantly, like all the snow falling off the metal roof at once. She had to gulp and hide her face while she let him pass her to come inside with the various packages he toted.

"I hope you like Italian." He held up two large to-go bags and stepped inside.

Are you Italian? she nearly asked. "Uh-huh." Dumbly, Tabitha followed him into the kitchen, where he set things on the counter like he owned the place.

"Mario's marinara won him a James Beard award a few years ago. Trust me, I made sure there's marinara. Don't tell me you haven't tasted it yet." He lifted two containers from a tall paper bag with handles. "If not, you're finally going to start living. Tonight."

Something in the way he said it, and in the way his gaze penetrated to the depths of her soul, made it sound like he wasn't talking about the marinara sauce anymore.

She just bit her lower lip a little too hard. Sam gazed at her mouth for a moment, and then he met her eyes.

She cleared her throat, as if that would help clear the crackling air. "Do you want to eat first or sing first?" *Or make out first?* No! Such thoughts needed to be corralled! This was not that kind of date. This was dinner and prep for a service project.

"I'm pretty hungry," he said, still staring at her lower lip and moistening his own. "It's been a long time."

Uh-huh. It'd been a really long time for Tabitha, too. Far too long. "Mmm," was all she could intone. He was so near, and he smelled so good, like the Christmas candles from his bookstore, and whatever pine-and-spice cologne he was wearing. Or maybe that was just his natural scent. It sailed around in her brain, wiping out a lot of her self-restraining thoughts.

"I'm starving, actually." He reached for the bag, but his arm brushed against hers, bumping her high-heeled boots off balance, and she caught herself by grabbing for the countertop, but not before she'd landed against him.

He reached for her, pulling her close. "Steady on, Tabitha."

Steady? His gaze was steady, his arms and chest and shoulders were truly steady. But Tabitha was not steady. Nothing about this moment was steady. It was all a huge, balance-threatening swirl of chemistry and marinara and anticipation.

I'm not just going to kiss this guy, I'm going to fall for this guy.

Chapter 17

Sam

With Tabitha in his arms, he couldn't even smell the manicotti anymore. She'd high-jacked every sense. This was moving a lot faster than he'd expected, or even dared hope. Conflict warred in him, though. He was blocking her deal with her client by hanging onto that book, and yet he was trying to woo her with Mario's delicious food?

He'd better slow down and think this through.

"Shall we watch the manicotti's cheese string out?" he asked, releasing her from his embrace. "As we eat?" Hint. They were going to eat and practice singing, not just collapse into each other's arms.

It's been so long since I've held a woman in my arms, though.

Tabitha stepped back, opening her eyes. They were so deeply green tonight. Emeralds laced with fire. "Watching cheese string out is one of the great joys of life."

Like having a soft, sweet-scented woman in his arms. "I couldn't agree more." Sam pulled the foil pans from the tall paper bag.

Tabitha produced some vintage Corelle dishware with an embossed floral pattern around the edges in dark gold. It matched the house, which was decorated like a 1970s time capsule.

Tabitha joined him on a barstool at the island and they said grace on their food.

"I like this house a lot." He spoke through bites. "Very warm and homey."

"Right? It's perfect just the way it is. All the appliances still work, even though they're decades old, and I am really hoping Grandma never even considers updating it. If so, I'll stage a protest."

"Against your grandma?"

"I guess not." Tabitha lifted a bite but didn't put it in her mouth. "Is it wrong to be terrified that someone would turn everything so-called *modern*? I'd die if that happened. And I have to be ready to purchase the house if she ever decides to sell. I'd also die if this place fell into the wrong hands, believe me."

It wasn't wrong to be terrified of decorating changes. Different, yes. Wrong, no. "You appreciate things with a history."

"Oh, sure. Not piles of historic cookbooks, mind you."

"Glad I can like those in your stead. Pick up the slack."

"They're all yours, without prejudice. Or pride. In fact, I think there was a copy of *Pride and Prejudice* in one of the Lincolntown estate boxes."

"I saw that." He held his fork suspended in the air, watching her. "Are you going to taste it?"

"Right." She finally took her bite of her ricotta-filled pasta drenched in Mario's famous spiced tomato sauce. Her eyes rolled back in her head, and she sighed in what sounded like ecstasy. "This is … just … words fail."

Sam stamped out the naughty voice in his head that said he'd like to see her repeat that sentiment after a truly good kiss from him. "I'm glad you like it," his brain managed to get his mouth to say instead.

They ate on in mostly silence, since Mario's deliciousness demanded it.

"I do like old books," Tabitha said after she'd cleared most of the pasta from her dish and dragged a breadstick through the sauce.

Good thinking. Sam followed suit. "Any old books in particular?"

"Victorian, actually. Though I don't get worked up over first editions like some bookstore owners or book collectors. I just like books. I'll even take e-books."

"Heresy." E-books! They couldn't be hefted or sniffed.

"Sorry." She gave an apologetic shrug. "I like to read books in the dark. E-books let me do that."

He pictured her in bed at night with her e-book aglow, lighting her face and making her eyes sparkle. Ahem. Picturing her in bed was not the best course of action if he was going to slow his chemical roll. "Victorian, though? Which authors, for instance?"

"I like Charles Dickens, Anthony Trollope, and Elizabeth Gaskell.

There's a lot more delightful description in those stories than twentieth century writers' works."

Dickens, huh? That was the second Dickens reference Sam had encountered that day. First from Mr. Milliken, and now from Tabitha. "I'm less versed in Victorian authors, so steer me to a favorite book."

She listed about twenty—with verve. From *North and South* by Gaskell, to *Great Expectations* by Dickens, to *The Eustace Diamonds* by Trollope, and then she winced. "Whoa. I didn't mean to douse you with a tidal wave." She blushed—quite prettily. If he were a Victorian author, Sam could have waxed verbose describing that blush.

They moved their dishes to the sink and went into another room with a piano and a long orange velvet sofa.

Sam sat down, right in the center. "Funny you should mention Dickens. I learned today that the plot of *Angels Landing* closely resembles the plot of a novella Charles Dickens wrote as a follow-up to *A Christmas Carol*." He told her about *The Chimes,* in thumbnail, as described by George.

"Interesting. *Angels Landing* is so coveted, it must be quite the story." She sat beside him. Not too close. *Not quite close enough.* "Can you tell me what it's about?"

For the second time that day, Sam gave a synopsis. This time, he had it down better, since he'd practiced. With one arm across the back of the couch to turn himself toward her, he included the highs and lows. When he described the prose and the pacing and the characterization, he may have lapsed into similar rhapsodies as hers over descriptions of clothing in Victorian novels.

She seemed to watch his face through the whole retelling, as if she were hanging on his every word. "And so she was that close to death?" Tabitha's brows pushed together, and her chin trembled. "Her circumstances were that terrible, that she'd resort to …" She seemed unable to speak the final words.

"The angel came to her, just in time." Sam lowered his arm and slid his fingers toward her free hand resting near his. The side of his little finger brushed against hers. "He gave her perspective. She was able to go forward—and to stop looking back."

"And instead of falling to her death, and to the death of her child, she had an angel's landing instead," Tabitha whispered.

"Yeah." Exactly. Although, Sam hadn't ever created that connection in his own mind before. *Tabitha saw the title's meaning. Instantly.*

"Beautiful," she sighed.

"Yeah." Tabitha was so beautiful, insightful. She made him want to reconnect with life, with someone. Well, with her. "Good insight into a book you've never even read."

"The way you told the story, it's as though I didn't read it, I lived it." She placed a hand over her heart. The silver necklace she wore twisted around her thumb. "You are a storyteller, Sam. You've got a gift. Have you ever thought about writing?"

The ground shifted beneath him, or maybe it was one of the frequent coastal quakes.

Or maybe it's Tabitha's words, rocking my foundations. "Me?" he said, his voice almost cracking. "I'm out of practice."

"I'm not just saying this out of flattery. You should be telling stories. Writing or speaking or ... something. If you don't, it's like you're not living up to your calling in life."

His calling in life. Ha-ha.

Or was it an *a-ha*? Adelaide had said the same thing, over and over. And now, Tabitha. She was so different from the other women he'd tried to date and feel something with since Adelaide—to no avail. Tabitha was disorganized and emotion-driven. She said things off-the-cuff. She lifted a hand like she would karate-chop him in public. She got teary-eyed when he recounted the plot of *Angels Landing,* accepting the characters as if they were real.

Just like they are to me.

No, Tabitha bore almost no resemblance to the few women he'd taken to dinner in the past five years. Women like Tonya, the office manager who wanted to talk about maximizing her 401(k) funds at her corporate offices, but who never wanted to discuss stock investments even though Sam had a good head for options trading; or Nadia, the charming but narcissistic magazine writer who never once asked Sam if he liked to write; or Sharon, the geneticist who reveled in obscure scientific discoveries, but never asked Sam his opinion on them, though he'd read every book in his store on the subject.

None of them, for all their bright minds and similar preferences, had understood Sam.

Then, there had been the others, like Elise. *The Deep-fakes,* as Andrew had referred to them. *For good reason.* Elise, who'd taken the back entrance into his life by researching him first, by ingratiating herself into his extended family. Who'd made comprehensive lists of his likes and dislikes and then pretended to mirror them. Only when he mentioned Adelaide did she gain a conscience and leave him alone. Or maybe she'd realized that Sam wasn't ever actually going to allow her into his world. Not with Adelaide still occupying all the space in his heart.

Meanwhile, by sharp contrast, there was Tabitha. Twice-failed businesswoman. Drove the wrong car in the winter. Aggressive bidder at estate sales featuring lava carvings from Easter Island. Full of street-smarts and a sharp wit, if (as she claimed) not book smarts. How could someone so free-spirited, instead of studious and staid, have such insight into not only the story he loved but also into Sam?

Plus, there wasn't a fake cell in her body. She was total WYSIWYG— *what you see is what you get.* Refreshing. Real.

And it allowed Sam to be real around her. Or it might. It could, eventually. *I might even tell her about Adelaide sometime.*

"I know why *Angels Landing* is important to you now," she hummed, as if proving his internally stated point. "It's planted itself in your soul."

"Then you understand why I can't sell it to you or give it to you or let it go."

"I understand." She blinked up at him. "But you understand, too, why someone I know wants it so much."

If it had to do with preserving things, making connections, allowing angels in personal lives, he did understand. But it didn't change his mind about giving it to her. "It appears we're at both an agreement and at an impasse."

"With regards to the book, yes." However, she inched closer to him. "But maybe not with regards to anything else. On other topics, it's possible that we might be in perfect agreement."

Please let that be true. He reached for the side of her face and touched a pin curl where it rested on her cheek. It was smooth and perfectly round. Her eyes closed for a moment at his touch. A shiver ran up his hand and arm.

"You're different, Tabitha." He leaned in close. She smelled like citrus and cinnamon, luring him nearer, despite everything looming between them. "I'm not sure how I feel about this."

"About this what?" She hooked her pinky finger around his. All the defenses he'd been shoring up could fall with the tiniest encouragement. *Can I let them?*

"About this." Keeping her finger hooked around his, he leaned in, placing his other hand around the back of her neck, and gently moved her face toward his. "I can't keep being with you and not kissing you. I'm afraid of coming apart at the seams."

Her warm breath feathered across his lips, tempting him, drawing him like a will-o'-the wisp's light through a dark forest. Her large green eyes beckoned to him, and her zest for life awakened a vibrancy in him, passion that had lain dormant so long he'd almost forgotten it existed.

"Tabitha," he whispered. "I'm not sure."

She halted. Then, slowly, she placed her fingertip on his lips for a long moment. Then, she removed it, drawing it softly across his jaw line. "Sometime, I'll let you kiss me." With gentle pressure from her fingertip, she turned his cheek to the side, and then placed a supple kiss just above his eye. "When you're sure."

Oh, he was sure, all right—about the kissing. Just not about the implications. He patted his pocket for the typewriter key. It was gone.

I can't do this right now. Not yet. I should tell her about Adelaide. But I can't. Not yet. Soon.

The air quivered between them, and a grandfather clock down the hall struck the hour, and the mood lightened. She was right. He should be sure about kissing her and meaning it.

Sam Bartlett wasn't a man who could kiss without meaning it fully.

But could he mean it fully? Soon? With Tabitha, perhaps he could.

"We should sing, or at least decide on some songs for tomorrow." He

107

leaned back, out of her gravitational pull a bit, and reached for the stack of sheet music he'd brought and left on the coffee table. As he tugged it, something on the lower section of the bi-level tipped over with a thwack.

When Sam bent to straighten it, he saw it was a photo album, one of the kind where the outside cover had been padded and quilted in festive fabric and lace appliqué. Sam's mother had created a few of those when Sam was a kid, and—

"What's this? A photo album?" He pulled it into his lap. "May I?" He opened the front page when she gave him a nod. "Is this your mom's family?"

He tipped through the pages. There was a younger version of Collette Honeycutt, and a man who must be Mr. Honeycutt, standing in front of this house, flanked by three teenage girls in retro hairstyles and dresses. Their socks were folded down, and their knees looked knobby.

Tabitha slid closer to him and looked over his shoulder. "My grandma looks so young and posh. She's always had shampoo commercial hair."

Now that she mentioned it, yeah. "Are these your aunts?"

"Charlene and Charlotte, yeah." She pointed to the two smaller girls. "And that's my mother."

"She looks like you."

"You think so?" Tabitha asked without looking up. "I don't see it, but Aunt Charlene says I have Mom's mannerisms."

"You don't remember her?"

Tabitha shook her head, taking the photo album and turning the page to the center. "This is my memory of her. It's the thing I'd save in a fire. That, and my mother's journal, which I recently found."

In the photo, a youngish Charmaine Townsend held a baby in her arms, looking down with that one-of-a-kind love, baby worship. Beside her, a man had his hand on her back, but he was looking elsewhere, as if speaking to someone off-camera. The picture was obviously taken somewhere in this house, from the décor and the furniture. This very couch, perhaps. A huge Christmas tree dominated the background of the photo, and the baby looked serene.

"That's you?"

108

"My mom and dad split up when I was still a toddler. He wasn't as attentive a husband as she would have hoped, or so Grandma Honeycutt puts it. But after reading Mom's journal a little, I now know there was more to it."

Inattentive husband, huh? That was likely a kind understatement, knowing Collette Honeycutt. "You do look like her."

"Maybe. I have had a few experiences like hers, it turns out. I wish I'd known her. I wish I could ask her some things. How to navigate life's challenges. You know, that kind of thing. She died—in a wreck—soon after their divorce. Dad remarried not much later."

"So, you were brought up by a different mom. How was that for you?" Sam had always had his own mom. They weren't close, as in daily contact, these days, but she was still his mom, and Dad was still Dad.

Tabitha didn't answer right away. "They had other children," she said finally. "Dad was always looking for chances for me to come to Sugarplum Falls in the summers and at holidays."

The forgotten one.

How could anyone forget Tabitha? "This photo is precious, then."

"Very." She ran a finger over the cellophane that covered the photograph, as if to caress her mother's long hair. "I want to freeze it."

"The moment? The photo? The memory?"

"Yeah. And the house. It's perfect like this. Mom's in it like this."

Tabitha gazed a little longer at the picture. Sam took in this moment, Tabitha's movements, her facial expressions, her loving glow.

Much as he'd wanted to kiss her a few minutes ago, this moment might be worth a lot of kisses. Tabitha was someone different. She had a deep love for preserving the past and a serious commitment to other people's happiness. She valued these things in spite of her obvious deep wound at the loss of her mother, as well as her father's marginalization of her. And yet, she maintained an understanding attitude toward him and lack of judgment toward people in her life who made mistakes. All while keeping a giving, happy outlook.

Yes, she was someone who'd need a kiss to be a hundred percent sincere. A kiss that meant something confidently real.

A woman like her deserved nothing less.

"May I?" Sam took the photo album off her lap. "Can you hand me your phone?" He snapped a photo of the picture of Tabitha with her mother. "Now, what if you email it to me? Then, if anything ever happens to your album, or to your phone, there's a backup."

He handed back her phone and she looked at him like he'd just negotiated peace between eternally warring factions. "Thank you." She tapped her phone, and at the same time his chimed that he'd received a message. Then she put hers away. "Really, Sam." Her eyes went glossy. "Let me do something in return. Could I?"

She could. "Actually, sure. Remember that photo album I mentioned, and you said you wanted to help me find the owner?"

"Yeah. I might not have been a year-round Sugarplum Falls resident, but I have sleuthing skills." She sat back, closing the cover of the book and setting it back on the coffee table. "You didn't seem like you have time for it right now, so I didn't push."

"I'm going to make time, especially if we're doing it together."

Chapter 18

Tabitha

Tabitha sat in The Cider Press staring out the window at the swirling powder-snow. Despite the swoon-inducing moments she'd shared with Sam, including his sweet idea to preserve the picture of Mom, their service project at the nursing home had glowered like a dark cloud on Tabitha's horizon all morning, threatening humiliation and doom. How on earth could she possibly sing aloud in front of anyone? Even the stone-deaf residents might complain the second she opened her mouth.

Worse, Sam had a great voice. When he'd offered a few bars of different songs as examples of what they might perform, he'd sounded like Michael Bublé and Robbie Williams had a shared nephew, and it was Sam.

Meanwhile, Tabitha had avoided adding her own voice during practice by changing the subject to literature. And just as well. Once Sam heard Tabitha's screeching, he'd break into a dead run to escape before his ears started bleeding.

This wasn't going to be okay. This was going to be a holiday disaster.

"We'll finalize at lunch," he'd said as he was leaving last night. "Do you have time?"

"Okay." Lots of time, but not if it required singing. Still, he drew her like a magnet to steel. Like a Wise Man to a manger by the power of a magnificent star. "Where do you want to meet?"

Frankly, she'd been dying to kiss him last night, in the force of that pull. It had required all her willpower not to close that final gap between their faces after he'd been so vulnerable and beautiful and made her neurons hum like she'd been hooked to a twelve-volt battery.

But despite chemistry's demands to the contrary, he obviously wasn't ready for her, and Grandma's words had echoed. *Don't hurt him.*

Sometimes kisses could hurt. At least kisses poorly timed could. They

111

could be a death knell to something that could potentially thrive—just like too much Miracle-Gro dumped on a seedling could burn it up.

Instead, he'd poured Miracle-Gro on her connection to him by getting her to open up about Mom.

I shouldn't have told him about Dad. It sounded like Dad didn't love me. But Dad did, just ... after Dad's own fashion: a little (lot) distracted by Pamela and the girls.

Tabitha stirred her apple cider with orange and cloves and stared out at the snow, wishing things had been different for a moment.

But then I wouldn't be here. In Sugarplum Falls. Falling in love with Sam Bartlett.

Maybe bad things could happen for a good reason. Maybe getting bumped off life's obvious highway put her onto a side street or a country road that could take her somewhere happier than the highway's destination.

"What are you doing for lunch today?" Poppy asked, dropping into the seat across from Tabitha. "Please say you're going to spend it giving me hints as to who my mystery-gifter is, since you seem to know all."

"Not today. I'm meeting Sam."

"Ohhhh." Poppy nodded. "You guys went on your third date last night, I heard."

"How would you hear a thing like that?"

"Mario's Italian. I stopped by in the afternoon, and the sous chef told me he was making something special for Sam Bartlett who was going on a third date."

"You didn't tell him it was me, did you?"

"No, but I don't think I needed to. Everyone in Sugarplum Falls knows Sam Bartlett hasn't been on a date with anyone but you lately. And not on multiple successive dates with the same woman since Adelaide."

"Adelaide? Who's Adelaide?" A girlfriend? Gasp—a wife? Tabitha's mind raced. Of course, it was possible. With his movie-star good looks, and those Paul Newman blue eyes, women always noticed him. And there was no reason he wouldn't notice back. Except for that miles-thick shield around him. Could it be caused by the loss of someone he loved? Someone named

Adelaide? "Tell me, Poppy. Right now."

"So, here's the deal, Tabitha. I'll tell you all about Adelaide sometime—
if you'll tell me what it was like to kiss Sam Bartlett."

"Poppy!" Tabitha looked over her shoulder. The only other person in the
shop was a teenager with over-the-ear headphones on. Still, Tabitha lowered
her voice. "I'm not going to talk about that."

"Come on. It's written on your face that you were hoping to kiss him."

Maybe. But that wasn't the point right now. "Who is Adelaide?"

Alas, a group of cider-thirsty patrons entered, pulling Poppy away and
leaving Tabitha in the dark.

There were apparently more reasons Sam needed time to trust Tabitha
before kissing her.

What was his history with Adelaide, whoever she was?

Chapter 19

Sam

After that chemical overdose in Tabitha's living room last night, Sam didn't have a prayer of falling asleep. Instead, he'd lain awake for an hour, just letting the blood rush in his ears and the beat of his heart occupy his thoughts.

No doubt, this woman had awakened him out of hibernation. Her aliveness. Her insight. Not to mention that insistent pout begging him to kiss her.

Since he hadn't told her about Adelaide yet, thank heaven above he'd resisted.

Sort of. She'd been the one to press on the final brake.

When sleep eluded him, he went down to his garage and pulled out his snow shovel, then resumed his rounds. He'd missed Mrs. Langford's house the other morning, but she didn't have her dialysis appointment until Wednesday and didn't get out much otherwise, so he'd gone to Collette Honeycutt's first. She had Pilates and Bunco on Mondays. Mrs. Langford only lived around the corner, so he trekked over there through the snow and began pushing it aside in the moonlight.

Every scrape down to the concrete cleared his mind a little more. By the time he finished, he'd almost purged his arteries and veins of the cocktail of Tabitha's near-kiss. No cold shower required.

But, back at home, after he put away his shovel, his mind hadn't followed suit. She was still in there, her green eyes wide and inviting and urging him to action.

Instead of writhing in regret, he went to his roll-top desk and turned the key. When he slid open the lid, each slat folding away inside the top, there sat his pen and his incomplete novel. He switched on the desk lamp, sat down, and stared at the untouched stack of papers.

His story. With Adelaide. It sang somewhere between his ears and the back of his chest. Usually it called for him to complete the manuscript, give it an ending with closure. And always he'd ignored that clarion call. However, tonight, in the wee hours of his post-date adrenaline rush, the lyrics of its song had changed dramatically.

Don't finish me, it said. *It's time to write something new.*

For a long minute, Sam sat still. The skin of his face tingled, and so did his fingertips. He gazed at the unfinished stack of printed pages, stalled at the false high of the midpoint.

Then … he opened the center drawer and placed the manuscript inside.

From a compartment at the front of his desk he pulled out a clean sheet of paper. So clean, it didn't even have lines on it. He set it before himself and stared at the blank page. A picture formed in his mind, images of something brand new.

Sam lifted his favorite pen and began to write.

Hours later, the day dawned, and Sam found himself asleep at his desk, his head on his folded arms, resting atop five pages of handwritten prose. He rubbed the side of his face, and went to the bathroom, where the mirror showed proof on the side of his face that he really had written something last night. In fact, the transfer from his pen to his face reflecting back at him in the mirror made it perfectly legible instead of backwards. Even if it did lean at a horrible slant.

Huh. He tilted his chin to reread the blurry handwriting while he brushed his teeth. Not bad. The adjectives were a little flowery and could use some paring back, but for a long-out-of-practice effort, the visible sentence had merit.

Tabitha did it. She encouraged me to write.

And he had.

Tabitha Townsend. If she were here right now, he wouldn't dither and say he wasn't sure. She'd unlocked a door inside him that had rusted on its hinges. And—he was going to see her today at lunchtime at the art gallery's solarium. Yes, they were supposedly discussing music, but this felt so much bigger. He had to tell her about his breakthrough, right?

Unless, it might make her feel pressured.

Again, the uncertainty.

But much, much less.

Someday he'd tell her. Someday he'd kiss her.

"You're chipper today." Mrs. Milliken gave him a sly smile. "Did the marinara sauce work its love magic on your date?"

"Gracie!" George called from the back room. "Lay off the guy. He's not beholden to inform you of any of his dating activities. It's not like he's one of your students. He's your boss."

"Sorry, boss." Her smile didn't dim. "I'll just get back to work on setting up this display of handmade Christmas ornaments. If you need someone to rehash your date with, though, I'm all ears."

No doubt. "I'll keep that in mind." He headed for his office where he worked until lunch. Then he said, "Going out. I'll be back in an hour."

"Take as long a break as you need." Mrs. Milliken and her eye-glint. Ugh. "We're just thrilled you're taking a lunch."

Oh, brother. "Yes, I'm meeting Tabitha, but we're only finishing up our preparations for the nursing home performance tonight."

"You're taking that photo album instead of the sheet music?"

The sheet music was in his car. "I'm looking for the owner. There's someone I think may be able to help me with that."

"Does that someone have red hair and a mouth like a china doll's?"

"Gracie!"

If she must know—"Yes, as a matter of fact."

Mrs. Milliken's gasp was cut silent by the shutting of the door behind him.

With the photo album under his arm, Sam headed over to the Sugarplum Falls Art Gallery to meet Tabitha.

Chapter 20

Tabitha

Sitting at the little metal table, Tabitha resisted the urge to pull her knees up to her chest and curl into a ball. Sugarplum Falls Art Gallery's solarium was probably not the most popular place to go into fetal position. But any second now, Sam was going to walk into this poinsettia-laden room, where an orchestra playing soothing holiday jazz floated through the speaker system, and he'd insist they plan a song together.

Or three.

To sing. Out loud. In front of people.

How could she possibly hide her angry-chimp-like singing voice in a room with a soaring ceiling and ridiculously good acoustics?

Except, in he walked, and Tabitha's gasp bounced around the glass room.

Bless his heart! In his arm wasn't a pile of songbooks but that fabled photo album.

"Hi." Sam's face was red. Was that from being out in the cold?

Heat crawled up Tabitha's neck, and she tugged at her scarf. "It's good to see you." She started to rise from her wrought-iron chair.

"Don't get up." He plunked the photo album down on the aging metal patio-table with its green patina. "It's probably not important what songs we pick for tonight. This is more pressing if we're going to find the owners before Christmas. I hope that's okay."

Was it ever! "You're right. We might need every day we can get."

"Good." He shrugged off his coat. "I checked with the front desk. They said they'll bring our lunch as soon as the kitchen has it ready. I hope you like soup and sandwiches."

"Thank you." How nice. "I didn't realize we could eat here." Art galleries usually had strict *no food or drink* policies.

"Really? Hasn't anyone told you about the best bakery in Sugarplum

117

Falls?"

"You mean Sugarbabies Bake Shop?"

"They're good for sweet things, but the art gallery's kitchen wins hands down on all things made with yeast. Their sprouted wheat bread is the stuff of legends."

"Sounds delicious." As did Sam's voice, and pretty much everything he said and the way he said it.

"Ready to check it out?" Sam pushed the book toward her and then moved his wrought-iron chair around to her side of the table, its legs scraping lightly on the flagstone floor. "Warm in here, eh?"

Really warm, at least when she looked at the future kiss that hid at the edge of his lips. Pheromones floated off him, pulling her in again. "Much warmer than I'd expect in an all-glass room in winter." She tugged at her scarf again pulling it away from her too-warm neck.

He did have a heating effect on her.

For a second, his gaze lingered on her exposed neck, but then he opened the cover of the photo album, as if reminding himself why he was really here. "It's hard to imagine you're going to know who these people are, since this album seems to be older than you are."

"Maybe, but I spent summers and Christmases in Sugarplum Falls growing up, and Grandma invites everyone over for her card games and social clubs. I might recognize a feature or two on a face as someone local's relative."

"I'll give you that. However, I already showed my intrepid staff of two. If Mr. and Mrs. Milliken don't recognize them, chances are strong these aren't pictures of Sugarplum Falls locals. That's the problem I'm up against."

"People change, though. Some more than others." Tabitha opened the cover and began thumbing through the pages. "Look at this one. Everyone has matching plaid pajamas. And this one with a toy train set up around the tree. And this one with the dog attacking the train." Dozens more precious moments were captured in the pages, but Sam was right. Not a single face rang a bell. "I'm sorry. I'll see what I can find out through other avenues, though. Can I take photos of the photos?"

"Sure."

"Notice I'm not asking you to loan me the book. I'm aware you already don't trust me with certain *other* valuable books." She arched a brow. Tension between them tightened until she broke into a grin.

"Of course not. But that's because you would want to give it away to someone I've never met. I might never see it again."

"True enough." She pulled out her camera to begin cataloging.

"Did you come to Sugarplum Falls between college semesters?"

"Me? College?" She gave a dry laugh. "After a year of repeatedly missing classes and assignments, I realized it wasn't a good fit for my personality and I dropped out. *Long* before getting that juris doctorate Dad always said would make him proud of me." Her face was officially on fire. "Why am I telling you all this?"

"Don't worry about me." He turned a page for her when she finished snapping pictures of all the photos on the current spread. "I didn't finish either."

Gasp. "Really?" She steeled herself from sounding overeager. "But you own your own store and are so ... educated."

"It was my grandpa's general store, and I happened to be the only grandchild who would want to inherit."

"But you have this professor thing going on. Forgive me for being taken off-guard that you're not a college man."

"To your other point, it's possible to be educated outside of a classroom, especially if you surround yourself with good books. And read them. Come on, I've heard you speak and tried sparring with you in bidding wars. You've outsmarted me time and again. Don't give me that *not smart* stuff based on a piece of paper." He rolled his eyes. "I've never met a woman who would show up at a storage unit with a drone to outwit the whole assemblage of people. You're brilliant and you know it."

Every cell in Tabitha's body tingled. Her face was both on fire and numb at the same time. Sam couldn't mean that. No one thought Tabitha was smart.

But ... I did have strong kung fu that day.

She'd consider his words more later, when she wasn't busy being electrocuted by them anymore. "But you at least started at the university."

119

He sobered and nodded. "Some things happened around the beginning of my second year of college. My life's plans changed." He traced the curlicues of wrought-iron painted white on the tabletop.

"Oh?" What could dissuade a man like Sam who exuded intellectuality and brilliance from finishing college? In Tabitha's case, it made sense. She and the classroom were not friends. She was more of a hands-on, trial-and-error, make-mistakes-until-you-get-it learner. But Sam was probably born with a book in his hand. "Is it something you can talk about?"

He lifted his eyes. "You'd actually want to know?"

If he had any idea how long she'd pined for his attention, for a connection with him on any and every level! "I—I want to know everything about you, Sam."

Chapter 21

Sam

T he wrought-iron chair grew cold against his back as Tabitha's invitation wedged itself in a crack in the mortar between blocks of his emotional wall and expanded. *Trust and openness are what I want in a relationship.* But by opening up about Adelaide, he'd really be letting Tabitha onto sacred ground. He'd thought he was almost ready last night. Was he?

The air was fresh with pine scent. Christmas hymns played so softly through the sound system they were like a prayer, and the sun shone bright and warm through the dome of glass, almost as if Adelaide herself could descend and tell him, *It's all right. Tabitha can know about us.*

Really? If he did this, he'd be moving forward. Away from Adelaide and toward something new.

Here goes. It all poured out.

"I started college with lots of plans, and they all included my high school sweetheart. We'd known each other all our lives, but we became a couple after sitting by each other in sophomore English class. Adelaide was always arguing with the teacher about everything, and I told her to put a sock in it one day, and she brought a sock the next day and gave it to me. We were together after that."

There was more to their emotional bonding, of course, but that was how it had started. Tabitha probably didn't want to know all this. He looked up from the table and glanced at her. Since they'd slid their chairs side by side, it would have been easy for her to avoid eye-contact, but she was fully gazing at him, as if prompting him to go on.

"We both signed up for classes at the private college in Darlington, but approaching Christmastime and finals, she was having trouble getting to class, staying out sick most days. I thought maybe she had mono, or a flu. She didn't want me to, but I called her parents. They came to check on her, and that was her last weekend at college."

"What was wrong?"

"Advanced leukemia." Even now, the words were spikes. "I had a front row seat to her life. I should have noticed sooner."

"You did notice. You called her family."

Yeah, too late. "When school started again in January, I didn't have the heart to leave her. She was in treatment, and I couldn't exactly say, 'Well, bye,' and head back to school."

"You stayed by her side."

I even married her. But it didn't help. "She mostly wanted someone to read to her. TV gave her a headache. Only books took the edge off."

"What did you read?"

Of all questions. Not a follow-up to know what became of her, or anything like that. Instead, Tabitha asked about the books.

"Anything she wanted. *Ella Enchanted* was her favorite, but she also loved everything from spy novels by John Le Carré to space operas by Yardley Gregson."

"Did you write any stories for her?"

Sam stiffened. "How did you know that?" He turned toward Tabitha to read her face. Only innocence and sorrow were there.

"I didn't." She shrugged backward a little. "I just thought, you know, after hearing you tell me the story of *Angels Landing* last night that you would have been a good storyteller for her during that time."

Thoughts of the manuscript sitting in the closed desk drawer dragged through his mind. "After a truly novice first-attempt as a teenager, which will never again see the light of day, I did write a little something of value. It's not finished."

"Oh. Because she ..."

Died. It echoed in the silence.

"Yeah." Sam drew a deep breath and let it out slowly. "She wanted me to write something else. She made me promise."

A million little memories with Adelaide flashed through his mind, each a unique star twinkling. Their first date, their first kiss, opening their college acceptance letters at the same time at her parents' house and jumping for joy on the trampoline and sleeping out under the night sky with the Milky Way stretched above. That was the first time he'd told her he loved her. *I still love her.* So what if their marriage had lasted a month? A month could hold a lot of emotions. A lifetime of them.

"You'll write it, Sam." Tabitha placed a hand atop his. The cool brush of her skin was feather-light. "Whatever it is," she said, looking at her fingers, "and whenever it happens, I bet it will be amazing."

Tabitha tilted toward him and rested her head on his shoulder. Instrumental strains of "What Child is This?" filled the otherwise silent room. The sun shone down through the glass into a setting still and reverent enough for an angel to land.

Chapter 22

Tabitha

What should a person wear to a potential scene of public mortification? Was there a dress code for such an occasion? Certainly not one's favorite dress, or one's favorite anything. Probably something already despised, so as not to taint an otherwise perfectly good article of clothing.

Grandma popped her head in the door. "What's that?" Her upper lip curled at the mess on the bed and floor.

"A pile of discarded outfits?" Tabitha offered, wincing. Grandma didn't love slovenly ways. "I'll hang them all back up when I get back from Sweet Haven tonight."

"Not the clothes, Tabby dear. The book."

"Oh, that." Tabitha stepped out of the dressing area of her bedroom wearing an outfit she would have chosen for one of those paint-a-picture date nights. "It's a photo album."

Sam had changed his mind about letting her borrow it, after his story about Adelaide had taken up too much of his lunch hour for her to finish inventorying the pictures.

But I wouldn't trade that half hour for the world.

"Yes, but I don't see anyone of your generation creating that kind of book. Padded, quilted, and embroidered?"

"Yeah, it's older even than ours downstairs. Probably from the nineteen seventies."

"Uh-huh." Grandma reached for it, but then she looked up, and her gaze took in Tabitha's whole appearance—and her upper lip curled even further. "You're not going to the nursing home wearing that, are you?"

"What's wrong with it?" Tabitha looked down. Ah, that was what was wrong with it. "I'm just so worried about how I'll sound when I have to sing."

124

"So, in self-defense, you're trying to dress like some sort of rodeo clown to distract the listeners? That rainbow-striped sweater is the loudest thing I've heard since we used to get sonic booms from the Air Force Reserve base up yonder way." Then, Grandma's face softened. "Dear, what's really going on?"

Tabitha flopped down on the chair at the vanity, with a huge exhale of breath. She might as well ask someone who knew. "Did you know Adelaide? The girl Sam dated a long time ago?"

"Sure. Adelaide Johansen. He married her."

Married her. Of course he did. Because she was sick, and he was Sam, and Sam did noble things.

Tabitha leaned against the vanity, while Grandma perched on the corner of the clothes-strewn bed and told the story. "Adelaide's parents lived here until about five years ago. It was such a shame when they lost her so young. But they faced it with faith, and they've been able to move forward. Why? Did he tell you about her?"

Tabitha grimaced. "Yeah. A little."

"I think you should count that a very high honor."

An honor that he was in love with another woman, and that he would never *see* Tabitha?

"From what I understand from his extended family, he's never really opened up about her to any of them in all these years. Why do you still look sad?"

She shouldn't. Grandma was right. But, "I know I shouldn't feel like I have to compete with a man's memory of his first love, but somehow, I know I'll never measure up, so it makes me want to give up trying." She put her head in her hands. "He married her, you say?" That made her ache all the deeper—on his behalf, and on her own.

"Just a short time before her death, yes. Since then, he's dated very little, some a few years ago at his family's insistence, but none of his relationships amounted to much."

Which proved Adelaide was still obviously lodged in his heart. End of story. Tabitha could take her bows and exit stage right.

Except now, how to get through one more event with him before closing that door, or risk getting her heart mangled? "I'm not sure I can do it, Grandma."

"He'd be worth the patience."

"Oh, not that." True, Sam would be worth the patience. No question. He was one of the best guys she'd ever met, if not the best. He'd even restrained himself from kissing her when he sensed it might not be good timing. That was a great guy. But she'd never be enough for him. Especially after he heard her sing. "What I meant was, I don't think I can sing tonight. You've heard me try to warble out a tune, right?"

"Don't take this wrong, but you're not a good candidate for one of those TV show singing contests, except maybe as comic relief."

"Legends say the Honeycutts have the gift to make neighborhood pets howl."

"Yep. And it's been legendary for three generations, starting with Grandpa. Your aunt Charlotte may have been the worst, but you're a close second."

"When your grandma tells you that you're a terrible singer, no one can doubt it. Could you, maybe, call Mayor Lang and tell her I'm sick?"

"Not happening. I'm not going to cross Lisa Lang." Grandma slapped her thigh and gave a silent laugh. "Points for creativity, though—except, however, not for the creativity applied to what you're wearing."

"If I look clowny enough, the audience will just think I'm there as a joke, right? And I don't have to sing well."

"Maybe, but are you sure you ..." Grandma shook her head. "Never mind."

"No, say it." Tabitha bounced her knee. "Am I sure what?"

Grandma half-grimaced. "Are you sure you don't want to look like a knockout for Sam?"

Oh, that. Even if Sam would never see her as a viable possibility to replace Adelaide, Tabitha admittedly did want to look like a model for one of those designer perfume commercials for him.

Too bad facts were facts, and limitations were limitations. "I'm more on the *look cute* side than the knockout side." She placed her hands fingertip to

126

fingertip beneath her chin with palms down and batted her eyelashes and smiled. "See? Cute?"

"Cute, yes. But don't underplay your hand. You're not the type to give up on something good."

Wasn't she? Tabitha had abandoned two tanked businesses and dropped out of college. "Are we talking about me, here? I'm Tabitha, remember?"

"I remember, believe me." Grandma laughed. "Look, I may have an idea for your singing problem. You do your best knockout imitation while I go upstairs and look through a few of your grandpa's old things." She stood up and then came to give Tabitha a side-hug. "It's going to be fine, Tabby-girl. You're doing better at this *life* thing than you know."

Sure, she was. Humph. She went back to the closet and peeled off the Bozo outfit. At the back hung a sparkly silver sheath she'd worn just once to a college formal dance. Not while *she* was in college, but her date had been. They'd met at church, and he'd asked her to the dance. It had been her one and only big college memory. Tonight, the dress seemed to be begging for another holiday outing.

If Grandma said to stop trying to underplay it, maybe a broad swing in the other direction was better. It couldn't hurt to show Sam she valued his opinion of her.

The dress still fit well. She added jewelry, fixed her makeup with a sultry eye-shadow, the kind other people could always manage, and for some reason Tabitha was magically able to achieve today. The *smoky* eye. It actually looked good for once. She applied a darker red lipstick, because … the holidays.

Yeah, this was a much better tack to take: when she sounded awful, at least she could lean on that old line, *But you look marvelous.*

"Knock-knock." Grandma stood at the bedroom door beaming, holding something in her right fist. But when Tabitha turned around, she gave a low whistle. "And you said you didn't do knockout. Yowza, young lady. He's going to be down for the count."

"It's just a service project. It's too much, right?"

"No such thing."

"What do you have?"

Grandma tiptoe-jogged forward. "I found it." She beamed again. "It's going to solve everything."

Tabitha looked down at the cylinder in Grandma's hand. It took a moment to sink in, but soon Tabitha nodded. "I do believe you're right, Grandma dear. This *is* going to solve everything."

Chapter 23

Sam

Late. After everything that had transpired between him and Tabitha in the museum, he'd been floating on air and losing track of time all afternoon, and now—what would she think of him? *What had she been thinking all afternoon about his confessional session?* Would she be more distant from him, now that she knew his past?

Sam speed-talked into the phone. "I'm so sorry, Tabitha. We had a last-minute customer rush at the store, and I couldn't leave Mr. and Mrs. Milliken in the soup. I'm just pulling into your driveway now."

He parked and jumped out of his truck, jogging up the front steps of the vintage ranch-style brick home. Lights clung to every straight line of the house and were crisscrossed over every juniper bush. Just as he raised his finger to ring the doorbell, the door swung open, and Tabitha stood bathed in light.

"Whoa." He grabbed the iron porch rail. "I mean ..." Words fled. If sparkles were to morph into human form, they'd have been Tabitha Townsend in that moment. Every inch of her caught the porch light, from the shine of her hair, to the gleam in her eyes, to the smile that weakened his knees. And that dress! That silver fabric draped over her elegantly, highlighting all the right places. Tonight Tabitha belonged on a red carpet, not Sugarplum Falls. *Yet it's for my eyes only right now.* And he basked in it. "You look incredible."

"Thank you." Her eyes dipped, and he was slain all over again.

"Shall we?" He offered his arm. She pulled a black wraparound coat over her shoulders, covering up that gorgeous ... everything.

"What time are they expecting us?" She wasn't letting on how she'd felt after processing his story at lunch.

"Is that a different shade of lipstick?" He tried to sound casual. The deep red of her lipstick was going to ruin him. Sam helped her down the steps, which were blessedly already swept, since she wore a pair of very sexy heels.

"Do you like it?"

Did wise-men ride camels? "I'll be the envy of the night. The ninety-genarians will be fighting me for a place at your side." He helped her into the car, and he pulled out onto the winter roads. *Does she think of us as being side by side?* Still, no clues from her tone. She wasn't sitting any closer or any farther from him. No body-language hints, either.

He was dying.

"Is that a word, ninety-genarians?" She pointed to a house. "I love how they put lights on every single branch of every single tree."

"That's Mrs. Langford's house."

"The widow with a walker? How ... ?"

"She's always loved Christmas lights, so the teenage boys from church always come and do up her trees for her."

"How sweet. Reminds me of another ongoing kindness someone has been performing for my grandma for years. Anytime it snows, there's a lone shovel-man who clears her driveway. She can never seem to catch him in the act."

Sam gripped the wheel like his life depended on it. He kept his tone steady. "Ah, the phantom snow-remover."

"Exactly. It means so much to me. If I knew who he was, I'd probably give him a really big kiss."

The truck jerked to the right, its wheels rolling off the pavement onto the shoulder, and Sam righted it, narrowly avoiding a skid. *The first clue?* "Sorry about that. Slick road."

"I see you don't like it if I mention kissing another man." Her tone had a playfulness, like she knew she was tormenting him. Did she know? And—did she like him?

"It's not that," he said darkly. "It's ... never mind. Here we are. Only three minutes after our scheduled performance time. If we rush, they may still be wheeling the patrons into the gathering room." He came around and helped her out of the truck, but he paused. "Hey, Tabitha? About our discussion this afternoon—"

"There's not really time now. Let's go."

While they signed in and applied stick-on name badges, he whispered, "I can't believe we're going to wing this. Just tell me which three songs you like most or know the lyrics best, and that'll be our show. You decide."

"Don't worry about me and lyrics." For some reason she patted her pocket. "As long as we choose familiar tunes, it'll be fine."

For a short moment, concern prickled at the skin on his neck, but a coordinator bustled toward them, gathering their coats. "I am so glad you're here. We are so ready for our guests. What will you be singing? Or is it a surprise?"

Yeah, even to themselves.

"Just introduce us as Sam Bartlett and Tabitha Townsend." He took Tabitha's hand and helped her stay steady on the slick tile floors. Those heels looked deadly in more ways than one.

And when her wrap went to the coat closet, Sam had a hard time remembering what day it was, and his name, and up from down. That dress, those curves. Good night, nurse!

"And now, ladies and gentlemen, Sam Bartlett and Tabitha Townsend!" The coordinator announced them the second they stepped across the threshold of the spacious room. It was filled wall-to-wall with elderly people, crocheted or quilted blankets across their laps, in various states of wakefulness. "They'll be singing holiday classics for you tonight. Take it away, Sam and Tabitha."

A few meager claps rose from the audience.

Sam looked at Tabitha. She looked much calmer than when they'd been discussing the topic all-too-briefly earlier. "What do you want to sing?"

"You choose. But just so you know, I'm not—"

"Townsend! Isn't she a Honeycutt? She *looks* like a Honeycutt." A gruff voice hollered from the second row of the semi-circled wheelchairs and recliners. "Oh, Barbara, you didn't bring us a Honeycutt, did you? Quick, everyone. Turn down your earpieces—before it's too late."

"Honeycutt!" another person's voice cracked. "Not any relation to Lanny Honeycutt, please. Nurse? I'm not feeling well. I need to go to my room."

A grumbling rose everywhere in the room, taking Sam aback. He side-whispered to Tabitha, "What are they talking about? Who's Lanny Honeycutt?"

131

"My grandpa. He died about ten years ago."

"But all these folks are talking like he's liable to loom up and attack them."

"Attack them with his bad singing, they mean. He *really* couldn't sing. It was the stuff of local legend."

"This is Sugarplum Falls. Everyone can sing."

"Everyone but the Honeycutts. Mayor Lang must have forgotten, but apparently the older generation is still smarting." Tabitha didn't look nearly as worried as she should have, considering the mutiny brewing in front of them. Knitting needles could be used as deadly weapons at any moment.

"*You* can sing, though, right?"

"Depends on how you define it."

"Why didn't you say anything?"

She looked down at her toes and then back up at him. "Because ... I wanted to spend time with you."

In that moment, if Sam had been a hunk of gruyere cheese in a holiday fondue pot, he would have reached the perfect melting temperature instantly. *Second clue.* "So you were willing to ..."

"Humiliate myself? For your sake?" She pulled a wan smile. "I have it handled. My grandma came through for me." She held up her fist, and some kind of metallic tube peeked out from either side. "How about some of the less-reverent songs, though? Hymns might not go with my plans as well, unless they're really upbeat. Although, I guess 'Joy to the World' might work."

Meanwhile, the crowd had gotten restless.

More than one chair was jockeying for position at the exit, the spokes potentially getting caught in a neighbor's wheel brake, like a bad remake of *Ben Hur.*

"Marge and I are getting out of here, and you can't stop us, Julio."

"Make room for me, Willis, or I'll stab your wheel's tire and pop it." Marge wielded a knitting needle in earnest, like Sam's prophecy being fulfilled. "You coming?"

"Nuh-uh. You ladies can leave," Willis said. "Julio and I want a look-see at Collette's granddaughter. She's mighty glowing tonight. We'll just turn down our hearing aids."

"You're insane. And I'm telling you, you'd better get out of our way." Marge held up a rolled magazine.

Yikes. Things were turning violent—but, hey. Good singer or not, Tabitha did not deserve this rudeness.

"Enough!" Sam hollered, and all the chairs halted. "Now, roll it back, everyone. Tabitha and I have something great planned, and I guarantee you're going to love it."

Tabitha looked at him with pure amusement—well, maybe not pure. There could have been some admiration mixed in there, too. The red lipstick accentuated her smile and set off her straight white teeth to advantage. He could almost taste the spiced honey of her lips now, and—

"And if we don't love it? What of your guarantee then? Will you bring us each a book of our choice from your Angels Landing store?"

"Absolutely." In fact, he could do that anyway. "Now, settle in. This is happening."

Tabitha said, "I'm ready. Hit it, Sam."

Sam broke into "Joy to the World." He hadn't warmed up, and his voice wasn't as clear-toned as it used to be. That's what came of disuse. "Let earth receive her King!" he sang—at which point, Tabitha joined him.

With a kazoo.

The first heckler from the second row burst into laughter, and then a second heckler started to clap, and then they were all laughing and clapping.

The remainder of the verse and chorus, she hum-buzzed through the tune. Yeah, she was slightly off key, but with a kazoo, who cared? Clearly not this crowd. They were eating it up.

When it ended, they erupted in applause with as much energy as a crowd this size—and age—could offer. Tabitha bowed like she'd just performed *La Traviata* in Milan, and the naysayers ate it up.

"She's the prettiest kazooist we've had here all season," one lady said far too loudly. "I couldn't hear a sound, but she's right gorgeous. Has she been on television?"

"No, Tillie, that was her grandma who should have been on TV in a shampoo commercial. Hair the stuff of legends."

"What?"

This banter continued for a full minute until Sam realized he'd better move things along. He broke into "Rudolph," and then finished up with "Jingle Bells," which he invited everyone to join in singing at the end. They did, in syncopated disharmony.

Whew. That was over—or was it?

When Sam turned, wiping his brow in mock sweat-level exertion, Tabitha had departed his side and was crouching beside a recliner while a crocheting woman placed a hand on her shoulder and smiled, talking loudly, though Sam couldn't make out the conversation for the din of the other residents.

She looked like she might be visiting for a while.

Maybe he could try that, too.

A woman in a walker approached him. "You, Sam Bartlett, sound as good as you did back in high school when you and my great-grandson Donny sang during his freshman year and your senior year. Good young men. Nice voices. I'll always remember."

Donny Kingston. That was right. Good kid. "Thanks, Mrs. Kingston. You're very kind to remember me."

"Now, stop, you handsome devil. I can't believe you remember my name." She pinched his cheek. "I sure did love that sweetheart of yours, Adelaide. We all felt for you. She was a darling. It's so good to see you're finally making another friend." She emphasized the word *friend.*

Oh, brother. The matchmakers came in all ages and varieties. Not that Sam minded as much tonight. He could use that kind of a *friend.* A gorgeous one. An ingenious one. Who wasn't afraid to laugh at herself.

The director came and took Sam by the arm. "I can't believe you saved the day like that. How on earth did Mayor Lang forget that Tabitha was a Honeycutt? Close call, but brilliant save. Come back again anytime. But don't forget the kazoo!"

Nearly all the residents were being wheeled down halls now, and although Sam and Tabitha offered to help, they were shooed out. "I bet you haven't had dinner yet, and your date is dressed to go somewhere nice." The director winked. "Don't let that outfit go to waste."

"I won't." He accepted their coats, helped Tabitha into hers, and they exited to the parking lot. "That was incredible. I had no idea you were hiding such talent." Her kung fu had proved very strong tonight.

"Such *lack* of talent, you mean, of course."

"Your gifts are varied. Including brilliant problem-solving."

"I have to give credit for that to my grandma."

"Sometimes the brilliance comes in recognizing other people's brilliance." He helped her into his truck, sneaking a glance at the sheen of her stockings. "Where would you like to go to dinner? I'm starving." *And not just for dinner.* The feel of her head on his shoulder at lunchtime today, the empathy rolling off her like a warm quilt at a cozy fire, and the scent of her skin played through his mind.

Tabitha wasn't Adelaide. But she *was* Tabitha. And she made him want to write. And sing. And talk to the elderly residents of Sweet Haven. And be a better person who didn't just hide with his books all the time, but who got out and talked to people outside the bookstore.

"Anywhere without karaoke," she said with a grin.

That left a pretty narrow selection: Mario's, which they'd eaten last night, and the Sugarplum Falls Art Gallery, which was closed this time of day. There were also a few out-of-the-way places that wouldn't call for silver dresses. Not much else. "How about the drive-up burger and shake place?"

"Ding-ding-ding! I think we have a winner."

"Unless you want to go up the canyon." There was the very nice restaurant at Frosty Ridge Lodge. "You're dressed for surf and turf." Sam, however, was dressed for turf only. Chinos and a red sweater; although, the wait staff at the resort would only have had eyes for Tabitha in that silver number and not even noticed who was on her arm other than to be horrifically envious in passing, so his clothes wouldn't matter. "Have I told you that you look amazing tonight?"

"Thank you. You think so?" She glanced down at herself. "I'm glad you like it."

"You're surpassing, like the glow on a rosy ocean. Glittering."

"Ah, you should be a writer." She squint-smiled.

"That was Lord Byron's metaphor, not mine. But actually, I did take your nudge."

She turned toward him, her hem hiking a few inches above her knee and risking another near-run-off-the-road. "You're writing something? When would you have had time?"

"Last night." Sam tore his eyes off her legs and forced them back to where he was going. "A little something came to me when I couldn't sleep."

"You couldn't sleep either?"

"Not a wink."

They pulled in at the burger and shake drive-up and ordered—cheeseburgers, fries, and two chocolate shakes, gluttons for cold punishment that they'd both turned out to be. "You sure you want a shake? It's cold tonight."

"I can eat ice cream any time of year." Tabitha took a big sip through the straw.

Sam drove to the best view in town—the overlook of Sugarplum Falls.

"Look! We got here in time for the light show," she said. She tuned his radio to the shortwave station that played the music for the show. Down below, different holiday scenes projected in colored lights onto the tower of frozen waterfall, made from the Sugar River flowing from Sugar Lake, changing to the beats of the music on the radio—everything from Santa in a sleigh to a nativity scene complete with sheep and donkeys and shepherds at the manger.

"Which scene in the light show do you like best?" Sam asked. The show was mostly the same every year.

"Believe it or not, I've been here every winter and never watched it."

"Really?"

"Well, Grandma has a strangely strong preference for white lights, and any colored lights, even in a show, are the glass-and-filament equivalent of persona non grata—so the Waterfall Lights is not on our holiday rotation."

"You're missing out on some very good laser-projected vignettes, I must say." He took his burger and ate a bite. "So, you've never seen the light show, and I'd never met you before this winter—even though you said you've been here every Christmas. Help me out. How have our paths never crossed?"

"They've probably crossed."

"Don't tell me … you have known who I am and not the reverse." He sounded like an idiot. Moreover, he sounded like an idiot begging for compliments. "You noticed me."

"You're hard to miss when you're out scraping my grandma's driveway—and all the other widows' driveways—every snowy morning."

She knew! Sam's face must have gone as pale as those snow piles on the banks of Sugar Lake. "Who else knows?"

"Don't worry, sneaky snow-plow man. Your secret's safe with me." She nudged him, sliding a little closer. "I get it that everyone celebrates Christmas in their own ways. Me, I do gifts."

"But, how did you find out?" Was he not-so-stealthy in his ski mask?

"It was a long time ago. I stayed with Grandma the first Christmas after Grandpa Lanny died. She was sad to the level of being paralyzed, so I just sat with her, watching Christmas movies alternated with crying jags and bowls of soup. It snowed a lot, and then you came along."

Right. The year Lanny Honeycutt died. That was the first year Sam had begun it. Part of his grief process. *If I help people, I won't feel as sad.* That had been the reasoning. And Adelaide's dislike of driving in snow. It fit. "I didn't wear the ski mask until the second year."

So, Tabitha had known him—for a long time. Admired him, maybe? Appreciated, anyway. Sam sat back. How come she hadn't said anything?

She knows what it means to give in secret.

In fact, that was what her entire business was based around—giving in a way that others could take the credit. A sweetness coursed through him.

Tabitha sipped her shake. "Maybe I shouldn't have ordered ice cream after all. I'm going to start shivering until I fall into a million sequins."

Sam adjusted the heater so it blew hot and directly on her legs, which he was having a hard time not staring at. As everything about her grew more and more attractive, he was in a massive fight with himself to keep his hands off her. But did he need to? Really?

Just until he knew what she thought of his past. "Today, when we were talking in the glass room of the museum, I told you some pretty heavy stuff."

"You mean you *trusted me* with it."

True. "How—how are you holding up under the weight of it?"

"The question should be, how are you doing now that you've shared some of the burden of it?" Her gaze was tender. It gave him hope. It gave him permission.

"Better," he whispered. "Have I told you how beautiful you are?" He set his milkshake down and slid on the bench seat toward her. "Or how much you revive me?"

Tabitha dropped her french fry. In the starlight, she was exquisite. And she was looking at him like she could belong to him.

"I'm going to kiss you, Tabitha."

"Are you sure?" she whispered.

Tonight, yes. He was sure. He hadn't been this sure of anything in a very long time.

Chapter 24

Tabitha

She never expected her first kiss with the man of her decade-long crush to happen while she had a lap full of fries, or while she quivered uncontrollably from drinking a chocolate shake on a winter's night. Off in the distance, Sugarplum Falls danced with color and festive scenes of reindeer and a Christmas star rising up a frozen waterfall, and scores of other cars were parked all around them to watch the light show.

But when Sam said, "I'm sure," in that soul-strumming voice, only Sam and she existed. They could have been at the North Pole or on the moon.

With three fingers, he brushed salt crystals off her mouth, tugging her lower lip slightly open. Her tongue nipped out and tasted the salt from her upper lip.

Sam groaned. "Go easy on me."

"Hmm?"

"I mean, do that kind of thing and you turn my blood to fifty percent kerosene."

So, he was liable to go up in flames, too? Shivers of heat and cold alternated across her skin. She pressed her hand to her stomach to try and quell the tremors. "I'm freezing, or else I'm …" What? Trembling at the thought of his impending kiss?

"Funny, I'm way too hot." He lifted her hand and pressed the back of it to his forehead, and then to his cheek, and then to his neck, curling her fingers around his. "See?" He placed her fingers across his mouth. Then he pressed his fingers across hers, and slowly inched their hands aside, leaning in, his lips finally connecting with hers.

At first it was gentle, just a brush. Like the first flakes of the first snow of winter. Or a breeze off Sugar Lake. Cool, fresh, dotting her skin with chills and excitement.

Then, the crystals of his snowfall gathered, falling in clusters, gracing her lips with tingling points of stimulation. Each of her ten million neurons stood at attention, and she was both in a trance and as awake as she'd ever been in her life. His snowfall became a blinding blizzard, every sigh and touch a storm of ice and fire churning her into drifts high enough to obscure her view of anything else in all the world ever again.

"Hey, Crouching Tiger," she whispered between assaults. "Your kissing kung fu is strong."

"I bow to your prowess, Hidden Dragon." He placed an expert kiss on her collarbone, practically cutting her to the quick, and then kissed her long and deeply.

"I think I like date-six first kisses more than date-three first kisses." She sighed as he drove her home, sometime after the light show ended and all the other cars were gone.

"Maybe we should talk to Mayor Lang about that." Sam headed for Grandma Honeycutt's house. "We could demonstrate the difference for her."

She stayed snuggled up beside him for the remainder of the drive, until he pulled in at her house. "Thanks for shoveling Grandma's driveway all these years." And for saying Tabitha was brilliant. And a problem-solver—not a problem creator.

Fact was, ever since she'd started on this quest that took her to Sam's store daily, her business acumen had improved. That, or she'd finally hit on a business idea that harnessed her talents, and she was using them. And not failing. Well, mostly not failing.

"Thanks for keeping my identity a secret." He put the truck in park. "Can I see you again soon? As in, tomorrow? How early do you wake up?"

He sounded so eager to see her, it raised a giddy flame in her chest. "I'll come by the bookshop. We can research the photo album more."

"You're luminous." He leaned in and gave her a parting kiss, sweeter this time. Tender. Protective. Possessive. "Good night, Tabitha."

"Good night, Sam."

Luminous. That meant full of light. A synonym for brilliant. Bright. Maybe he really didn't think of her as the dolt everyone else seemed to.

Around him, she wasn't one.

A loud knock sounded on the passenger side window of the truck. Tabitha jumped, knocking her now-melted chocolate shake and nearly spilling it down her shin. "Jumping Jehoshaphat!" Who would do such a thing?

The windows were too fogged over to see, but the voice sounded loud and clear.

"Tabby-girl! Tabby! Where on earth did you get this photo album?"

Chapter 25

Sam

Kissing Tabitha had made him lose track of time—and brain cells. Here he was, a thirty-year-old widower who should know better than to make out in a truck instead of offering her a classy first-kiss on the porch. Geez. His windows had a serious telltale fog to them, and his lips probably bore the stain of Tabitha's irresistible burgundy-red lipstick. Collette Honeycutt would know exactly what had been going on between him and her granddaughter.

Tabitha opened the truck door and alighted. "That album belongs to Sam. Do you know anyone in it?"

"I certainly do!" She waved the album.

Sam cut the engine and jogged around to their side of the truck to help both women across the wintry driveway. "Is it a relative or a friend of yours?"

"Yes. It's like jumping in a time machine. I'm sorry I snooped, but people your age just don't have photo albums, especially not like this and—"

"No, Grandma! Don't worry about that." Tabitha put an arm around her Grandma as they reached the porch. "Let's go inside where it's warm." They headed into the house.

"Sam Bartlett, how did you end up with my friend Della's family photo album?"

"Those pictures are of Della?" Tabitha gasped. "The friend you were talking with the other day? My heart is leaping, Grandma. I can't believe it."

Sam's heart jumped as well. "Your friend is in the photos?" Hallelujah! A Christmas miracle. "How I got it is a strange story …"

Inside, in the rear of the house was a sunken living room with a massive hearth, a huge Christmas tree to eclipse the sizable one in the front room with the piano, and a roaring fire. Two stockings hung on the mantel, one labeled *Grandma* and the other *Tabitha*.

And yet, some of the same items filled this room as had been in the photos Tabitha had shown him of herself as a babe in her mother's arms. A chair here, a wall-hanging there. Like a time capsule.

"Tell me your strange story." Mrs. Honeycutt chose a brown tweed recliner and perched on its edge.

"I stumbled across it at a … in an acquisition I made recently."

"He stole it from me, Grandma." Tabitha shot him a playful glare. "Okay, he bought it from me after I won it in the storage unit auction."

"Oh, that. I heard about that." She pulled an afghan off the back of the couch over herself. "I play Bunco with Gracie Milliken."

Of course that was where the news came from. "Suffice it to say, we were surprised to find the album in a box labeled Inglewood Cookbooks."

"She called me the other day, out of the blue." Mrs. Honeycutt shook her head as if sore amazed. "I hadn't been able to track down Della for years, and she hung up in a hurry before I could get her address, but still, we had such a good visit, reliving the past. You know, she had all the best ideas for mischief when we were in grade school, got us into a few near-serious scrapes."

"Scrapes?" Tabitha asked. "What kind of scrapes?"

"I wasn't always the decrepit lump you see standing before you today."

Ha. Hardly. She looked more like she could have starred in one of those vitamin commercials for women over sixty, where the woman was shown riding a bike up a mountain with her hair flying behind her and her activewear hugging smooth, crêpe-free skin.

"Della and her sister Edwina and I ended up doing some crazy things. Let's leave it at that."

Edwina? What a misfortune of a name. Sam moved a step away from the too-warm fire. It smelled like hickory in here, very homey.

"You'd deny us the stories, Grandma? No. You have to tell." Tabitha rubbed her hands together. "How about this: if you aren't able to reach her, I'll use my super-online-sleuth skills to track down your old friend to give back this photo album—on the condition that you tell us about three of the scrapes."

Tabitha's grandma's escapades with Della and Edwina involved making log rafts and floating them down irrigation canals, collecting water snakes and placing them strategically in neighborhood front-porch milk delivery boxes, and even nearly jumping off Sugar River Bridge up above the falls.

"It's a good thing Edwina talked us out of that, or we could have been seriously dead." Grandma Honeycutt giggled. "And there would be no Tabitha here today to help you fog up the windows of your truck on a frosty night."

"Grandma!"

Sam shrank to two feet tall. "Mrs. Honeycutt, I—"

"Don't worry. Lanny and I were young once, too." Mrs. Honeycutt gave an exaggerated wink, complete with the open mouth and the scrunched side-of-the-face.

"Grandma," Tabitha said, "can we call Della now?"

"Sure. Let's do it." Mrs. Honeycutt pulled out her phone. "Let's see, we were talking the other day, and ..." She pressed *dial*. "This should do it."

Everyone held their breath. Well, Sam did. Getting the album to its rightful owner this year instead of waiting until next would make his Christmas so much more meaningful. Less commercial—which it was by nature as a shop owner.

A tinny voice came through the receiver of Mrs. Honeycutt's phone. Her face fell.

"It says the number is out of service." She winced. "I guess I shouldn't be surprised. Della did tend to have her chaotic times."

Disappointing. Sam let out his breath. "Do you have any idea where she's living?"

Mrs. Honeycutt frowned. "It should have been the first thing we talked about, but she wanted to reminisce and then tell me about her grandbabies. Her daughter ended up having seven children, and they all are grown now with babies of their own. She's got quite the posterity, believe it or not. I'm so happy for her. And she sounded happy. I bet she'd love to see this album more than anything, and share it with her kids."

Sure, but how?

Tabitha cleared her throat. "If there's one skill I've developed to the point of obsession, it's scouring the internet for difficult-to-find items." She cringed. "Not that your bestie is an *item*, but you know what I mean."

Tabitha to the rescue! Sam gazed at her. She really was brilliant. And luminous. A light in his room. She'd slid the dimmer switch up, and he didn't have to squint at the text in his book of life anymore. She was there. "You're wonderful," he said.

"Is it okay, Grandma? Can I act like a sleuth and find Della?"

"Of course! Yes. Thank you, Sam. Thanks, Tabby. You're wonderful." Her smile rested on the center of his chest and melted into his heart. No, she wasn't upset with him for bringing Tabitha home in that well-kissed state. It almost seemed like she'd been hoping for it.

Tabitha stood and kissed her grandma's cheek. "Your kazoo idea was a hit."

"It was your grandpa's idea, actually. I'm glad I hung on to it." She sighed. "Now, if you're able to locate Della or Edwina or anyone from the family it will be a great gift. It's been too long."

"Do you remember when they left Sugarplum Falls?" Tabitha asked, taking the photo album back and setting it on the mantel.

"Years ago. Almost fifty now. Not long after Della's antics got her into actual trouble. She and I grew apart in high school because I started dating Grandpa Lanny. Unfortunately, Della found a high school football player boyfriend. Boy, he was a mean one, but Della refused to drop him, even when everyone told her he was bad. They got married right after graduation, had a baby girl—just one. And shortly after that, something happened. Not sure about details, but I do know her family had to do the olden-days equivalent of an intervention to get Della away from him. She was very unhappy, I do know that. And later, she and Edwina had a horrendous fight. I don't think they've spoken. I can't imagine a decades-long rift in my family like that."

Very sad. "Maybe that would make these photos all the more precious." Sam ran his hand over the top of the album. "We'd love to help you find your friend again."

Mrs. Honeycutt looked at them with pleading. "I really hope you do. Maybe the album will do something to help Della bring her family together again."

Chapter 26

Tabitha

The Cider Press hummed with activity. There was no chance of a private visit with Poppy today. But, look-a there at who was reading the *Hill Street Journal.*

"Andrew Kingston, right? Merry Christmas."

He pulled down his paper to peer over it at Tabitha. "Hi?"

It was one of those many situations where Tabitha knew someone better than that person knew her. Nature of her work. She had to research people without their knowing.

"I'm Tabitha Townsend."

"I know who you are. Poppy's friend." He didn't look friendly. He looked like he'd rather prosecute her for parking tickets than chat.

"Nice to meet you," Tabitha squeaked, and her greeting sounded more like a question. Maybe this was a mistake. "I saw you at the Hot Cocoa Festival with Poppy."

"Yeah?" A tiny light sparked in his eye at Poppy's name. "And I saw you there, too."

Perfect. Tabitha had to do this right, had to manage it in such a way that he wouldn't detect that Tabitha was helping Poppy discover his ideal gift. The gift to end all Andrew Kingston gifts. More than the pewter cider-stirrer, for sure, although he did have that resting in his cider mug today.

Cute.

"That was a good night. You were there with Bartlett, I recall."

"Uh-huh. Sam." Ooh, she couldn't start thinking about Sam or she'd get starry-eyed, and she had work to do. "So, can I ask you for help? I'm trying to think of a present for my good friend back in Darlington. He's a lawyer, and about your age, and I'm really racking my brain. Christmas is almost here, and I'm stumped. Can you help me? What do lawyers want for Christmas?"

146

He looked a lot less interested in this conversation than in the mention of Poppy a second ago. And talk about *not stealthy.* Tabitha was totally losing her touch. "Never mind. I will just come up with something."

"What's your friend's name in Darlington? I know a lot of the attorneys over there."

"Uhhh," she blanked. "Steve?" There could be a hundred lawyers in Darlington named Steve, right?

"Steve who? Steve Marsden?" All of a sudden Andrew, sat forward. "As it turns out, I get a little kick out of gift-giving—when it's a gift for the right person." His eyes strayed toward the cash register, where Poppy stood. The spark came back.

"It's nice to meet a fellow present-enthusiast." Her phone began to vibrate in her purse. She reached for it. *Ooh, I hope it's Sam, letting me know when he can get together on the photo album owner update.* Tabitha had some excellent news to share with him—Della wasn't too far away! Maybe they could go together to Reindeer Crossing to meet her. It would be kind of romantic to give the gift of happy Christmas memories side by side. Maybe he'd even kiss her again on the ride home.

Mmm. Samson Bartlett had the nicest kiss in the entire world.

The phone buzzed again. "Excuse me," she said to Andrew Kingston and answered.

"Miss Townsend!" The impatient voice of Mrs. Barnes crackled through the line. Tabitha stood and faced the wall, but there wasn't any other place in the shop to go to take the call. "I have been waiting for your call. Why haven't you updated me on your progress? That book is everything to me. It's almost Christmas. Why aren't you keeping me in the loop?"

There wasn't any loop to keep her in. Tabitha turned away from Andrew, who lifted his newspaper to shield her. How polite. "Yes, Mrs. Barnes. I'm so sorry. It's definitely a work in progress."

"I'm not *interested* in works in progress. What I need is results. Tell me exactly what you are doing to make this happen. Are you even meeting with the current owner?"

"Of course I'm meeting with the owner. We've been in serious talks about the transfer of the book. However, he does have ownership at the moment, and like I said, isn't interested in selling."

"Don't you understand? Everything is at stake." Tabitha pictured her pinching the bridge of her nose to summon patience. "Tell me what you're doing to persuade him."

"I have spent time with him every single night, ma'am."

"As in, you're seeing him?" Mrs. Barnes shouted, probably loud enough that the whole Cider Press clientele could hear. "Romantically?"

Tabitha covered the receiver and tried to move outside, but the massive line to Poppy's register had her blocked in. "Well ..."

"You're dating him in order to get the book? Astute move. I hadn't thought you'd go that far in sacrifice for this project, but I do appreciate your resourcefulness."

That wasn't it. Not remotely. "Can we just say I'm doing everything I can to finesse the book away from him." All of which efforts were probably useless.

"And by *finesse,* I assume you mean you've kissed the man." Mrs. Barnes snorfled. "I'm impressed."

"I don't think I'm conveying accurately how things are working out. The owner loves the book."

"Make him stop loving it. Pull out all the stops. Cry if you have to. Beg. Kiss him into submission. Kiss him *blind.* And while he's blind, get my book."

The air in The Cider Press turned red. Tabitha's teeth clenched. It was like Mrs. Barnes had gone off the rails. Sure, she'd always had the potential for a meltdown hovering just at the edges, but up to now, she'd controlled it. Now, yikes. "Mrs. Barnes, are you feeling all right? It's a Christmas gift." A book, not an organ donation situation.

"We had an understanding, Tabitha."

They had. And Tabitha wanted to fulfill her side of it. "I'm going to enormous lengths, personally and professionally. Beyond ordinary modes of conduct."

"Just ... get it." Mrs. Barnes hung up, driving off any Christmas Spirit in a ten-block radius.

Tabitha's nose stung, as did her eyes. When she glanced around, everyone in The Cider Press was looking at her uncomfortably, including Andrew Kingston, who had dropped his newspaper. He wasn't smiling.

"Sorry, everyone," she mumbled. She had to get out of here. Going next door to see Sam felt icky, like she was using him, but she still had the information about the photo album to share. Plus, she missed him. His hug could comfort her.

Where was her bottle of headache medicine when she needed it? And her extra Kleenex for her leaky eyes?

Poppy appeared at her side with a little pile of Cider Press napkins. "You all right? That was a really loud phone call."

"Angry client." Plus, idiotic businesswoman who should have turned down the volume.

"Can you fix things with her?" Poppy asked. "I thought I overheard some yelling. Don't tell me she's firing you. And … did you really kiss Sam? You haven't told me any of this! I'm so excited and mad at the same time that you haven't kept me informed."

This was not the time or the place to discuss her love life. Way too many Sugarplum Falls citizens' ears were tilting in their direction.

"I have to go. Can we talk later?"

"Sure, sure. I have a crowd anyway. Call me?"

Tabitha buttoned her coat up to her neck and nodded a grim goodbye to Andrew, who was still eyeing her skeptically. Who wouldn't, after such a display? How humiliating. Tabitha should have just gone outside to take the phone call—or not answered. Or *anything* else.

Now, she was stuck with a a huge broken promise to Mrs. Barnes and a large financial debt to repay, if she valued Sam's needs over her own.

Which, yeah. She was starting to, no matter what she'd foolishly guaranteed Mrs. Barnes.

As long as she was breaking promises, maybe she should breach confidentiality. Because if she told Sam what was going on, he might have some kind of a good solution. He had offered a few ideas for a win-win solution, but none of them involved giving Mrs. Barnes the book, so Tabitha couldn't accept any of them at the time.

Her phone rang—again.

"Tabitha? Could you come home for a few minutes? I'm in a pinochle wrapping paper panic. They'll be here in a half hour and I'm still twelve gifts out."

Oh, right. Grandma had all her pinochle group's gifts to wrap today by noon for their holiday luncheon. "Sure. I'll be right there."

Talking with Sam would have to be put on hold. His store would probably be slammed for the lunch hour anyway, what with so few shopping days remaining. She sent him a text that she'd be in a little later with her news.

He replied. *Can't wait.*

Chapter 27

Sam

Sam rubbed the glass display case with a cloth. Someone with sticky red-and-white fingers had admired the case's silver hand-bells quite a lot, apparently.

"Mrs. Forger's grandkids were in here earlier." Mrs. Milliken brought the bottle of glass cleaner, handing it off to Sam. "Sorry. I gave them each a candy cane."

"Several of the bells are gone."

"She bought one for each child. I think she's trying to start a hand-bell choir, a few at a time."

Good for her. "Is something wrong?"

Mrs. Milliken was pacing. "I—it's only a few days now, Sam. Until the Christmas Eve author event. We've been advertising it on the radio, and online. That young man Declan has been diligent in getting the posters we finally printed up everywhere—from the grocery store to the ski resort and lodge."

"All the way up at Frosty Ridge?"

"He rode his uncle's horse."

That was ingenuity. "Impressive."

"I'd be a lot more impressed if"—Mrs. Milliken looked at the ceiling—"if we actually had an author coming."

Every single author he'd called had turned him down for the Christmas Eve event. That had never happened in the past. "I'm going to get someone."

"Who?"

He didn't know yet. "I've got a lot of feelers out." Feelers and feelings, make that. Growing feelings about Tabitha.

"Sam!" Mrs. Milliken used her English teacher voice, the one reserved for kids who were tardy for the third day in a row. "The time for *feelers out* is passed. We have a crowd coming to this 'mystery event,' and they're starting to talk in mutinous tones. I can't even go to pick up my dry cleaning without getting ambushed by curious patrons. They're sure you're holding out on them and lining up someone as famous as Mark Twain."

"Mark Twain ... is dead." Or Sam would have called him, too. "I've had half a dozen book and then cancel. It's like I'm ice fishing on catch-and-release day at Lake Sugar."

Mrs. Milliken huffed in obvious exasperation, slapping her forehead. "Sam! We're going to break trust with our patrons if we don't have an author to feature at the author event."

"I'll get someone." Of course, could he actually find anyone on such short notice, willing to come all the way to Sugarplum Falls on the day before Christmas? He'd called so many people already, and he'd come up with zilch. It really started looking impossible. "Look, you know I'm not usually like this."

"Which is the only reason I haven't wrung your neck before now." She made a gesture like wringing out a rag. "You've been preoccupied—for very good reason. Is she coming by?" *To distract you again?* was the unspoken end of the sentence. *Don't forget the store! Get an author!*

"Tabitha texted and said she'll be here after lunch. Wrapping paper emergency."

Mrs. Milliken shook herself. "Which authors are on your short list? Has anyone responded? Has anyone expressed mild interest, and could we lean on them? Sweeten the deal?"

No one. It was crickets. Which was weird. Most of the time, authors jumped at the chance to be spotlighted and make some book sales. It didn't make sense. "I'm coming up empty on every front. Do you have any suggestions? It doesn't have to be someone famous, as long as it's someone *interesting,* you know? Someone with even a faint connection with Sugarplum Falls could excite the locals."

George walked up. "They're looking for you, Gracie, to help with the candy jars, but hey, I overheard. *Not* because I was eavesdropping."

"This time," Mrs. Milliken ribbed. "Any ideas?"

"Why not the author of the book you named the store for? That E.B.

Grandin person?"

"Ed Garnet, you mean?" Sam said.

"Yep. That was the name. Was *Angels Landing* the only thing he ever wrote?"

Mrs. Milliken left to go help the customer in urgent need of old-fashioned candy, and George remained, leaning against the glass case, getting fingerprints on it again.

"As far as I know. I looked it up once, a while ago, but all signs point to Ed Garnet being a one-and-done author."

"Shame. The story takes place in a town suspiciously like Sugarplum Falls. It's got the bridge, just like the one over the Sugar River, and the waterfall, and the whole Sugarplum vibe."

Now that George mentioned it, yeah. Maybe that was part of the reason it had resonated with Sam so deeply. "Ed Garnet wrote so long ago. He might not even be alive anymore."

"Sam." George leaned closer. "Gracie hasn't been in this much of a bunch since we had an invasion of sugar ants in our pantry. Do me a holiday favor, kiddo. Find an author. Even an aspiring one. Who cares? It will make my home life so much better." He pulled one of those pleading faces, a mix between a frown and a wince.

"I'll take care of it. In fact, I'll go look for Ed Garnet again." He accepted George's hearty fist-bump. "As a personal Christmas gift to you."

"Ho-ho-ho, Merry Christmas." Mr. Milliken placed a hand on his round belly. "And my advice is to check in Darlington first."

Good call. Ed Garnet would be perfect, if he existed. Having only written one book, the guy was probably not inundated with requests for appearances and might be the one author who wouldn't turn Sam down at the last minute.

He headed back to his office, sat down, and dug into online research for the elusive Ed Garnet yet again. All the sites, even the police-references, turned up nothing. Not even the Social Security Death Index for his state.

Unfortunately, nothing but the connection with *Angels Landing* came up, and even that contained scant information, since the book was not in wide circulation, by anyone's definition. The few people who had reviewed it online recalled it fondly and with great gushes of praise, but there weren't more than twenty readers in online book forums who claimed to have read it.

Frustrating.

Maybe Ed Garnet was a pen-name. The front matter of the book did note that the story was based on true life experience. Perhaps not only the names of the characters in the story—like the main character Elda, and her friend Lettie—weren't the only disguised identities.

That would make it significantly more difficult to hunt the guy down.

Darn it! Didn't Sam already have his hands full with hunting down the owner of the photo album? This whole Christmas season was getting highjacked by missing persons. Maybe he should have been a private investigator instead. Perhaps a shared company with Tabitha, since she apparently had all the skills, what with news already to share with him about the photo album, or so she'd hinted. Why hadn't she come yet? How long could a wrapping paper emergency last?

I crave her company.

The door jingled out front, and Sam snapped upright. In fact, lately, every time the bells jingled at the entrance of Angels Landing, Sam looked up in hopes of seeing her. However, Andrew Kingston, local lawyer and sometimes Sam's shoveling buddy after a really big snow, strode in instead, slapping his mittens loudly against his thighs.

"Hoowhee. Cold out there." He looked a little lost, probably since he'd rarely set foot in Angels Landing. "Sam, old friend. I need to talk to you privately. You got a second?"

"Sure, Andrew. You all right?" He looked like he'd seen a bad wreck. Or like he'd been assigned to prosecute the girl of his dreams again like happened a few months ago. "What's going on?"

Kingston shifted his weight and aimed a look at Mrs. Milliken. "Can we talk in private?"

"Bookseller-client privilege. Got it." Sam waved Andrew back through the store-room to the office. "Have a seat?"

"No, that's okay." Kingston looked even more uncomfortable now than he had out front. "Look, I know I have a reputation as a hard-nose, so nobody

154

has a reason to listen to me, including you."

"What are you talking about? We've been friends for … how long? And you helped me shovel at the Langfords' house that time, during the polar vortex. You've earned my listening ears."

"Sorry. I know that. It's just … lawyers get a bad rap. I usually have to preface stuff with excuses in real life outside the courtroom."

Sam shrugged. "Most of the time they're doing their job."

Andrew's stance softened. "Thanks, man." He sat down in the chair after all, across from where Sam was sitting on the edge of his desk. "I overheard a conversation next door, and it involved you, I believe. Are you officially dating Tabitha Townsend now?"

"Sure. She's great." He tried to keep his face from registering any emotion, like worry. Because Andrew had him worried with the whole fear-demeanor thing going on. Andrew didn't usually ratchet things into the discomfort level. "Everything all right with her?"

"Not sure. Have you ever heard her talk about someone named Steve? A Steve Marsden, maybe?"

Never. "I'm not following."

Kingston's mouth flattened into a grimace. "According to her conversation, she's dating you in order to get something you own."

"The book? Do you mean *Angels Landing*?"

"Yeah. Probably." He looked surprised. "Well, it was about getting a book." Obviously, Andrew Kingston didn't know the title of the book shared the name of the store, so he must not have specifics. "She spoke to a client about it, saying she was trying every means possible to get it from the owner, who I assume is you."

Sam swung his leg. "I appreciate your help, but I'm aware of that. She's never hidden her interest in that book."

Kingston cleared his voice and lowered it. "What about her *every means possible* methods of getting it from you?"

"How's that?"

"With my own ears, I heard her tell her client she's dating you, kissing you, fooling you, to get the book."

155

Ouch. But Sam didn't buy it. There'd been too much sincerity in her kiss, and they'd discussed all this. Tabitha had even agreed it played an important role in his life. "Believe it or not, she and I are pretty open about this whole thing."

With a shove of hands outstretched and palms up, Kingston said, "Is she open with you about her attorney boyfriend in Darlington, the one she's buying a special Christmas gift for? Steve somebody?"

Boyfriend! Ten knife-tips stabbed simultaneously into Sam's back.

"Ah, I can see I've finally got your attention."

"Where is this coming from, Kingston?" No wonder no one trusted him. He was a snake. "Did you overhear this, too?"

"I'm not like that. Think about it. Pretty much the whole town knows my dating history, so you surely understand I'm not just meddling here. I'm here because I have your back."

True enough, Andrew had been nearly engaged to that summer-resident girl who cheated on him, stringing him along to the point of buying a ring and taking her to the Kingston family orchard to propose in front of his family, all while hanging on tight to a big-city boyfriend back home.

When Andrew proposed, the girl found out he wasn't inheriting the orchard. Then she refused the offer of his hand in marriage and ran back to her boyfriend in Caldwell City.

Yeah, Andrew wasn't coming from a meddling place. He was protecting Sam—from outsiders and cheaters.

"She has a big-city boyfriend, Sam. Believe me on this." He frowned, his voice getting tighter. "She's not what you think. She's ... a Deep-fake."

Tabitha? Hardly! She was as real as they came. Still, the word troubled him. Andrew wouldn't use the term lightly.

Sam crossed his arms over his chest, if only to ward off the knives that had made their way around from his back and were sticking him in the ribs near his heart. *Boyfriend!* "Tell me how you came to this conclusion."

"Because she told me herself. I was sitting in The Cider Press, and she sat down beside me and started quizzing me on what I would like for Christmas, and said she was trying to buy a gift for a *good friend* back in Darlington who was my age and also an attorney. Named Steve. I'm guessing it's that Marsden sonuvagun I can't stand from law school. What would a guy like me want as a gift, she wanted to know."

All the stuffing went out of Sam, and his arms uncrossed and hung limp at his sides. "Oh." Sam searched Andrew's face for any sign of insincerity or dubiousness about his own assertions, but there was nothing like that—only what looked like genuine protective interest. "You're sure about this. You couldn't have misinterpreted anything."

"She told me his *name*. It's a guy I've met, man."

A fake? Tabitha? Little edges of the pages of his soul began to burn and curl. "It's not possible."

"We've been friends a long time. You haven't known Tabitha Townsend for half a year, even."

Sam couldn't answer to contradict him.

Andrew got up, as if it leave, but he paused at the office door. "I don't mean to be the Anti-Santa. But there's this, too: I remember Adelaide. She and my older sister were in the same dance classes. She was a nice girl, and I know she wouldn't want you getting hurt."

Andrew left Sam and his myriad painful realizations reeling in the back office of Angels Landing.

Ten percent of him wanted to shove it right back in Andrew's face. But ninety percent of him couldn't deny those claims. Andrew wasn't exactly a town gossip or interfering character in the community. And with his history, he'd have his defenses up and his radar for cheating going strong. Besides, Tabitha had asked him *personally* about ideas for a gift for a boyfriend—with a name—back in Darlington.

The biggest problem was, Andrew had zero motive for inventing such a story.

Fake? The whole thing had been a lie? Just like Andrew's out-of-town girlfriend that summer, and like Elise when she'd had stars in her eyes about Angels Landing bookstore?

Nausea sloshed in Sam's gut. Was it true, then? Tabitha really had only been dating and kissing him to get to the book? She had someone else on the side, and everything she'd said to him was deception?

All the evidence stacked up strongly against her.

He sent her a text. *I heard you met Andrew Kingston today.*

Great guy, she responded. *Reminds me a lot of someone I know and admire.*

Sam's heart lurched, and a sickening heat crept up his neck to his cheek. Her text confirmed it: Tabitha was using him for the book. Everything else was all a sham.

Chapter 28

Tabitha

Finally, the present wrapping with Grandma finished. It took a long time to wrap twelve nutcracker dolls.

Tabitha raced back to downtown Sugarplum Falls. She had to take it easy on the icy corner of Apricot Avenue and Orchard Street. A little roadster was truly impractical in a town like Sugarplum Falls, considering how many months of the year it snowed to excess.

If I'm going to stay here long-term, a vehicle with four-wheel drive might be a good idea.

If things continued the way they were going with Sam, she couldn't imagine leaving. She could much more easily picture sharing his truck in the winter and her sports car in the warm months, taking canyon drives in the fall with the top down; buying Grandma's house from her someday, and making brand new memories in it with Sam.

For sure, something real was growing between Tabitha and Sam, something good and unexpected considering their differing temperaments. His staid quietness steadied her, while her enthusiasm seemed to fire him up. The kisses they shared were certainly fire. There was a lot more to discover between them. Because for Tabitha, it could very easily turn from crush-interest into love.

I have to stay. But to do that, I have to figure out a way to make Mrs. Barnes happy. Because until I do that or pay her back, I'm in arrears on my debts.

A big payday might come this year from the clients she'd amassed, but after the holidays, shopping would definitely taper off. It wasn't like Tabitha could expect to earn enough to both reimburse Mrs. Barnes *and* continue running the website and the advertising and all the other overhead during the off-season.

Despite the fact that Mayor Lang had spread the word on Tabitha's behalf, and she had three more good potential commissions lined up, even those wouldn't cover the exorbitant outlays from the *Angels Landing* quest. If only she'd kept some of those purchases of books from estate sales, she could at least offer them to Sam to sell in his store. Of course, when they hadn't contained her quest, she'd donated them to thrift stores or thrown them away.

Short-sighted fool, since Sam might have let her sell them on commission.

Hindsight.

No, Tabitha would have to shut down Twelve Days.

When it came to business, she did everything—*everything*—wrong. At least she was better at choosing men than she had been in the past. Sam was the best of every other guy she'd ever met rolled into one, and none of the mega-flaws. All her previous relationships had ended with the guy walking away on some simple misunderstanding, that if they'd just taken time to hear her out, things might have worked out.

But then I might not have come to this time and place to have a chance with Sam Bartlett.

So, maybe things did work out—in love, if not in business.

Or, would they? Because unless she got that drattedly rare book and the commission, she couldn't stay here in this time and place to be with Sam Bartlett anyway. The cold truth was that she'd checked the job listings and there wasn't other work around here for Tabitha's skill set—or lack of skill set. She had zero remaining capital to start yet another business. Twelve Days was her final shot before she'd have to return to Darlington or Caldwell City and take a job where her lack of organizational skills were highlighted even more.

And go right back into her humiliating get-a-job-lose-a-job cycle.

She needed to keep Twelve Days alive. Somehow. There had to be a way. Even without *Angels Landing*. But nothing came to mind, not even a tiny, snow-crystal-sized idea.

At the bookshop, about ten cars lined the front curb. Sam's store looked swamped. Good for him. Local businesses received tons of love from Sugarplum Falls shoppers. Man, there were so many things to love about this town.

Including Sam's kiss.

"Hi," she said as she came through the door and met Mrs. Milliken nose to nose. "Is Sam here?"

Mrs. Milliken's usual smile was gone and had been replaced with a dragon's gaze. Ooh, so that was why everyone said her English-teacher stare could ice a victim's veins. "He's with a customer."

"Okay. I'll wait. Or … do some shopping." Tabitha pulled a smile and made a beeline for the glass display cases. Maybe they held something Poppy could give to Andrew Kingston.

The store was packed with customers as always. She browsed the handmade greeting cards, the carved bone-handle letter openers, the knitted caps. If only she hadn't been interrupted this morning when she was so ham-handedly interrogating him about his interests, she'd know better what to recommend Poppy give him next. It was going to be so fun when they each figured out the other was the gift-giver! That moment would be so sweet, Tabitha half-wished she could witness it.

Well, Poppy would describe it in detail after the fact. That'd be almost as good as being there.

"Tabitha." Sam's voice rumbled down her spine, and she turned to face him. "You have something to say to me?" He looked—and sounded—so stern. "I'm waiting."

"Uh, yeah." She set down the hand-painted tile she'd been considering. "I found my grandma's friend Della. She's in Reindeer Crossing. I haven't contacted her, since I didn't know how you wanted to handle that, but I've got her number. We could get Grandma to call her. Or maybe you and I could drive over there together and give the album to her personally." She faltered under the weight of his frown. "If you want."

Sam worked his jaw, his blue eyes cold and glowering. "Pass me the information, and I'll handle the contact."

Really? No excitement? Not even a thank you? "What's going on, Sam?"

"Look, Tabitha, I know you want the book *Angels Landing*."

Of course she did. "And?"

161

"And I'm guessing you'll stop at nothing to get it." His tone was steel. What was he getting at? Something was definitely wrong.

"I did have an idea about that, Sam. What if we were to sleuth out the author together? Maybe we could ask him if he has another copy." Even though Mrs. Barnes said no other copies existed, could she be a hundred percent sure without asking the author personally? Or his family? "Then we both win—and so will my client. I'm not a private investigator, but I've read a lot of mystery novels about finding missing persons. Mrs. Barnes may have said it won't work, but—"

"Who?" Sam interrupted, his head snapping toward her.

Shoot. His demeanor had thrown Tabitha off her game, and she'd breached confidentiality by stating the client's name. "Never mind." She scrambled. "As a bookstore operator, do you have insider access to author profiles or publisher contacts? That might be a place to start." It seemed like her words were bouncing off him and landing with clatters on the wood-plank floor. "Is everything all right? I'm getting a weird feeling from you right now." Decidedly not the Christmas Spirit.

"The book is mine, Tabitha. Stop asking for it."

"Sam?"

"Who's Steve?"

Steve. Steve. She racked her brain.

"Hint: he's someone you admire."

Sam's real name was Steve? "I'm really lost here, Sam." Slowly she shook her head while searching his face for clues. None surfaced.

"Maybe you'd better leave." His words sounded forced, like they were pushing back emotion. "Text me the information about your grandmother's friend."

"No, Sam. I'm not leaving unless you tell me what's going on."

He sighed like he'd just been through divorce court. "I'm tired of the insincerity, Tabitha. Can we just end the pretense? Now?"

"What insincerity? Sam!"

"Ask Steve." His face hardened, and he turned away from her and went to the cash register, where a customer was waiting to purchase a large coffee table book about angels.

I need an angel right about now—to come down and tell me what just happened.

Reeling, Tabitha went out to her car. It was like she'd turned into Cindy Lou Who, rising on Christmas morning and expecting to see all her joyous presents, only to find they'd been stuffed up a chimney by a fake Santa, never to be seen again.

Everything around her went from hope's shining star to nothing but dashed expectations, pulled-out rugs, popped red balloons in a latex heap at her feet on a dangling string.

Nothing but tears stinging her eyes.

Seriously, who in tarnation is Steve? Her head started pounding. *Why is Sam turning on me?*

Had something happened when Tabitha texted him? She'd meant it as a compliment—saying she admired Sam. Did he have something against Andrew Kingston that he didn't like the comparison?

If so, this was a wild overreaction.

Massive misunderstanding.

Another one. *Like the misunderstandings that set off avalanches of all my relationships' breakups.*

Irritation blossomed. She would march back in there and demand he explain, but with all the crowd gathering in the store, this was no time for Tabitha to get to the bottom of it. She should preserve at least one shred of her dignity. For now.

Irritation died on the vine, everything draining out of her as her deepest suspicions about herself were confirmed. Once again. *I must not be a girl worth taking the time to unravel a simple mystery for.*

Eerily, it echoed what Dad had said to Mom when he left her. Tabitha had found it written in Mom's journal: *You're not worth the effort anymore, Charmaine. It's just too much work.* And with no more than that, Dad had left. Just like Tabitha's other boyfriends had left.

And now Sam. *I thought he was different.*

She drove around town for a while, her various feelings ebbing and flowing. One second a tide of despair rolled in, another second it was gone and replaced with a tidal wave of fury.

Honestly! Tabitha should just give up on trying to win the hearts of guys who looked stable and steady, who looked honest and true. Instead, she was going to date some kind of amateur dirt-bike racer, or a nomadic lumberjack, or an unemployed guy who played video games in his mom's basement to glom onto. Then her expectations could stay low and always be met—which might actually be nice for a change.

Yep, she'd work on that after Christmas, or maybe as a New Year's resolution.

After her fuel ran low, she pulled into a parking lot near the playground at the orchard and sat a long time before pulling out her phone to forward him the information about Della.

And, great. She had a voicemail waiting for her—from Mrs. Barnes. "Please, Tabitha. You promised. If kissing him isn't enough ..." She made a suggestion wildly outside Tabitha's standards. Outside Sam's, too, if Tabitha read him right. And, in fact, outside Mrs. Barnes's standards. The woman was clearly losing her grip.

Tabitha placed her face in her hands and her forehead on the steering wheel. Sam wasn't talking to her and had kicked her to the curb. Mrs. Barnes was going berserk and having a massive personality shift. Twelve Days had about twelve minutes to live.

I can't leave Sugarplum Falls. I'll be leaving behind my only tangible memories of Mom.

How had her day gone from cheery holiday hope to this broken glass Christmas ornament in shards on the ground?

Chapter 29

Sam

The rush eventually calmed down in Angels Landing. They'd sold twenty-six of Mrs. Inglewood's cookbooks in three hours, but Sam couldn't bring himself to rejoice. He managed to stay standing long enough to make his way back to his office and grab his keys.

"I'm heading home for a few to grab some protein," he said to Mr. Milliken, who was lugging an armload of boxes out front to replenish the front shelves of Christmas cookbooks. "I'll be back."

George just chin-jutted and lumbered toward the sales floor.

It took all his willpower not to hit the gas and rev the engine through town. He gripped the wheel hard past Mario's, Sugarbabies Bakery, and all the other holiday-lit shops. Gravel peeled up from his back tires as he tore into his driveway and shut off his truck.

He marched into the house, stomped the snow from his boots and left his coat, hat, and gloves in a heap. Before even heading to the fridge for his roast beef sandwich, he marched upstairs to his study.

There, his roll-top desk sat open, like the gaping maw of a monster ready to chomp. Sam marched to the desktop and jerked the dozen or so handwritten sheets of paper he'd created over the past two weeks since he'd allowed Tabitha Townsend into his life. With two swift motions, he ripped them into four uneven quadrants. They landed in the metal trashcan with a thud.

Sam gave the side of the can a swift kick against the wall, denting it. He'd burn the remains later, when he had more time.

Then he went to eat his sandwich and seethe.

Chapter 30

Tabitha

In the driveway of Grandma's house a few hours later, Tabitha sat in her parked car, just sitting and staring, until the air in the Miata grew cold and Tabitha's breath came out as steam but froze before it could affect the windows.

None of it made sense. But she should be used to it by now. Getting ghosted by a guy just when she thought things were heading in a good direction.

I have to let all of it go. A tear trembled on her lower eyelid. She pulled out her phone and dialed Sam. No answer.

She dialed again. A different number. Still no answer, but she had to say this. Tabitha took a quick intake of bracing-cold breath for fortification and left Mrs. Barnes a voice message.

"Mrs. Barnes? This is Tabitha. You won't like this message, but I have to leave it for you anyway. It's that I've pressed the owner of *Angels Landing* enough."

So much that he'd seemed wounded the last time Tabitha had seen him.

"If you would like to ask him yourself for the book, please do. I'll forward his contact information to you now. I'm sorry to have failed you about the book, and about Twelve Days. You trusted the wrong person with your investment. Again." She had to stop talking to slurp up an errant tear. "I'm closing up my business immediately and won't be offering personal shopping or gift location services in the future." She heaved a shuddering breath. "For what it's worth, thank you for all you did for me. I'll definitely pay you back over time with income from my next job."

Click. By text, she sent Sam's contact information to Mrs. Barnes.

Then, she sent Sam Della's contact information.

Grandma needed it, too, so she wrote it down on a sticky note to put on the fridge.

Everything was tidy, as in tied with a bow. Or at least it was as tidy as Tabitha ever made anything in life.

Twelve Days gifts had all been distributed and paid for. The little chunk she'd managed to keep would get her moved to Darlington or Caldwell City, pay a deposit and first and last month's rent.

She could eat ramen for a few weeks. Or maybe there were a few pecan trees she could forage from. For protein.

Upstairs, she found her suitcases. Clothes, makeup, Mom's journal, the photo album from downstairs with photographic evidence that Tabitha did, indeed, have a mother who loved her. It all went inside.

When she couldn't stuff anything else into them, she decided to shove the rest into black plastic bags. It'd be fine. Somehow. Then, she flopped down on her bed with her laptop and did an internet search for *soulless corporate jobs in Darlington,* and a second for the same in Caldwell City.

Plenty of results popped up, none involving creating happy gift-giving-and-receiving moments for people in need of love, of course. However, Tabitha had a hard time reading which links to click on as her vision got too blurry from the salty tears flooding her eyes.

Chapter 31

Sam

It was hard to care about the Christmas Eve author event—based mostly on the fact that it would be a total bust. Yeah, chalk this up as his first official Total Business Failure since opening Angels Landing after turning it from a general store into a used bookshop. Maybe the community would forgive him, even if the Millikens never did.

Sam zombied his way through the remaining shopping days counting down, not even allowing the sales totals Mrs. Milliken brought him each evening to cause a blip in his mood.

The only thing he'd managed to accomplish since the blow-up with Tabitha the other day was contacting the owner of the photo album. Della Ruskin had seemed wary at first, but she eventually heard out his tale of the storage unit purchase. After some prodding, she'd confirmed that she'd known Mrs. Inglewood—and that the Inglewoods had bought Della's family home as an investment property when they moved away, and thus might have had possession of the photo album.

First mystery unraveled.

Now, Mrs. Ruskin spent her days tending grandchildren, so the soonest she'd be able to drive down from Reindeer Crossing would be Christmas Eve to inspect the photo album and accept its return.

At least there was that.

But there was nothing else.

Without Tabitha, he had nothing to write. Nothing to invigorate him. No one to watch the Waterfall Lights with, or sing badly with at the nursing home, or to kiss until his blood boiled.

No one to be in love with.

Truth be told, Sam was almost as empty without Tabitha as he'd felt when Adelaide had succumbed to her illness. One of those psychology-babble articles online that he shouldn't have read but did anyway claimed that a breakup could be as painful for a newly formed relationship as a longer-term one. Not just emotionally painful, but *physically*. Every time he pictured Tabitha's green eyes squinting in dismay when he asked her to leave, a new kick landed in his solar plexus.

Her kung fu, even in absentia, was strong.

Why had she used him so callously, when she had a boyfriend elsewhere? And who was that Steve person? It took sheer willpower, but Sam resisted stalking the guy online.

Sometimes not knowing was better.

On Saturday evening, after a late-night closing time the week before Christmas, Mrs. Milliken hovered. "I know I'm a broken record, and I hate to ask, especially since you're in that … condition."

Sam looked up from the accounting numbers he'd been vacantly staring at. "What condition?" He wasn't in a condition. "I'm not sick or anything."

Mrs. Milliken just frowned and cleared her throat. "Okay." She stepped into his office. "Then you won't mind my bringing up the fact we don't have a guest author for Tuesday."

He hadn't forgotten. There was just nothing he could do about it at this point. "Should we cancel?"

"Cancel!" Mrs. Milliken's gasp was drowned out because the phone rang.

Sam reached for it. "Angels Landing. This is Sam Bartlett."

Mrs. Milliken grimaced and left with a shake of her head.

"Hello, Mr. Bartlett. My name is Mrs. Edwina Barnes."

Edwina. Sam's neck pulled backward. A name like Edwina, Sam would of course recall hearing twice in a short time period. Wasn't that the same name as the sister of Della Ruskin? Collette Honeycutt had used it.

"Yes, have you heard about the book we found?" Della Ruskin must have reached out and told her sister the good news. Maybe Edwina had volunteered to be the errand-person to pick it up, due to the grandchildren-tending-schedule thing.

"Your acquaintance Tabitha Townsend told me about the book. I've been looking for it for a good, long time. I'm prepared to offer you a very liberal sum for it." Her words tumbled out, like she'd just run a race.

Pay for the photo album! Hardly. "I wouldn't dream of asking you to buy it back. It's yours. It's your family's story. If you'd like to have it before Christmas, I invite you to come and pick it up. I'd normally deliver, but I've got the shop to run, and my assistants are already overly generous with their time."

She let out a whoop. "I would most definitely like to have it before Christmas." Mrs. Barnes sounded thrilled to the point of giddiness. "And I must say, Mr. Bartlett, you're much more accommodating and generous than Miss Townsend described you to be."

Humph. At this point, Sam couldn't blame Tabitha for maligning his character, but hearing it still cut him to the quick.

"When would be convenient?" she asked. "Unfortunately, with travel and holiday busyness, the soonest I think I could come would be Christmas Eve."

Clearly, the sisters had talked it out and agreed that Edwina would fetch the album. "Then you could take it to your sister in Reindeer Crossing. She's of course anxious to see it as well."

"Excuse me?" Her voice sharpened. "What do you know about Della?"

"I apologize." Sam backpedaled quickly, having dealt with angry customers before and learned to smooth things over. "Christmas Eve would be just fine. We have a special event going on in the store at noon that day. Perhaps you'll arrive in time to enjoy it."

"Good night, Mr. Bartlett. I'll see you Tuesday."

Right. At the event for which he had no headliner.

Ed Garnet was nowhere to be found in any database. Maybe they'd have to change it from a *meet the author* to a … what? He had no ideas. No inspiration.

No Tabitha.

Chapter 32

Tabitha

On Christmas Eve morning, Tabitha tucked another pile of clothes into the second plastic bag. The only things left were odds and ends, or things she still needed for daily use. Her impractical little car was going to be wedged full when she took off for Darlington in a couple of days. She'd stay at Aunt Charlene's house on the couch until she found a place to rent.

Everyone who'd expressed disappointment when Tabitha dropped out of college was being proved right about her. She hadn't amounted to anything. Alongside her two prior businesses, Twelve Days was dead.

"Tabby-girl?" Grandma knocked twice softly and then cracked open Tabitha's bedroom door. "You in there?" She pushed it wide and gasped. "What's all this?"

"Grandma, I—"

"Are you telling me *you* knew about the remodelers coming, too? And you didn't tell me?"

"What are you talking about?"

"They'll be here Friday with a demolition team." Grandma walked through the room, inspecting the emptied closets and dresser drawers. "But you already knew that or you wouldn't be packing up. How did everyone keep this secret from me?"

Competing responses fought in Tabitha's throat for dominance. "Who is demolishing? Something is changing?" Tabitha's voice cracked.

"They're gutting the kitchen starting the day after Christmas. Your aunts gave me it as a gift. Plus, I've been saving up for years for a remodel. It's about time, you know."

"Remodel? As in …"

"As in the harvest gold everything is out the door. And hallelujah for it!"

171

Not hallelujah. No. Not hallelujah at all. Tabitha shrank into herself even further.

"What's wrong? Don't tell me you love harvest gold."

No, but she did love what it represented. *Mom's memory.* "I didn't know about the demolition, so that's not why I'm packed. I lost my business, Grandma. My business bank account is empty, and I have no capital to last even another week."

"Oh, no!" Grandma backed out of the dressing area and whirled around. "What happened? You had so many clients."

How could Tabitha explain accurately without sounding either peevish or devastated? "I guess my business model was faulty." As were her business practices, and most of all her assessment of her own ability to manage details of anything. "I've made some mistakes. Big ones."

"Everyone does. Even Grandpa Lanny did in his businesses. He owned five different ones over his lifetime, you know. Took a long time for him to get the right fit. But he was patient with himself."

"I don't have the luxury of being patient with myself anymore." Her last chance was over and done with. As was her independence.

"Sweetheart, you can stay."

No, she couldn't. She had to find a job. And she needed to get away from Sam. Seeing him around Sugarplum Falls was going to be too painful. He wasn't taking her calls, and he wouldn't explain anything. It was time to let him and the idea of Sam and Tabitha go.

"Thank you, but I'll be better off in a bigger town with more job opportunities." That she could swing into and out of like a revolving door.

Grandma bent down to look Tabitha right in the eye. "Can you give me details of what happened? Was it your big client? The secretive one?"

Tabitha nodded. Her throat was spasming, closing and opening. An explanation tumbled forth.

"I ran up huge expenses trying to find it. Then, it turned out I can't fulfill the request, since it was for something truly one-of-a-kind that couldn't possibly be replicated." At least she'd quit before she could be fired. There'd been too many firings in life already and too many yet to come. "I owe everything I make from now until I'm fifty in back payments to my investor. It's over."

"But you have other clients."

"Not enough. I have to get a job."

"Your business is a job."

"I mean a real one." Not a pretend one, where she was playing around like she knew people's secret hearts, or like she knew anything about what she was doing in life as a businesswoman. "So, I'm packing up to go."

"Sweetheart. If I'd known you were in dire straits, I could have helped. I could still help. I'm not terrible with bookkeeping."

It was so much more than bookkeeping here. "Let's be realistic. If I can't keep a personal shopping service afloat during the biggest shopping season of the year, I hardly think it's going to turn into a success during the rest of the calendar months."

"But … why do you have to go? That's drastic, especially with the way things have been going with you and Sam Bartlett."

Now the stinging really started in her eyes, prickling her nose, too. One spilled out, but she smashed it off her cheek fast.

"There isn't going to be any Tabitha and Sam." Before Grandma forced her to explain, she rushed ahead. "Financially, I don't really have a choice. There are a lot more jobs in Darlington and Caldwell City for someone with my skills." Lack of skills, she repeated to herself. And lack of education. And failed business history. "I've been checking out leads and sending out applications already. There's probably something where I can work as a filing assistant in an office."

Grandma Honeycutt tapped her fingernail to her tooth. "Tabitha, honey." She looked around at the remaining piles of papers and hair products and tufts of junk strewn through the room, with an eye lingering longest on the unmade bed. "Do you really think you're the best person for a job at organizing things like files?"

Cut to the bone! "I don't think I'll be the best. I know I'll be the worst." Great, she was going to cry again. She sniffled it all back up into her head. "But I can change. People can change." Sam had changed. He'd gone from the kindest, tenderest, most amazing man to … Tabitha's breath hitched. "I will really miss living here."

"Sugarplum Falls is a special town."

"I mean *here* here." Tabitha waved a hand around at the popcorn ceiling with the glitter, at the pink ceramic sink and the burgundy tile in the dressing area. "With you. In this house. It's really special, you know?"

"Lots of memories, and some more to come. Especially after we get rid of the avocado green."

It was too much. A constricted cry wedged its way through Tabitha's throat. "But it will change." She let out a sob, and the mental image of Mom holding Tabitha as a baby dissolved into confetti and floated away.

"Tabitha." Grandma looked alarmed. "Where is this coming from? I can't imagine you're attached to aging appliances and dated design."

"It's not that. It's …" How could she say this? "Don't you sometimes feel my mom here?"

"All the time, honey." Grandma Honeycutt came over and placed an arm around Tabitha's shoulders. "And Grandpa, too. They may be gone, but their love isn't. It's all around us."

"But if you change the house …"

"What, honey?"

It seemed so lame to say it aloud, so she whispered, "It won't look the same as it does in the pictures in the album. Their angel spirits won't be able to come back and land here. They won't recognize it." A hiccup erupted in her throat. "My mom will really be gone." Forever.

Grandma pulled Tabitha into a full hug, rubbing her back. "Sweetheart. It's not the place they recognize, it's the hearts. The spirit. The love."

Tabitha wept until Grandma's shoulder was wet. Grandma rocked back and forth with Tabitha in her arms, like in the picture with Mom rocking her as a baby.

"Love doesn't end if someone dies. That's … the real promise of Christmas."

Tabitha pulled away and dabbed at her eyes and nose with her sleeve as the import of Grandma's words sank in. "You mean that?"

"Are you going to be okay? If you really won't, I'll call Manny and cancel."

"No, no." Not if Grandma had been planning and saving, and it was Dad and everyone's gift to her. Gifts mattered. And Grandma had looked so excited. "You're right. I guess I just felt like I'd lose her all over again if we got rid of the orange sofa or the gold lamp."

"Honey. Sweetheart. You never lost her. None of us did. Her love transcends all that. Grandpa's does, too." Grandma smiled. "When it's real love, it's strong. The strongest thing."

Tabitha tried to smile back, since Grandma was talking about Grandpa Lanny. The strength of their love lived on in Grandma's smile, in her kindness, in her never forgetting him.

I can still smile and be kind and never forget my mother.

"Speaking of real love, and strong love." Grandma folded her arms and tapped her chin. "Are you going to tell me what happened between you and Sam?"

"Honestly? I don't know." Except that it couldn't be real love on his side, no matter how Tabitha might have grown to feel. She'd typed up texts to him a hundred times but erased every one of them without sending. There was no right way to phrase the question *Why are you icing me out?* Especially when she probably didn't want to know the answer—that she wasn't worth the effort to clear up whatever was bothering him.

Or which he may have forgotten about by now—along with Tabitha herself. Tabitha, the girl no one fought for. The girl not worth it.

"Well, you ought to find out." Grandma stood up and tugged Tabitha into a hug. "He's not one you want to let get away on a simple misunderstanding."

Ouch. Could Grandma's incision into Tabitha's wound be more precisely calculated to cause pain?

"Sorry, Grandma. I couldn't make him fall in love with me. If I could turn back the clock and fix things at whatever juncture I went wrong, I would." *Why can't I go back to that moment and get some divine intervention? Some messenger from above to stop me from saying the wrong thing or hurting him or whatever—so I can have my happiness back?*

Grandma smoothed Tabitha's hair. "What makes you think you're not standing at that juncture right now?"

Uh, because she didn't have the job or the man she loved? "What should I do?"

Grandma pulled back slightly and took Tabitha by both hands. "An honest conversation is often a good place to start. Does Sam know how you feel about him? What you'd give up to have him in your life?"

Ah, that. For instance her giving up *Angels Landing* for his benefit, and thereby losing her business? It'd be better to let that sacrifice go untold. No sense burdening him with it.

Grandma got up to leave but paused at the door. "Ah, I just remembered. Gracie Milliken contacted me, sounding panicky, which isn't her usual mode."

Oh, dear. Was something wrong? "Is Sam all right?"

"Sam apparently has a huge event today at the bookstore, and something has gone wrong—she didn't say what. Anyway, she asked you to please bring the photo album down to the bookstore by noon. The owner is coming by to pick it up."

Any wispy, ghostly vestige of Tabitha's fantasy died all over again. The one where she and Sam drove over to Reindeer Crossing to deliver it in person. They'd never have the joy of standing proxy for two of Santa's elves and watching the look on Della Ruskin's face when she opened the album and saw her family young again.

"I should have dropped it off the other day." When Sam requested it. But she'd been too gutted to do much of anything, other than pack. "Grandma, why don't you go? You could be there to hand it off to Della." Tabitha couldn't imagine setting foot inside that store ever again. "After all, she's your childhood friend."

"I wish I could—more than anything in the world. Believe me. But it turns out I've got that volunteering thing scheduled today at Sweet Haven Nursing Home—not singing, mind you. Just some crafts and decorating individual rooms for the patrons whose families haven't come by yet. It's Christmas Eve and no one else signed up to be there for the residents or I would absolutely postpone it for the chance to see Della." Grandma smiled.

176

"You found her number for me, so I'll meet up with her another time. Besides, you love giving meaningful gifts. That's your 'gift.' Since you're the one who found Della, won't it be satisfying to be the one to deliver her the photographs?"

The last gift of Twelve Days. "All right. I'll take it down there."

Chapter 33

Sam

The front bells jingled on the shop, and Sam reflexively looked out between an opening on the shelf of sports how-to books. A fist closed around his heart as Tabitha entered, her arms laden with the now-familiar sight of Della Ruskin's photo album. Or her sister's. Whichever one—he didn't really care. They'd both be glad to get it.

Mrs. Milliken ambled over to greet Tabitha instead.

Sam didn't jump in. For one, he wouldn't know what to say. *How's your lawyer boyfriend in Darlington?* He'd sound peevish, jealous, juvenile. *How are you? I've missed you.* He'd sound desperate, lonely, and in love.

Either option would lay bare his true feelings, on both sides of the spectrum.

Better to hang out in the sports-books shelves with *How to Improve Your Golf Swing* and *You and Your Rotator Cuff* than to risk letting Tabitha see how broken he'd become since he discovered her lies. The sole thing he'd accomplished was to take the residents of Sweet Haven each a book of their choice from his store. And even then, every conversation and gift-giving had been laced with Tabitha in his thoughts.

"Thank you. I guess you got my message from your grandmother. Are you staying on to meet the owner of the book?"

Tabitha's voice was muffled. Sam slipped into the next row of bookshelves to hear better.

"I considered staying," she said, "but it's Christmas Eve and I have a lot of packing to finish."

"It's a little late to be mailing things. Or perhaps you mean wrapping, not packing?"

"Packing. I'm heading to Darlington, day after tomorrow."

Bah. Probably heading over to the city to meet up with her secret boyfriend Steve. The peevish side of Sam took ascendancy. Sam straightened a few copies of books about container gardening and tried to keep himself from throwing any on the floor.

"Do you have family in Darlington?" George asked. Apparently he'd joined the conversation, too. "I assumed you'd spend the whole holiday week with your grandmother."

"They're gutting her kitchen to remodel, and I'm ... changing jobs."

Gutting the house! But ... but that would gut Tabitha. Sam nearly lurched out to go hug her. Luckily, he stopped himself.

"But I thought—" Mrs. Milliken's gasp sounded like she'd seen an F on her report card, and Sam peered around the corner to try to catch Tabitha's reflection in the glass of the display case. It wasn't visible. "I thought that you had a thriving business as a personal shopper. I've seen your diligence firsthand. Besides, I heard *such* good things about you from Mrs. Toledo, and Shelby Forger. Not to mention Mayor Lang's staff Christmas party gifts. Why walk away from that? Are you sure you have to go?"

"I'm sure." Tabitha took a quick look over her right shoulder toward the display window, toward the copy of *Angels Landing* on its big bookstand surrounded by an angel and white organza and twinkle lights. "Not everything works out like you think it's going to, and sometimes you give something your all, but your all isn't even close to being enough."

Ouch. No matter whether she had a secret-attorney-boyfriend, the wistfulness in Tabitha's voice made his own breathing tighten.

"I wish my grandmother could have come in to make sure Mrs. Ruskin receives the photo album from someone connected to the book and to her past." Tabitha ran a smoothing hand over the cover. "They were childhood friends. But she's busy at Sweet Haven. It would have been a more personal touch that way." Was there a hitch in her voice? "At least Sam will be here to greet her with a friendly smile."

"Sam? Smile?" George guffawed. "I doubt it. He's a wreck."

Excuse me? Sam nearly burst out of his hiding place and outed himself as a grumpy, heartbroken eavesdropper. Instead, he crouched. He really should move out of earshot. Out of misery.

"Truth be known, so am I."

"It'll be all right, dearie. Things work out." George patted her shoulder. Traitor. "But do come back to pass along the photo album, would you? Please? Since you're Collette's granddaughter, that'll be a much more personal touch."

Tabitha didn't commit but gave a little nod and then exited the shop, making the jingle bells chime off key, sad instead of merry.

Wait! Sam should run after her, tell her why he was a wreck, ask why *she* was a wreck, find out everything about this mystery boyfriend straight from Tabitha instead of accepting Andrew Kingston's word alone as truth, without double checking.

It had sounded so true, and Andrew had heard it straight from Tabitha, and then that text—the guy she admired in Darlington. A lawyer. Named Steve.

So, he didn't.

He let her go.

Didn't the fact she was heading back to Darlington confirm that she must have someone there waiting for her? Any guy lucky enough to have her wouldn't be fool enough to let her go. Attorney-Man Steve probably pestered her a thousand times a day to come home to him. In fact, Attorney-Man Steve probably wanted her back in Darlington so he could be inspired to write his own novel. All attorneys seemed to have a novel-writing project on the side.

"Look at you, boss." Mrs. Milliken walked down his aisle of shelves, her arms piled with books on flower gardening tips—a wishful topic for the dead of winter. "I take it you heard all of that?"

"All of what?"

"Don't be coy. She's closing her business. Because of you, I'll wager."

"Me?" Sam hadn't made Tabitha close her business. "She's just moving on. Going back to Darlington and people there. People move on all the time."

"Not when they love their grandmothers the way that girl does."

And her grandmother's home and its irreplaceable memories. "So, I don't get it. How did I cost her her job?"

Mrs. Milliken frowned. "Fine. I'll spell it out for you, as if you weren't a grown man but one of my freshman English students, the first quarter of school." She slid her glasses onto the tip of her nose and peered over them at him. "She obviously needs the book in the window for someone she is working for. You are not letting her have it. Without it, she can't keep her business open. She let you have it and stopped pestering you because she's smitten with you—which at this point seems like a grave error."

"So you don't think she has a secret boyfriend in Darlington? You don't think she was using me?"

Disgust dripped from her tone, as if Sam were a three-day-old fish in the middle of her Christmas dinner table. "Get it together, Sam. I heard what that attorney said to you. It was poison, and you didn't take the antivenin of simply asking her side of the story."

"Why didn't you tell me this earlier?"

"Because I foolishly assumed you had a brain in your head and were just working up the courage or the right words for broaching the topic. If I'd known you were letting something real and good like Sam-and-Tabitha fizzle, I would have leaped in with my unsolicited advice-giving superpowers and managed things."

"Mrs. Milliken." Sam blinked. "I can't believe I'm going to say this, but I wish you'd told me what to do about a woman."

"Would you have listened? No."

She was a hundred percent right about that. But what was he supposed to do now that so much time had passed, call Tabitha up and ask her to come back in here, have a heart-to-heart, on Christmas Eve? He was probably much too late for that, considering she was packing to move. Plus, she'd lost everything. Which might be his fault if everything Mrs. Milliken said was true. "Should I text her?"

Mrs. Milliken shrugged. "If that's all the effort you're willing to put forth."

"I can't think! I mean, I want to swoop in and give her the world and tell her everything will be fine, but do I know that? What's the truth? Is she going back to a boyfriend? I am not used to any of this. I'm an old man."

"You're *thirty*." Mrs. Milliken crossed her arms over her chest and peered over her reading glasses at him. "Be a man." She headed back to the counter and handed him the photo album. "Put this aside so it doesn't look like it's for sale or a display piece in the meantime. The customers will come streaming in for the event, and we don't want to have to explain unnecessary things." She narrowed her eyes at him, laser-like. "Don't text, but you're on the right track. You're a writer. Use your words."

A writer. Ha! One who tore up his words and stuffed them in trash cans, more like. One who sent half-baked, juvenile novellas to big-city publishers and then burned the manuscript when it was returned unread. *It's okay that I wasn't good enough the first time. That book needed to come out of my heart, and it did, thanks to Ed Garnet and* Angels Landing.

Mindlessly, he flipped open the photo album as he walked it to his office in the back room. Christmas lights, rocking horses, Schwinn bicycles with banana-shaped seats and streamers on the handlebars. Kids wearing grins of ecstasy and footed pajamas.

All photos he'd never be taking of a family of his own.

What am I going to write? Nothing came to him, so he flipped another page. Then, on the next page, a gap-toothed child wore a t-shirt that read, *The Garnet Family.* As did a younger child who had obviously cut her own hair in front at a severe angle. And the parents.

A label beneath the photo read: *Nina and Joe and daughters Edwina and Della.*

Edwina? He'd heard that name lately. But he couldn't place it. Life was too stressful, and it was just a haze.

One thing, however, was clear: Sam now knew exactly what he needed to write for Tabitha—and even though the author event was slated to start in an hour, and without an author it was almost time for Sam to march toward his noose, he couldn't afford to waste a single minute.

Chapter 34

Tabitha

In Grandma's kitchen for one of the last times it would look this way, Tabitha put the final touches on Poppy's gift for Andrew. It had just arrived in the mail, barely in time.

Things were going to be okay. This meaningful gift, plus the one for Della Ruskin later today, would speak love. Twelve Days wasn't a complete failure if it had given someone love, if it had given someone light, even for a brief moment.

There. Done. She'd have to go to The Cider Press to give it to them, which meant being next door to Angels Landing, but that was the breaks. Tabitha could tell Poppy goodbye, if no one else. Besides, leaving Sugarplum Falls didn't mean she had to stop loving her friend Poppy.

Grandma had taught her that.

So downtown she went, venturing out into the snowy Christmas Eve day.

"Tabitha." Poppy crossed her arms over her chest and leveled a stern look when Tabitha stepped in the door of The Cider Press. "If you're going to place the CLOSED sign in my window at the lunch rush on one of the biggest shopping days of the year, you'd better have a very good reason."

"Oh, I do. Believe me." She gave Poppy the best smile she could under the circumstances. "I've got your final gifts compiled."

Poppy uncrossed her arms and clasped her hands at her throat instead. "For my mysterious gift-leaver? What is it?"

"Well, first, this one is for your niece." She presented the crystal thimble with the gold-leaf *K* on its top. "For Kate."

"You remembered! And I'm going to see her tomorrow. Wow." Poppy lit up. "It's perfect. How did you find it?" She cupped it in her hand, admiring it and looking like she might break into tears. "She's going to love it so much. Finding perfect presents is your superpower."

"I've had a great time." This chapter was closing, but at least it was closing on a high note. She'd have to explain that later to Poppy. Right now, they were basking in the gift glow.

"You said you have two things?" Poppy clapped quickly and bounced.

"It's something I think you'll both enjoy." She pulled the opaque-tissue-covered basket off the chair where she'd set it and placed it on the largest table in the empty shop. Only one particular patron would be allowed past the CLOSED sign, although he hadn't appeared yet.

"But, how would you know that?" Poppy asked. "I did get a little note of thanks from him when he left his most recent offering, a tiny Eiffel Tower made of carved bone. He mentioned he loved the signed baseball glove. Your idea. Still, should I trust you? This is big."

"You should."

"Wait a second. You know who he is! I have been watching for the pewter stirring stick every day, and I still haven't seen him. Her. Him. Him, right?"

"Him. If I'm right. I have a ninety percent gut feeling I do." More like ninety-nine, but she downplayed it by nine percent for dramatic effect. "He's supposed to be here soon."

"How did you contact him?"

"The same way you did when you left him the presents—by stashing the request to meet in the same place as he left you a present that day."

"Sneaky. Smart." Poppy bounced up and down. "To tell you the truth, I'm as excited as I used to get on Christmas Eve as a little girl. I'm even more excited than if I were going to meet Kang Jin-Wook."

Good. That was exactly what Tabitha wanted to hear. Where was he? Tabitha checked the clock on the wall. He was a little behind schedule. Outside, a huge press of people covered the door to the shop. Ah. Maybe they were waiting to get into Angels Landing for that Christmas Eve author event. Who was coming, Charles Dickens's ghost? Anyway, the man should have been here by now.

"I can't believe I'm going to meet him. Maybe I'll go put on some lip gloss." Poppy disappeared into the back room, leaving Tabitha to worry and wait.

The gift basket loomed large. She'd invited Andrew to meet Poppy and reveal his identity on Christmas Eve, saying that Poppy had a special gift all picked out for him. When that conversation Tabitha had had with Andrew Kingston the other week had gone sideways—the day Sam had more or less dumped her—she'd lost all fire for the deed to go pick out something lawyer-related. Instead, she'd settled on something they'd both enjoy together.

Fingers crossed.

The front door rattled, and Tabitha turned around.

"You." Andrew frowned. "Please, don't tell me you're the one in charge of this, or that you somehow got confused into thinking I was interested in you."

Whoa there, cowboy. Hold the holiday rudeness with the side order of scorn. "Hey. Poppy doesn't know you're the one who's been leaving her gifts, but I do. She wants it to be you, since she had such a good time on your hot chocolate date, et cetera, but if you're going to be salty to me, I can just remove her gift to you and end this right now."

"Because you're the guru of all dating relationships?"

"It's Christmas Eve. What is wrong with you, dude?"

"Let's just say I don't like it when women think they're pretty enough to two-time good men like Sam Bartlett." Every word was laced with tiny shards of glass, cutting her a thousand times.

"I—I have no idea what you're talking about." She swallowed hard, but there was a fist in her throat that wouldn't go down. "Two-timing?"

Poppy emerged from the powder room and strode over to stand at Tabitha's side. "Excuse me, Counselor Kingston. My friend here is not on trial, and you are neither judge nor jury. And I don't take kindly to accusers who are completely free of solid evidence for their accusations. Tabitha here has not had a boyfriend for *years*." She turned to Tabitha. "Sorry, babe, but you're the one who told me that, even if it's embarrassing."

Poppy turned back to Andrew, putting her hands on her hips menacingly. She took a stomp toward him. "And the last thing she'd do is mess over the man she's been crushing on since she had braces and a side ponytail."

Oh, but that visual. If only it weren't so accurate. "Poppy—"

"I can't believe you're defending her." Andrew didn't back down. He narrowed his eyes. "I love that you're loyal. It makes you even more crazy-attractive, but you're misplacing it. This *strumpet* here not only flirted with me, but she also bragged about having a boyfriend in Darlington who was just like me and was a lawyer. Named Steve. My money's on Steve Marsden, which she didn't deny."

Steve Marsden. Who the heck was Steve Marsden?

Good grief. Sam had used the name Steve, too. Where had any of this come from?

Andrew forged onward. "*Then* she proceeded to gush over the phone to some screeching woman about making out with Sam Bartlett just to get him to kowtow to her nefarious plan to get a certain book from him. Isn't that right, Tabitha?" Her name left his mouth with a razor blade attached.

Tabitha crumpled against the wall. "I didn't—" Except … she had. "You completely misread that whole situation."

"Dimwit!" Poppy jumped in. "She wasn't talking about some boyfriend of her own in Darlington, duh. She was trying—and failing horribly—to be sneaky in asking *you* about *your* interests." When Tabitha's head popped upward and she met Poppy's eyes, Poppy shrugged. "Sorry, hon. I can hear every word of every conversation in this place. There's an acoustical miracle going on in this building. I've known ever since then that Andrew was my mysterious gift-giver."

"You knew?" Both Andrew and Tabitha gasped at the same time.

Again, Poppy shrugged. "Merry Christmas." She reached into the pocket of her apron and pulled out a miniature wooden gavel, which she handed to Andrew. "I carved it myself. But after your performance today, and your sheer rudeness to my good friend Tabitha Townsend, who was only trying to help me out, I'd like you to use that gavel and pop yourself right in the eye."

Andrew pressed a hand to his forehead. "You were really trying to do this for Poppy and me?"

Tabitha nodded. "I do not now nor have I ever had a lawyer-friend in Darlington. He was a fiction. And I don't know anyone named Steve there."

"But you said his name was Steve."

"No, I didn't. I wouldn't."

"Sorry, babe." Poppy threw her arm around Tabitha's shoulder. "Andrew's not wrong. But you were a little flustered. I can see how you'd forget the white lie from the adrenaline of the moment."

Steve. The fictional lawyer's name. That was right. Couldn't the floor just open up and swallow her whole? "I'm such an idiot."

Apparently, Poppy still thought Andrew was the idiot, though, because she went off on him again. "And another thing, pal. Tabitha didn't kiss Sam Bartlett to get at his stupid book. If you knew anything, you'd know she told the client to figuratively go jump off a bridge. Fitting, considering the plot of the book the client wanted so badly. But now, Tabitha ended up not getting paid by the client, so she's shuttering her business—all because when she quit trying to get that book from Sam the client got mad and refused to pay any of Tabitha's *many* expenses in her efforts to get the book."

Poppy knew all that, too? Well, yeah. Everyone probably knew by this point. Since Grandma knew and talked to everyone else in town.

"It wasn't exactly like that," Tabitha mumbled. "I told her she could try to convince Sam to give up his book, but that I was finished hurting him. I only wish I knew why he dropped me so hard." Hard enough it felt like Tabitha had made the bridge jump onto a frozen river and bounced.

Andrew slid the hand from his forehead down the side of his face and looked at his hands. "I, uh, am afraid I may have had something to do with that."

"What did you do, *Andrew*?" Poppy looked ready to swipe the mini-gavel out of his hand and use it as a deadly weapon. "Don't tell me you …"

"Uh-huh. But I had a really good reason. I swear it."

"Why you …" She whirled around and yanked the still-wrapped gift basket from Tabitha to her chest. "I don't know what's in this, but since Tabitha arranged it for us, I *know* it's good. She's the best, most-intuitive gifter I've ever heard of. And I'm *not sharing* it with you." She turned around and marched it to the kitchen, and then returned and flipped the front door's sign to OPEN and swung the entrance wide. "You all can come in now," she shouted

187

to the crowd. "Come out of the cold while you're waiting to get a spot in Angels Landing. Hot cider for anyone who needs it. On the house. Merry Christmas." She didn't sound merry at all.

Poppy turned around and gave Andrew a glare that would make Rudolph's red nose stop glowing and the light go out altogether. "Except for you. You'd better leave."

"But Poppy!" he said.

"Go on." She shooed him off, and he left in a desolate trudge through the crowd.

Tabitha scooted out of the way of the influx of cider sippers. "You didn't have to be so harsh on him. It was an honest mistake. I'm the one who lied."

"White lied. Anyway, it will make him do the right thing. And I know him well enough to know that he's a guy who likes a challenge. He doesn't want a sweet, cloying girlfriend. He wants someone who's not afraid to tell him when he's wrong. That's what happened when I was in court with him. It took me a while to piece it together, but after I yelled at him in the hallway of the county courthouse for a solid fifteen minutes for his ridiculous behavior toward me, he started coming in here and looking at me with the big puppy-dog eyes."

"You knew before he started leaving gifts that he liked you?"

"Yeah, but I thought he was a dirt-bag until we got matched by the magical Santa hat at the Hot Cocoa Festival. Then, I decided to just embrace the dark side. Er, you know what I mean."

Yeah, Tabitha knew. That hot cocoa night had been a turning point for her, too. "Well, I am sorry this little reveal turned into a breakup rather than a get-together for you and Andrew."

"Don't worry." Poppy got a gleam in her eye. "I think it will be all right between us again soon. Did you see what he left for me under the croissant cloche?" She reached in her apron pocket and pulled out a diamond keychain.

"Oh, my gosh. Are those real diamonds?"

"I don't know, and I don't care. They're seriously sparkly, and I'm in love."

"With him or the keychain?"

"Do I have to choose one or the other?" She giggled. "Now, I have to get serving cider. Can I peek at what's inside the gift basket now, or should I, you know, wait and share with him?"

Tabitha shrugged. "Up to you."

"Thanks, Tabitha." Poppy gave her a quick side-hug. "I'm sorry Andrew destroyed your relationship."

Yeah, Tabitha was sorry about that, too.

At least now she knew why Sam thought of Tabitha as scum of the earth. It gouged like a reindeer antler in the flesh that he thought her capable of such deception. No wonder he'd avoided her so completely. Why blame him, if that was what he'd been told?

But … he should have asked her personally for her side, not just trusted Andrew's word.

Then again, Andrew had strong evidence—having heard the words from her own lips—and as an attorney, he definitely would have the power of persuasion. More than that, he was a disinterested party and would have no ulterior motive in telling Sam about her perceived falsehood.

No, she couldn't blame Andrew for thinking it, for telling Sam, or blame Sam for believing Andrew's claim, mistaken though it was.

Or, could she? Didn't Sam know her better than that yet? After all they'd talked about and done together? What about the photo album and all the effort she'd put into finding Della, or what about the things she'd told him about her family, and the way she'd let him into her life and heart? Did none of that count for anything?

At the same time, Sam had turned out to be just like every other guy who had let her go based on a simple misunderstanding.

Not willing to fight to find out her side of the story.

That was what stung the most.

Man, she was so conflicted. It wasn't his fault, but at the same time it was. And it wasn't Tabitha's fault either, or Andrew's, but at the same time it was all their fault, and the pain had yet to be washed away.

She pushed her way out into the snowy day and through the crowd of people lined up at Angels Landing for the author meet and greet. Who was the author? Despite all the ads, she'd never heard particulars. Not that Sam would want her dropping in today when he had a million business details to handle. He wouldn't want to deal with her or with any of the feelings that would crop up around a woman who he believed had betrayed him.

No, she dodged the piles of snow on the curb and made her way past the holiday crowds to her car. There, as she fumbled to find her keys, she paused and took a longing look at Orchard Street. Sugarplum Falls really did have the most wonderful charm, and it was at its most glorious during Christmas.

I'm going to miss this place. She could barely breathe.

Chapter 35

Sam

What was that lawyer doing here in the bookstore again? Sam always tried his best not to shoot the messenger when someone gave him bad news, but in Andrew Kingston's case, it was impossible for Sam not to get his neck muscles twitching on sight of the guy.

"Sam, I need to talk to you." He cut the line and came right to the counter.

"Sorry, Andrew. Not a lot of time here." Sam handed a customer a bag of books, each festively wrapped in the signature Angels Landing gift paper. "Come again soon. Merry Christmas."

"No, Sam. This is important."

Although Andrew looked gray with worry, Sam couldn't get distracted. "So is completing last-minute shopping for all hundred and fifty people in line here." He took the next family's purchases and began scanning the bar codes. "These look like great choices." He smiled at the customer, but then sneaked a frown at Andrew. "How's tomorrow? Can you come back then?"

"On Christmas Day?" Andrew looked shocked.

"It would actually be more convenient, dude."

"But it could be too late. She's leaving Sugarplum Falls."

"Who is?" Sam knew, though, the second he asked. "Back to Darlington? To Attorney-Boyfriend Steve?"

"Yes and no." Andrew made two fists and released them. Then he turned around to the crowd in the line. "Folks? Merry Christmas!" he shouted. A few murmured greetings echoed him. "I know you're all in a rush to get through the line and get home, but I need to borrow the owner of this shop for three minutes. Can your gift to him for being the best bookshop owner in Sugarplum Falls be three minutes of your time on Christmas Eve?"

191

A murmured assent ensued, and Andrew grabbed Sam by the arm, dragging him away. "I'll bring him right back."

As soon as they were in the storeroom, Andrew exploded with words. "I was wrong. Totally wrong. She doesn't have a boyfriend in Darlington. She was only asking me a bunch of questions to figure out what Poppy Peters should give me for Christmas. I misinterpreted it, which wasn't totally my fault, but she wasn't cheating on you. The Steve thing was a white lie gone wrong. Moreover, she did kiss you, but not to get the book. She actually liked you, and probably still does, but she's moving to Darlington because she had to close her business because, one, she couldn't give her client that book and, two, the expenses from trying to locate that book were too high, and now she's taking some kind of position there that she will hate, and it's all my fault. And sort of yours."

"Whoa. Slow down." Sam didn't actually need Andrew to slow down. Adrenaline made him process everything at lightning speed. "And you know this how?"

"Poppy and Tabitha straightened me out, so I knew I had to come over immediately and tell you. I was wrong, and you were misled. By me, no matter the good intentions. I'm sorry, man."

Sam blinked. Could he believe it all?

She didn't have a boyfriend. She did surrender the book to me, and she gave up her business—and her home. For me.

The enormity of it pressed down on him, almost buckling his knees.

He stiffened both his joints though, as well as his upper lip. Sam stuck out a hand for Andrew to shake, which he did. "Thanks, Kingston. It takes a brave man to admit when he did the wrong thing."

"I always appreciate it when a suspect who's guilty pleads guilty. That's when the plea bargains and the fun begin."

"What's your bargaining chip, since you're guilty?"

"I ask your forgiveness—and that you don't waste time before reaching out to Tabitha Townsend. She didn't deserve my interference any more than you did."

That wasn't exactly a bargaining chip, but Sam would consider the advice.

Mrs. Milliken popped her head through the swinging doors. "What in the name of St. Nick are you doing back here? The crowd is going crazy."

Uh-oh. "Have them sign up for a raffle for a big gift card." That would keep them busy for a while. "And tell them whoever shares most on social media about the store will get a free book every week for a year."

Mrs. Milliken raised a brow. "Sure, but it's not just that. There's a woman here, and she demands to see you."

"Did she give her name?" Oh, dear. Everything hit at once. "Is it Edwina Somebody?"

"She didn't say."

Sam turned to Andrew. "Here's my bargaining point, Guilty-Guy. Can you find Tabitha for me? Bring her here. Tell her the woman is here for the photo album, and I need to talk to her. Don't take no. You're very good at that, I hear."

Andrew nodded and headed for the back exit. "This will be faster. I'm on it." He turned back when he got to the door. "Thanks, Sam. And good luck."

He'd need it, after the way he'd been treating Tabitha—completely undeservedly. He'd been blindly selfish, to her great detriment.

Sam just prayed Tabitha would allow him to prove himself. He grabbed the photo album from his desk and headed out into the fray.

Out front, he signaled to Mrs. Milliken, who was at the register. "I'm so sorry, but can you keep ringing people up while I get the photo album passed off to its owner? Then I'll be back to help you."

"Photo album?" a woman's voice said. "I'm here for a photo album." A short, stout older woman with dark hair pushed her way through the press, her hand stretching above the heads of the shoppers. "I'm Della Ruskin," she said as she emerged. "Someone told me Tabitha—Collette Honeycutt's granddaughter—found our pictures and said I could come get them."

"Yes, thank you for coming. I'm the one who contacted you."

Della was so sweet-looking. Friendly. Very different from how her sister Edwina had been with him on the phone.

"Sorry it's such chaos in here." He extended the photo album, but before

193

she could accept it, up walked another woman, much harsher in countenance.

"Della!" The taller woman glowered. "What on earth?"

Mrs. Ruskin gasped. "What are *you* doing here, Edwina?"

The taller woman—Edwina—glared and then turned to Sam. "All right. Hand over my book."

"Gladly." Sam offered the photo album approximately halfway between the two women. They could sort out between themselves who would get the album. Clearly this wasn't a warm greeting between the sisters. "The photos are great. I think you'll enjoy the trip down memory lane. So many are of family Christmases."

"Not that book." Edwina's upper lip curled. She lifted her palms and stepped back, as if he were offering her roasted chestnuts straight from the fire, burning hot. "*My* book. The one I wrote. Tabitha said you have it. *Angels Landing.*"

It hit him all at once: Della/Elda. Edwina/Ed. Even the Collette/Lettie connection from the book fit. This was …

He whispered it. "You're Ed Garnet."

Chapter 36

Sam

"Technically"—Della shouldered forward with an index finger in the air—"*Angels Landing* is *my* book. But it would have been much better had it been no book at all."

"Della," Edwina, the older sister, growled. "What are you doing here in the first place?"

"I have a right to shop anywhere I want on Christmas Eve."

"But …"

Out of nowhere, up walked Tabitha. "I think I can explain."

"Tabitha!" Sam gasped. Andrew must have found her and sent her in. Good on him. He had so much to tell her.

Please say I'm not too late.

"I'm Collette Honeycutt's granddaughter, Tabitha." She clasped Della Ruskin's hands. "She's dying to see you but had an unbreakable commitment."

Edwina scoffed and spoke under her breath. "Unbreakable. Since when is there such a thing in life as an unbreakable commitment?" She clocked her head toward Tabitha and glared.

Seriously? Tabitha had given up everything for the woman, including her livelihood! "Tabitha, I don't think you—" began Sam.

But Tabitha ignored both Edwina and him and continued speaking to Della Ruskin. "Sam found your photo album, and I found you—with Grandma's help."

With her engaging smile aglow, Tabitha briefly explained all about the storage unit auction, the photo album, and the great find of *Angels Landing*. At last, she turned to Edwina, who wore a sour expression. "It's nice to see you again, Mrs. Barnes. Merry Christmas."

"Merry Christmas," Edwina Barnes said tightly, but she did say it. "You actually did find my book, so that's something. I knew you would. Something told me so."

"It's my book," Della said, but not in an angry way. "Remember? My story?"

Whew. That could have gone the direction of far too many past Middle East peace talks, but Tabitha's warm ways had won the day. She really was amazing.

And to think, she probably hates me.

He sent up a combination prayer-and-Christmas-wish that he would be granted an opportunity to explain, and that she'd be gracious enough to forgive.

"Thank you for the photo album." Della finally took possession of it from Sam's hands, and then turned to her sister. "But I still don't understand why you want a copy of *Angels Landing* so badly. That's not why you're here, is it?"

"Mr. Bartlett said I could have it free of charge, since it's mine."

Wh-what? "Wait a second." He held up his palms. "Are we … uh? Weren't we talking about the photo album on the phone?" Except, obviously not. "I'm afraid there's been a misunderstanding."

"Yes, Mrs. Barnes." Tabitha stepped in. "It's like I told you. The book actually has Sam's name in it. But that's not the only reason he wants it. It's a very special book to him."

"But it's mine!" she said.

At the same moment, Della asked, "Is that so?"

They shot each other irritated glances. So much for the brokered peace.

Mrs. Barnes huffed and crossed her arms toward Sam. "Explain."

Mrs. Milliken popped her head into the aisle where they were standing. "You're blocking all of the Christmas recipe book merchandise. Can you reconvene somewhere else?"

"I want to see the book," Mrs. Barnes said.

Sam led them toward the store-side entrance of the window display, and they stepped up and inside. Mrs. Barnes, Mrs. Ruskin, Sam, and Tabitha stood in the front window among the long swaths of white tulle, beside the pretty white and gold book.

"Oh! I haven't seen a copy of this in so long!" Della made a little fist and held it to her upper lip. "May I?" She reached for it.

"Of course." Sam handed it to her, moving the bookstand out of the way.

"What are you doing?" Edwina demanded. "You're looking at that book like it's an old friend. I thought you hated it."

"I never hated it."

"Please." Mrs. Barnes rolled her eyes and snorted. Actually snorted. "You told me forty-five years ago if I didn't collect every single copy ever printed that you'd never speak to me again. There was only a print-run of a hundred. I found and destroyed the others. This is the final copy, and you don't know what I've been through to get it. I finally found and hired this ingenious girl, who already lived here in Sugarplum Falls, and she located it. But even she, with all her wiles and ingenuity, can't pry it out of the owner's hands." She shot Sam a look that would make the Ghost of Christmas Yet to Come shudder so hard he'd drop his scythe.

Sam sloughed it off and turned to Tabitha. "That's why you were so insistent on buying it from me? Because you were trying to help Mrs. Barnes make peace with her sister?"

Tabitha shook her head. "All I knew was Mrs. Barnes had to have it. When I'd promised to help … Well, I had a feeling in my gut that I should, one I couldn't shake. But I swear, she never told me anything about her sister." She turned to Mrs. Ruskin. "Can I ask why you wanted all the copies collected and destroyed?"

"It wasn't her story to tell." Della's mouth formed a hard line. "I'm the one who made the reckless choices as a juvenile that led me to holding my baby girl on that bridge. I'm the one whose life was touched by an angel's hand, and whose daughter was brought to a safe landing. Yeah, I know I never would have gotten around to writing it on my own, but I at least wanted a say in what she called me in the book. She used my *actual* nickname!" She turned to Edwina. "Don't you think Amanda would read that one day and put two and two together, that her own mother had at one point been willing to throw away her baby's life? *Her* life?" Her voice hitched.

Edwina looked repentant.

Della continued, "I couldn't have Amanda learning about what an irresponsible, selfish mother she had. After that angel came, I changed. We all did. I only wanted Amanda to know the me *after* the angel came. I can't imagine how much it would have hurt her to think her life had been worth nothing to me at one, solitary dark moment in a lifetime of joys as her mother. She had already lost enough not having a father in her life."

Right. The bad husband was this Amanda's father.

Edwina Barnes looked truly stricken. "Oh, Della."

The air grew thick with unspoken emotion. Sam and Tabitha caught each other's glance but waited silently for the sisters to speak.

Eventually, Edwina threw her arms around Della and sobbed. "I am so sorry. That was thoughtless of me. I only thought of how much inspiration hundreds or thousands of people could take from your experience of being saved by divine intervention. I only thought of how it could help someone on their worst day. I should have been thinking of the feelings of my own niece." She closed her eyes. "Of my own sister."

"I admit, I've actually told Amanda all about it at this point, but it was on my terms. She's forgiven me."

They hugged it out for a full minute, and outside, a light snow began to fall again.

Then Tabitha said, "Your story did have a profound effect, even in small circulation." Her eyes met Sam's again. "It changed Sam's life. I can tell you that much."

"It's true." Sam gazed at the book's white linen cover, now so familiar. "I discovered the book as a teen. Later, the story helped me through the lowest point of my life when my wife lost her battle to illness. Because of that book, I'd told her I wanted to become a writer. The prose and the turns of phrase made it more precious than gold."

"You truly love that story?" Della asked. "My experience helped you?"

"You loved the book. My words." Edwina's brows pushed together. "Enough that you were willing to defy the incessant wheedling of a girl as pretty as Tabitha Townsend?" She gave a dry laugh. "You must really like the book."

"I do. But not as much as I love Tabitha"—he only allowed his eyes to dart in her direction for a second, or else he might not be able to get the next words out—"which is why I'm willing to give you two this final copy. I assume you won't be destroying it now."

Tabitha gasped. "But, Sam!"

He shook his head and reached for her hand. "I've re-read it—even a couple more times over the past week. It turns out I had barely forgotten a word since first reading. It's imprinted on my soul." Like a mother's face on a baby's mind. "I'll be forever grateful to have found it again, like a long-lost friend."

"Like a long-lost sister," Della muttered. "I can't believe I let this come between us."

"I'm so sorry I didn't consult you before publication." Edwina wiped a sheen of tears from her cheek. Then she turned to Sam. "If it's okay with Della, I'd love to let you keep the book. It fits the store."

"That's right! You must have really loved the story. You even named your bookshop after it." Della's eyes grew wide. "I couldn't have told my experience well enough to inspire you, but my sister did, and I'm glad it helped your life. I expect you will write a truly moving book someday, young man."

Sam couldn't keep the book. He'd reread it, displayed it, and allowed it to bring Tabitha back into his life, and that was enough. He pressed it away, with great thanks for the offer. "I did recently start writing." *Again*, he should add. Luckily, he hadn't taken out the trash from his study before his words were lost forever. They were a good beginning to something, and he'd added to them since.

"You started writing?" Tabitha whispered. "I'm so happy to hear that. Adelaide would be so happy."

"I didn't do it for Adelaide this time." He smiled at Tabitha. She pulled what looked like a hesitant smile. "Thank you for coming back."

Chapter 37

Tabitha

The emotions were as thick as caramel sauce in Angels Landing. Tabitha almost couldn't breathe through them. Mrs. Barnes wasn't ready to throttle her anymore, the sisters' reunion made Tabitha choke up every time she thought about it.

And best of all, Sam was looking at her that way—like he'd forgiven her. Like he loved her.

She had to grab onto something, just to stay steady.

Instead, Mrs. Barnes put her arms around Tabitha's shoulder. It did the trick, but it wasn't what she'd expected. Mrs. Barnes wasn't the warm, embracing type. She led Tabitha aside, speaking confidentially.

"Technically, you may not have gotten the book for me, but you got me my sister back—which is what I wanted the most anyway."

"I wish you'd told me about the book's origin." It would have made things a little easier to explain, and possibly would have made Sam more willing to part with it sooner. "But I can see why it was so personal to Della."

"Yes." Mrs. Barnes coughed a little, as if the apology lodged in her throat. "I'm sorry I was so hard on you about this. Please forgive me and remember our past and our future, not this moment. You see, for years, I have needed Della back and couldn't see a way. I messed things up between us long ago, and without her, I got … crusty. I'm naturally terse. Terse people need fun people. Della always fueled the fun side of me, and that has been missing for far too long. To have her back—it's worth everything to me. Especially now."

"Why now?" She'd never explained. "Is something wrong?"

"I had … a mass. This summer."

A mass. The bad word no one wants to hear. "I'm so sorry."

"It put me on edge. Especially that day when Soccer Ball went missing." She gulped. "The day when you walked him for me and he went missing I'd been there, in the doctor's office, getting the news. From that instant, I knew I had to rebuild the bridge to my sister. Even though it turned out to be benign, I realized just how quick life can be, and that I'd wasted too much time already. But I had no idea how—until you said you were planning on looking for gifts for people in Sugarplum Falls."

Oh, Mrs. Barnes. "I had no idea. I'm so sorry I lost Soccer Ball. And on that day of all days."

"I'm not. If you hadn't lost him—which, I know that pup, and he definitely ran away of his own free will—then I wouldn't be standing here today with my sister. Together again. Thank you, Tabitha."

Then, the strangest thing happened. Mrs. Edwina "Winnie" Garnet Barnes embraced Tabitha warmly.

Tabitha hugged back.

Della came over and hugged her sister, followed by Grandma Honeycutt.

"Hello, all." She broke into a grin, and Della threw her arms around her. "I was at Sweet Haven, but someone pulled a fire alarm. I shouldn't count it a blessing to close down craft time early on Christmas Eve, but it let me be here with you."

They hugged it out. "I brought caramels for you, Lettie. But you have to promise to share some with your brilliant granddaughter."

Edwina Garnet Barnes reached into her purse and pulled out a checkbook, which she opened and scribbled in. "Here's your commission, as well as an amount I'm sure will cover any expenses." She handed Tabitha a check. The amount in the payment box was five figures—that didn't begin with a one.

Tabitha stepped back from it, pressing a hand to her heart. "Mrs. Barnes. This is too much! You already footed the startup cash for my business."

"I'm just paying you what you're worth, Tabitha. You should get used to asking for that from those who hire you."

"But I lost Soccer Ball."

"But because we found Soccer Ball, I found Della, remember?" It was as if Mrs. Barnes wouldn't be budged.

Her voice quavered. "It's too much."

"Not to me." She grinned in her sister's direction. "Della's back."

Chapter 38

Sam

Sam helped two more customers in the jammed store find the books they were looking for—*The Candy Kingdom* for Buck Sutherland for his kids; *A Gardener's Best Friend: His Square-Nosed Shovel* for Cardy McNair, the poinsettia-obsessed, newest gardening wizard in town— but he was desperate to get back to Tabitha's side, and to find out what Mrs. Barnes had said to her.

Weird, he felt so much lighter now that he'd given up *Angels Landing*. Sam paused to marvel. Maybe letting go of what he thought he wanted most was the best way to get the thing he needed even more. *I'll take a photo of the book on Mrs. Milliken's display. We can frame it and hang it in the store year-round.* Then, it would be like having his cake and eating it too. Or having his book and giving it too.

Whatever. There was something much more important to focus on right now.

He craned his neck to look for the one person he needed most.

The two Garnet sisters had taken their photo album and Grandma Honeycutt away toward a trio of armchairs in a back corner of the shop where they could look through their childhood. Together.

But where had Tabitha gone?

I know she came back to make things right with Mrs. Barnes, but now she's gone—and she hasn't let me make things right with her.

Sam straightened his necktie and looked around the store for her, giving a few customers the brush-off. Not his usual style. But this was an emergency. She wouldn't have up and left, would she?

Panic gripped him by the throat. He climbed one of the bookshelf ladders just to get a better view, peering everywhere for her distinctive red ponytail. *It's gone.* Now, his breathing got shallow. He reached for his phone to text her, but what if she'd driven away? Left, now that she'd set things right between the Garnet sisters?

"Have you seen Tabitha?" Sam snagged Mrs. Milliken's shoulder, but Mrs. Milliken just shook her head no.

He pushed his way through the crowd to the front exit. "Excuse me." He jostled a customer. He was losing it.

Outside, the air was so crisp it froze as it entered his lungs. "Tabitha?" he called into the milling crowd of last-minute shoppers on Orchard Avenue.

A roaring, cranking rumble sounded partway down the block. Sam would recognize that roadster's muffler anywhere in town. He jogged toward it—and found Tabitha's front bumper wedged in the snow. She was gunning the engine, but her rear wheels didn't make purchase on the slick asphalt.

Three taps on her driver's side window. "Need a winch?"

She startled, grasping her neck. A second later, her window rolled down a crack. "I'm not a wench. And … can you just let me get out of here?"

"Actually, no. I can't." Absolutely not. This was the woman who'd made everything right again in his life. Letting her go would be—

It'd be like losing love all over again.

"Sam, I think we both know that …"

"That I was a big jerk?" He opened her car door and fell to one knee. He reached for her coat sleeve and clung to it. "That I should have come to you first, asked for your side of the story?"

"Sam—" Tabitha looked pained and turned away.

"Whether or not it was a misunderstanding, I owed you more respect than that. I failed you, Tabitha. I should have fought for you. I need you." He inched closer to her, and he reached up and touched her chin, turning her face to him. "That I am in love with you."

Their eyes met, and hers widened. She sipped a swift, audible intake of breath.

"You are?"

"And I hope you'll give me a chance to do everything in my power to make it right." He gripped her upper arm. "Don't leave, Tabitha. Stay in Sugarplum Falls."

"Sam." Her voice hitched. "I'm—I'm in love with you, too." A gloss of tears filled her eyes. "I have been. For so long."

He leaned into her car and took her in his embrace. "Can you forgive me? Will you let me love you?" He pulled away long enough to see the answer in her features, and to swipe at the shining tear. "I'm yours, if you'll have me."

At the first sign of her shallow nod, Sam took her by both hands and lifted her out of the car, where he kissed her.

It wasn't the kiss of newfound passion. It was the kiss of newfound long-lasting love. The kiss of new beginnings. The kiss that breathed of *forever*.

When it subsided, Tabitha smiled. "How would you like to help me check on how things turned out with my final Twelve Days gift?"

***

They found Poppy and Andrew outside Angels Landing under the awning. Good. Sam needed a word with Andrew anyway.

"Tabitha! There you are!" Poppy bounced toward them. "Can I say? Best gift basket of all time! Not only are there the awesome Korean snacks like Milkis and O!Karto and Choco Pie, there's kimchi-flavored ramyun for dinner before the snacks." She rubbed her stomach and tilted her head in a cute, flirty way. "But the best part was the vial filled with *the first snow* that she packed for us in dry ice. You know what that means, right?"

Andrew raised his brows up and down like the two of them shared a delicious secret—that first snow means true love. "Besides the snow, I personally liked the gift certificates for the Korean restaurant and the K-Con coming to Caldwell City on Valentine's Day." He winked. "Saves me from trying to come up with the *best Valentine's Day ever* present, because it's already taken care of. Fighting!"

They smiled at each other, and Poppy grabbed his hand. "We can wear our matching hoodies!"

Sam pulled at his chin. "Matching hoodies, huh?"

Tabitha shrugged a shoulder. "They are screen-printed with the words *I turned off my K-drama to be here.*"

"What's a K-drama?" Sam asked before he realized he'd just uttered the most foul words in the known universe, based on Poppy's and Andrew's expressions. "Never mind. I'll get Tabitha to explain. Gently."

At that, Sam and Andrew met gazes. Andrew gave him a questioning look, and Sam gave him a thumbs up. Andrew gave it back.

They were cool.

"What was that thumb thing about?" Tabitha asked when she and Sam stood under the awning for a moment after the Korea-loving couple left. "Something to do with Andrew's penance for his mistake?"

More or less. "Tabitha, I'm the one who needs to do penance. But—I got the impression from Mrs. Milliken you weren't coming to give Della Ruskin the photo album."

"I decided to keep at least one promise. Besides, I really like giving gifts, and as of this morning, I'd assumed I wasn't going to get to anymore."

Mr. and Mrs. Milliken hurried out the door. "Sam? Are you out here?"

"Hey, we're all three out here." Sam shook his head. "Nobody's minding the store."

"We're scared, Sam." Mrs. Milliken's brow was a field of furrows. "All those customers are in there. They keep asking for their author to meet. What are we supposed to tell them?"

George grimaced. "They're getting restless. I'm worried chanting will come next."

No, no. Not chanting. "This is my fault," Sam said. "I dropped the ball and didn't arrange for anyone to speak or meet or greet or …" He huffed in exasperation. "I'll come in and tell them the truth, and I'll promise to make it up to them with a big discount on their purchases."

"But, Sam—what about profit margin? This year it's already pretty tight, and—"

Tabitha tapped his shoulder. "Excuse me, but don't you have an author in your store?"

He blinked a minute. "Ed Garnet?" Indeed he did—the most influential author in his life.

"As well as her inspiration? Couldn't they meet and greet the people of Sugarplum Falls?"

Indeed, they could. If Edwina "Ed" Garnet Barnes, author of *Angels*

Landing, agreed.

It turned out, she did agree, as did Della.

Within five minutes, both Della and Edwina were tag-teaming it at the microphone on the little platform he'd set up. They talked to a rapt crowd about their *co-authoring* of the book for which the town's favorite bookstore was named. "We're happy to announce that our long-out-of-print book, *Angels Landing*, will be available to read again as soon as a publisher is found."

The crowd clapped and cheered. Sam gaped. They were bringing it back? The world could have strength and help and hope from *Angels Landing* once again?

This was a great day. Sam may have had to swat at his eyes for a moment.

"Thank you, thank you." Edwina hushed the applause. "Finally, a big shout-out to Sugarplum Falls's own Sam Bartlett for bringing us together and making this happen today."

Three cheers went up.

But Sam was the one who needed to do the shout-out—to thank Tabitha for coming up with the brilliant, restless-crowd-assuaging solution to the problem he'd been facing for the past month. Where was she again?

Up came Mayor Lang instead. Uh-oh. What had he done this time?

However, she didn't wear her heat-seeking-missile expression this time. Instead, she looked almost gushing. "You're a marketing genius, Sam."

"Oh? How so?"

"You kept the identity of the authors for today's event under such tight wraps that no one—not one person—guessed who it could be. Not even I guessed."

Not even Sam, either. He scratched his neck, probably looking sheepish. "Glad it added some mystery to the Christmas season for everyone."

"Sugarplum Falls loves a mystery. Why do you think there were three hundred people lined up outside your store before the author event? Poppy Peters had to give them all cider to keep them from knocking down the whole line of stores on Orchard Street."

Apparently he owed Poppy a debt of gratitude as well. And probably free books for a year.

"We'll be wanting you to speak to the Chamber of Commerce about how you came up with this brilliant plan. It was a gift to the town."

Tabitha's gift, for sure. Tabitha might be all about finding gifts, but really … she was his gift.

Chapter 39

Tabitha

Tabitha spent the afternoon working with Sam and the Millikens in Angels Landing. Customer after customer thanked her for helping them find just the right gift for their loved ones through guidance of her insightful questions. She only slipped away for a few minutes to head to the bank to deposit her check—and to stop by Bijoux Jewelry to pick up the little gift she'd had them fashion for Sam.

Would he love it? He loved found items, right? He did own a used bookstore.

The store hours ended. "Head home," Sam told the two hardworking Millikens. "You've worked hard these past few weeks, and probably much too hard to do any holiday cooking tonight."

"True. We probably have something in the freezer we can warm up." Mrs. Milliken smiled and gave Sam a hug. "Merry Christmas. Today worked out beautifully." She said this while gazing at Tabitha.

"No freezer meals required. Mario's will be delivering your dinner in a half hour, minestrone soup and garlic bread."

"You remembered our favorite?" Mr. Milliken asked. "Thank you!"

"Credit goes to Tabitha." He winked at Tabitha. "She called Mario personally to ask him your preferences. She's an excellent personal shopper. Emphasis on personal."

"You're welcome. And you're worth it. Sam's lucky to have you." Tabitha hugged each of them. "Merry Christmas."

When they left, there was one final gift she held her breath over. Would he like it?

Sam followed Tabitha to Grandma Honeycutt's house, where they expected to relive all the excitement of the afternoon. However, upon arrival, Tabitha and Sam were the only two there.

Grandma had left a note: *Finished visiting with Della and Edwina. Last minute change of plans! Going to Darlington to Charlene's to spend the night. Back after the younger grandkids open gifts in the morning.*

"That's unexpected."

"Grandma is a social creature. If there's a party, she isn't going to miss it. Now, follow me." Tabitha led him into the kitchen on the way to the tree. "So, I guess I don't have anyone to spend Christmas with." *Hint, hint.*

Sam gathered her in. "How about spending Christmas with me?"

"Don't you have plans?" she asked. In all the hoopla of the book war between them, she'd never even asked him his family traditions or if he was going to travel.

"My parents are still doing their campground host thing in their RV on the coast, so I'd love nothing more than your company."

She would give it so gladly. "Let me give you your gift."

"You got me a present? In spite of everything?"

"Just because I hated you it didn't mean I stopped loving you."

"Love, eh?"

She nodded, and Sam took her hand, interlacing his fingers in hers. Sparks started in her fingertips and slid up her arms, lodging in her chest and igniting all over her body. Love sparks. The sparks of a cherished woman.

"The word love fits." She leaned closer, and Sam kissed her. Tenderly. The kiss of relief, of forgiveness, and of promises yet to come. Softly, and without releasing her from his embrace, he said, "Thank you for figuring out the solution to my author problem."

"It wasn't that big of a deal."

"It was to me. Huge. I could have lost credibility with my customers. And as a small business, that's paramount." He pulled away and looked straight into her eyes, speaking directly. "You may not believe this yet, but you will. I mean to make it happen."

"Believe what yet?"

"That you, Tabitha Townsend, are a brilliant woman—in every way."

Tabitha? Brilliant? "Not me."

"Problem-solving. Wit. Humor. Knowing what people need deep at their cores. You've covered all those bases, and probably many more that I can't wait to find out about."

Maybe she could do some of those things. "But I didn't go to school." Dad would never agree. "I'm barely employable."

"You're someone different. Someone that small-minded people can't wrap their brains around. Get used to that idea. Don't let it go."

Smart? Someone different—okay. Maybe she did do as her mom urged, and had found her own path in life. Not the school path. Not the oft-trod trail that Dad and Pamela wanted for *their* girls, but Tabitha had learned to give good gifts. And she'd kept promises, even when it was extremely difficult and came at risk of great personal loss.

Well, she'd done a few good things here in Sugarplum Falls lately. Okay, she might not be the dullest knife in the drawer, after all. It might take some time to believe him, but she'd try. *And Sam will help.*

"Thank you," she said, with a little gulp to clear the emotion from her throat. "I will try."

Sam embraced her. "I—I brought you a gift." He reached inside the pocket of his coat and brought out the crinkled papers, pieced together with tape. Added to them were twenty more handwritten pages, in much less of a state of disrepair. "It's a rough draft. As rough as the papers themselves look, so be kind."

"Sam?" Tabitha's gaze met his, which was filled with trepidation. "You wrote this? All of it?"

"Since I met you. Yes."

She pressed the pages to her heart. "I will cherish it. I'll memorize every word." But, no. She held it gingerly toward him. "Or do you want it back until it's finished?"

"I want you to be part of the story's journey, since you were the first step. Mrs. Milliken told me I was a writer and that I needed to *use my words* to show you how much you mean to me."

"And was it … for me?"

"For you and because of you. But do remember to go easy on it." He looked so unsure. Maybe all writers were like that, but in Sam's case the worry was needless.

"I'm going to love everything about it."

"I'm really going to do it." He pulled her to him and pressed a warm kiss to her forehead. "Because of you, I'm going to finish that book."

"I fully believe you are." No question. She rested her head against his chest for a moment, until she recalled the reason she'd brought him here. "Now, for the Christmas present I found for you." Tabitha placed the manuscript lovingly aside and pulled him toward the tree again. "Literally."

Sam quirked an eyebrow. "As in literally *found?*" He sat down by the tree beside her while she rummaged in the depths of her pocket for the box from Bijoux Jewelers.

"I mean, it kind of found me." A-ha. The gift. She pulled it to her stomach, not showing it to him yet. "Remember that day at Sugarbear Storage? It was snowing. I spotted something at the auction, and it made me think of you, so I picked it up and kept it."

"You were thinking of me, even then?" That old familiar glint flashed in his eye, sending a shower of sparks through her once again, only this time they just fell back into the glowing embers that he continued to fuel with his affectionate gazes.

"Sam Bartlett. If you had any idea how long I've been thinking of you, you'd blush."

"Is that right? Let me guess." He took her fingers and began to kiss them one by one. "Was it when you first beat me out of those books at the estate sale over on Bellwether Street? The one with the ugly porcelain ostriches?"

"Before that."

"Before that?"

"When a certain someone shoveled snow for an elderly woman who had lost her husband." She felt warm all over as his eyes shone with love. She handed him the gift.

Tabitha held her breath. Would he like it? Why such a small thing would speak to her as being perfect for him, she had no idea. But here it went no matter what. He almost had the box open. He was sliding the lid off, and ...

Sam stared wide-eyed, jaw-dropped, into the box, at the disc in the silver bezel lying on the cotton batting.

"It's a tie tack. Made from a typewriter key. Since, you know, you're a writer." Tabitha should keep quiet, stop explaining. But he wasn't moving. It was like he was paralyzed. "I told you I found something on the ground at Sugarbear Storage, and that was it. I thought of the A for Angels Landing. You had to give away the book, so can this still be a reminder for you?"

Sam blinked, not moving. "It's perfect," he whispered. "A. For Angels Landing."

"Do you love it?"

"More than I can say." His hand hovered over the open box for a long time, but eventually, he took it out and pinned it on his tie. "This letter A typewriter key is the whole reason we"—he choked up and then cleared his throat—"the whole reason I went back to the storage unit and met up with you that day. It's the reason we found the book."

"What?" Tabitha didn't follow. "You've seen that typewriter key before?"

Sam nodded. "It was a gift from Adelaide. I had it in my pocket at the auction. For luck." He gazed meaningfully into Tabitha's eyes. "I'm thinking it worked exceptionally well."

Thanks, Adelaide, our angel. Perfect gift.

Chapter 40

Sam

The bells signaling New Year's Day morning rang loudly in the Sugarplum Falls church tower, and Sam sat side by side with Tabitha at their Formica-topped kitchen table, her choice from the flea market where she'd outbid a fellow fan of 1970s chic.

Of course. As a consolation, Sam had offered the guy a paperback copy of his third book, the latest to hit the shelves, and the guy had said, *You're Sam Bartlett? The Sam Bartlett?*

Never dreamed that would happen. Without Tabitha it never would have.

"How many per page can we fit?" Sam asked, holding the stack of old-school-style printed photos, arranging and rearranging them on the page of the vintage photo album she'd found in one of her Twelve Days shopping hunts, but which she'd kept for their family instead of giving away. "This one of the twins in their matching baby Santa outfits when they were newborns last Christmas needs a page of its own."

They'd been pretty cute newborns, but Eddie and Della were a lot more fun now that they could giggle and feed themselves Cheerios and get into things. Fatherhood was a lot better than he'd ever expected.

Doing this project together was his gift last week to Tabitha for their fifth Christmas as a couple. It had been her request—his time, since time turned out to be her love language—enjoying the nostalgia of their life thus far together, quickly before baby number three arrived any day.

Clearly, physical touch was Sam's love language, and they'd spent quite a few hours in love in the back room at Angels Landing while she'd apprenticed with him.

"What if we do something like the Garnet family photo album for at least this little section and just choose Christmastime photos. Like time-lapse photography. First, here's one of our engagement three years ago."

213

"Wait. Do we have one of our first date to the Hot Cocoa Festival somewhere?" Tabitha found one. "Then our engagement. I love that you proposed to me in the snowstorm overlooking the frozen waterfall that next year."

"I love that you said yes."

"I love that we got married at Christmas the next year, and that our twins were born the following Christmas, the same month as I graduated with my business degree. We kind of have an *important milestones at Christmas* theme going on." She clutched her side. "However, this little inchworm is breaking the mold. She's … apparently more interested in making an appearance as the New Year's baby." Her voice was strained.

Sam knew that sound. "You're kidding, right? The baby is coming now?" But she wasn't due for another week or so. Should he spring into action? Grab the go-bag?

"If not now, soon." Tabitha's little pixie mouth pulled into a half-pained, half-thrilled smile. "By next year, we're going to have the most fabulous, hilarious family Christmas pictures to add to our album. I'm so excited. Three kids on a mall-Santa's lap. Envision it!"

She *should* be excited to be loading up and getting to the hospital, not thinking about more photo albums. But that was his Tabitha.

"Just a second," he said, trying to focus. "Are you saying the baby's coming? As in now?"

"Right after we add one more photo."

Sam dialed the on-call sitters, Poppy and Andrew, and told them their hour had come. They'd rush over.

Sam helped Tabitha on with her coat, kissed her, and said, "I think another angel is about to land in our family."

Tabitha grinned. "And we'll never be the same."

Epilogue

Claire

"**R**emind me why you're doing this again?" Portia sat on Claire Downing's kitchen counter swinging her legs and chomping on a stray piece of celery that didn't make it into the stuffing. "Thanksgiving was just a few days ago. Slaving all day to make a holiday meal—not on an official holiday, mind you—for people Mayor Lang told you to invite over? People we don't even know?"

Heavenly holiday scents of sage, thyme, and rosemary, along with roasting turkey, wafted through Claire's kitchen in her red-brick house on Apricot Avenue. It hadn't smelled this good in here since Mom and the girls moved out three years ago.

"We probably know some of them. I know you. You're bringing Owen. It won't exactly be a roomful of strangers." Other than her longtime best friends and Claire, it might not be a roomful of anyone. Despite good recommendations from Mayor Lang, most of Claire's invitations had gone unanswered. Seriously, who turned down turkey dinner?

All I need to do is meet a few new people.

"But remind me of the *why* again." Portia jumped off the counter and started scrubbing a few dishes in the sink. "It's a ton of work and expense, if you ask me."

Claire cracked the oven door and reached in with a turkey baster to help the bird stay moist and scrumptious for when her guests came. "The why is that my mother issued me a challenge"—after hearing Claire pine for family visits over the phone one time too many. "She insists I try something new."

215

"Then watch a horror movie or test out a new restaurant. Finally show the world your clothing designs, for heaven's sake."

Claire cringed. *Try something new* was Mom's code for *quit hiding your designs. Be brave.* "Not yet."

"Fine, but why the slaving all day in a kitchen to feed strangers—who may or may not even like watching your Christmas movies or putting on your Christmas-themed skits after the pumpkin pie is served?"

Pie! "Thanks for reminding me." Claire tugged two cartons of heavy whipping cream from the refrigerator. "Do you know how to whip cream?"

"Me?" Portia chortled. "I don't think you want to risk your cream investment on me."

Maybe not. Portia was more decorative than useful when it came to the kitchen, but she was fun. And Claire did enjoy decoration in life. It was nice, at least, to have someone around for when fun things went on.

Since her family had moved away and left Claire in Sugarplum Falls.

And sure, it was cool that Portia and Owen had gotten together. Great, even. To suddenly have her two best friends dating at least lessened the "third wheel" feeling Claire always seemed to suffer from. They'd invited her on picnics in the spring, to the fireworks in the summer, and spent most weekends hanging out at her house or near the falls or doing stuff together.

Claire whipped the cream. She also went over the skit ideas in her mind again. Would guests refuse to play along? Oh, maybe this whole thing was a terrible idea.

"Ding-dong." Owen banged through the back door. In one arm he held a large box labeled Kingston Orchards. In the other, he toted a sack from the grocery store, setting them both on Claire's countertop with his huge smile. "I come bearing apples. I hope you like Granny Smith. They're best for pie. And as requested, I brought ice. Is twenty pounds enough?"

Portia dove for him, affecting a swoon. "Owen Kingston, look at you carrying all those heavy things." She patted his biceps. "Take off that coat and show us those guns." She peeled away his leather jacket and more or less forced him to flex his muscles.

Yeah, they did strain nicely against the hems of his t-shirt's sleeves.

216

"Impressive," Claire said. "You must work out."

"I work out. Meaning I work *outside*." Owen put his coat on the same hook he'd used for almost twenty years. "What can I do to help?"

"You can use those *guns* of yours to pull the turkey out of the oven for me. I think we have about two minutes left until perfection." Claire handed Portia a water pitcher to add some of Owen's ice offering to. "And then carve?"

"Carving meat. Manly job." Owen chose a knife from the block. "Who else is coming over?"

Smirking, Portia shook ice into one of the goblets. "It's a holiday surprise."

With a tilt of his head, Owen asked, "Really, Claire? I thought—"

"I invited twenty, and I cooked for thirty." Just to be safe. Mayor Lang's list of people in Sugarplum Falls who might not have anyone to spend Christmas with wasn't very long, so Claire had just extended her invitation to everyone on it. "I probably should have asked for RSVPs or something."

"Ya think?" Portia snorted.

The oven timer rang. "When food is involved, yeah." Owen located oven mitts and pulled the turkey out. His muscles did flex nicely.

Better, Owen really was a great guy. In fact, he never even showed annoyance while he dated Portia Sutherland to have her less-sparkling sidekick in tow all the time. How could he ever advance the relationship with Claire always in the room?

Weirdly, Portia didn't seem to mind, either. Claire was the only one hating that she was preventing something good from becoming more serious.

This is why I need to find another batch of friends. Please, someone, show up for dinner.

"Seems like too much food, even for a Kingston family get-together."

"It's because Claire is *trying something new*." Portia handed Owen the platter for the carved meat. "Her mom *challenged* her. That's why we're stuck doing this."

"You're calling eating a gourmet turkey dinner *stuck* doing something?" Owen expertly placed the drumstick whole on the platter. Everyone loved seeing the drumstick kept intact. "I call it fantastic."

"You just like food."

"I'm a guy."

Still, *thanks, Owen, for the backup.* "Look, I'm appeasing my mom. It was her suggestion—a supper club. I'm kicking it off with a big meal, just to draw people in. Then, when people feel comfortable and get to know each other, we can all take turns hosting. I'm aiming for about a dozen people in all."

Imagine *twelve* friends emerging from the Sugarplum Falls woodwork. People who weren't already caught in their own families' obligations like everyone Claire already knew. How would that be? Imagine having people to actually go with to all of the amazing Christmas events planned in Sugarplum Falls. But every year it was the same at the holidays, with Portia spending every night at practice for the town Christmas play, and Claire stuck choosing to go alone or not at all to the Hot Cocoa Festival or the Waterfall Lights, or any of the other festivities.

That's why this supper club thing had to work—and why she'd finally caved to Mom's urging.

Owen expelled a sigh. "Man, I don't even get how people have time for friends. Other than you two, of course."

"Right?" Portia snitched a piece of the white meat. "Family obligations every single weekend."

"Look who's proving my mother's point." Ugh.

"Hey, remember that Sutherland status isn't all parties and laughter." Portia waved a *pshaw* hand. "Make Sugarplum Falls the *best.* Serve, serve, serve. It's exhausting. Do you know how much I just want to be like my uncle Zeke and be the black sheep of the family? I should go off to New York City and star in a musical. Or Los Angeles. Or anywhere."

Here came the old threat. Someday she might make good on it. Claire shuddered.

"For now, you get to star in the town Christmas play." Owen pressed a consoling kiss to her temple. It was still a little weird sometimes to see. "And you'll dazzle."

"Dazzle. In the town Christmas play." Portia guffawed. "Should I be the one to point out the elephant in the room, or does someone else want to? That play is smellier than bleu cheese."

"Yes, but it's the only play we have for now. Besides"—Owen placed an arm over her shoulder—"your acting elevates it."

Owen was so perfect for Portia. He could bring her down to earth when no one else could. Such a great guy. Not half bad as a friend, either, if not a boyfriend. Which, he'd never be for Claire. They'd friend-zoned each other for far too long.

"Elevate it. Ha! From negative level a thousand to negative nine hundred ninety-nine." Portia squirmed. "I really should have gotten brave and tried L.A.'s acting scene."

Owen enfolded her in his arms, guns a-blazin'. "I, for one, am glad you stayed." He pulled her head against his broad chest.

The public display of affection continued, and Claire looked away, but she was glad Portia had stayed, too. *Everyone I'm close to leaves.*

"Tell you what, Portia." Owen leaned back and forth with Portia in his arms. "I'll do whatever I can to help you be glad you stayed in Sugarplum Falls."

"You really mean that?" Portia looked up at him, her eyes shining. She really did have acting chops—probably because she felt every single emotion acutely. "I'm holding you to it." She grinned fiercely and gave a maniacal laugh.

Yikes. She'd better not be planning something terrible. Portia had planned a few terrible things in the past. It was how Claire had ended up eating a bug once. Luckily, she'd learned her lesson early—unlike Owen, apparently.

"Knock-knock!" A man's voice came from the front room, and the front door clicked shut. "Does this house that smells like Thanksgiving and Christmas dinners collide belong to Claire Downing, my high school friend?"

The stentorian bass voice was unmistakable.

"Archie?" Portia mouthed. "You invited Archie Holdaway?" Portia shot Claire one of those *nooooo!* looks she was famous for.

"Um … ?" Claire had just copied and pasted Mayor Lang's list and

219

printed labels, barely looking at them at all. She should have seen Archie's name and deleted it. Fast. "Hey," she said, hustling into her front room, where the Christmas tree blinked and a few candles burned. "It's so good to see you." She shook his hand heartily. "It's been a long time."

"I've been so buried in the high school teaching job I haven't poked my head out to see anyone since I got back to town in late summer." His voice lingered on the *anyone,* and his eyes lingered on Portia. "But I should have. Good to see you guys." He only looked at Portia.

Claire's mistake was a humongous oversight. This could go very badly. Unless—"Archie, you remember Owen Kingston?"

"Sure." Archie still gawped at Portia.

"He's Portia's boyfriend"—Claire emphasized *boyfriend*—"of about a year." Not quite, but since about the time Owen's Granddad died—and … the accident.

Archie tore his eyes off Portia and aimed the gaze at Owen. His face went from simpering to scowling. If ever she was short on funds, Claire should offer to have him over for poker night, just so she could clean him out.

"Kingston Orchards. Right."

The air thickened—unlike Claire's turkey gravy. This was so bad. Owen shot Claire a look that said *what do we do?*

She shrugged. *Help me?* she mouthed.

Owen nodded and threw his hands together. "It's a quarter after." A loud clap snapped everyone back to attention. "The turkey is carved, shall we sit down to eat?" He moved to the table and held out a chair. "Claire, do you have seating assignments in mind?"

"Anywhere you like." With twenty places set but only four guests, this wasn't turning out to be much of a club. Unless she called it The Awkward Dinner Reunion Club.

Portia sat down first, at the wall-end, as if to scoot as far from Archie as possible. Alas, Archie jumped and chose the chair closest to her—then slid it even closer. Now there was no way for Owen to seat himself beside Portia, and her annoyance showed. Archie slid even nearer.

Owen cleared his throat and shot Claire a droll look. Ugh. If only turkey drippings in the oven would set off the fire alarm and put them all out of their misery.

They found seats across from the others, Owen beside Claire. As he lowered into his chair, his shoulder brushed against hers, and she glanced down at it. The triceps were on full display. Working outside all summer in the orchards really did turn his upper arms into guns. The kind from action movies.

Not that Claire was scoping him out. Sheesh, he was dating her best friend. However, she could appreciate good form. Claire was a patron of the arts, including sculpture. Like Owen's musculature. *And let's not leave out his jaw line.*

"You're teaching at the high school?" Claire asked after they'd said grace. "What subjects?"

Archie had left Sugarplum Falls for the teaching college at the same time Claire and Portia had left for college. Now, running her shop, she didn't see many men. Men did not hang out at Apple Blossom Boutique. Well, other than Owen, who showed up now and then with Portia or to bring Claire a drink from The Cider Press if he was downtown.

"English, but they are trying to get me to start a drama department. I told them I had my hands full with the town Christmas play."

Portia's head snapped upward from staring down at her green bean casserole. "You're in the play? Auditions haven't happened yet. How—?"

"I'm not in it. I'm directing it. At Mayor Lang's insistence."

Owen chortled. "Yeah, the mayor of Sugarplum Falls can be insistent."

"Highly," Claire said. Mayor Lisa Lang kept hounding Claire about participating in her dating match-up activity at the upcoming Hot Cocoa Festival. Claire was ignoring her calls. "That's great, Archie. Maybe you can help it move along at a little faster clip this year."

Owen muttered something beside Claire that sounded like *Two hours of torture is what they should officially title it.* "Good for you, helping out the town," he said more audibly. "Anything I can do to help, let me know."

"Yes. Owen is great at everything. He used to own a construction company before he inherited Kingston Orchard last year," Portia said.

"I haven't inherited it."

Claire cringed for him. He hadn't inherited it yet. Owen's dad was still alive. Technically.

"I'm managing." To say more would be a buzzkill.

Not that there was much buzz to kill. This supper club was the most DOA thing in this house since Owen pulled Claire's turkey out of the oven.

"Try out for the play, Portia." Archie pointed his turkey-lanced fork at her.

"I don't know, Archie." Why was she playing coy? It wasn't like Portia Sutherland *wouldn't* audition for the only dramatic performance in Sugarplum Falls. "I've done it the last three years. I've starred, you know."

"I know!" Archie's turkey flipped from his fork under the force of his enthusiastic reply. It landed atop the cranberry jelly, which was still shaped like the can. "I need someone experienced!"

"There you go, Portia. Now you've got it—a reason to be glad you stuck around for the season instead of heading off to New York or L.A. or wherever." Owen took a forkful of stuffing and crunched the celery in it. "This is really good, Claire." He took another bite before finishing the first, a visible compliment.

"You were planning on leaving?" Archie looked stricken. "Are you serious?"

It was amazing how Portia, with nothing more than the bat of an eye or the lifting of a brow could convey almost any emotion. This time it was disinterest. "Like Owen said, I needed a reason to stay." She gave Owen one of those luscious smiles that no man could ever resist, at least not for as long as Claire had known Portia, which was most of her life. "As if Owen wasn't enough of a reason. You're too good to me, Owen."

Cue the red, wrinkling forehead on Archie. Geez, what was his problem? He was the one who'd dropped Portia back in the day. Regretting his decision?

"Owen," Archie muttered. "Owen Kingston. Geez."

Portia slammed her fork onto the side of her china dish—the good kind for special occasions from the upstairs cupboard. "Are you going to stop that forehead wrinkling or what, Archie?" The spoon clattered like an exclamation point.

222

"Stop what?"

"Stop being like that!" Portia got up and shoved her cloth napkin onto her plate. "If you're going to simper and be a beast, you can just forget about me trying out for the Christmas play." She stormed out of the room.

Archie chased after her. "Portia! Wait!"

So much for a friendly dinner.

Read the rest of Owen Kingston and Claire Downing's unintentional stage-kiss romance. Fall for how they go from best friends to something much more lasting in Sugarplum Falls in Christmas at Sugarplum Falls, *which features the most unlikely matchmaker of all.*

Author's Note

All stories in the Sugarplum Falls Romance series are clean, standalone holiday romances. **They're arranged in a loop**. Book 1 introduces characters from book 2, and so forth, until *Christmas at Gingerbread Inn* loops back to *Christmas at Holly Berry Cottage*. This means readers can begin at any point in the series and then complete the loop to fall in love over and over, while meeting the many recurring characters from the familiar and charming small town of Sugarplum Falls.

The Sugarplum Falls Romance Series

Christmas at Holly Berry Cottage
Christmas at Turtledove Place
Christmas at Angels Landing
Christmas at Sugarplum Falls
Christmas at Gingerbread Inn

For a short and sweet Sugarplum Falls Christmas romance, sign up for Jennifer's bubbly newsletter and receive *Christmas at The Cider Press* as an ebook for free. Email her at jennifergriffithauthor@yahoo.com and ask for the link.

Jennifer's other sweet holiday romance series include the Christmas House Romances, Snowfall Wishes, plus several standalone sweet holiday novels, and lots of romantic comedies set at other times of the year. Check out all her books on Amazon.

About the Author

Jennifer Griffith lives in Arizona with her husband, where they are raising their five children to love Christmas. She tries to put more lights on her tree each year, and she wholeheartedly believes the best way to kick off the holiday season is to sing Christmas songs with her husband's extended family for two to three hours on Thanksgiving night. Her favorite carol is "O Holy Night," and her favorite Christmas song is "Walking in a Winter Wonderland." She once sang a contralto solo of "Gesu Bambino" that wasn't too bad. The best part of it was her oldest son accompanied her on the piano.

13446901R00136